Praise for Sharon Sala's
Blessings, Georgia series

"Engaging, heartwarming, funny, sassy, and just plain good."

—*Peeking Between the Pages* for *You and Only You*

"A happily-ever-after that will make anyone stand up and cheer."

—*Harlequin Junkie* for *You and Only You*

"Sala once again shows why she is a master of the romance genre…an amazing story by a true storyteller."

—*RT Book Reviews* for *I'll Stand By You*

"Blessings sure sounds like a great place to put down roots."

—*Fresh Fiction* for *Saving Jake*

"There are not many authors who can write a story with such depth and emotion, but Sala excels and shines… Sala is magical!"

—*RT Book Reviews* for *A Piece of My Heart*

"With plenty of danger and passion, Sala will have readers flipping the pages."

—*RT Book Reviews*, 4 Stars for *The Color of Love*

"A strong and positive second-chance romance that fans of Robyn Carr and Susan Wiggs will enjoy."

—*Booklist* for *Come Back to Me*

Also by Sharon Sala

a RAINBOW
ABOVE *us*

SHARON
SALA

sourcebooks
casablanca

Published by Sourcebooks Casablanca, an imprint of Sourcebooks
P.O. Box 4410, Naperville, Illinois 60567-4410
(630) 961-3900
sourcebooks.com

Printed and bound in the United States of America.
OPM 10 9 8 7 6 5 4 3 2 1

We have no control over the family we are born into, and as much as we want to be loved by them, that's not always the case.

I'm dedicating this book to the people who have to find love and acceptance beyond the families into which they were born. No matter how long you have to search, you will eventually find your tribe. Just keep looking. They're out there, waiting for you.

Chapter 1

THE SKIN CRAWLED ON THE BACK OF BOWIE JAMES'S NECK as he pulled into Blessings. He'd sworn never to come back here, and yet here he was, and all because of Hurricane Fanny, and his love and loyalty to the last two people on earth who gave a damn about him.

He'd already called about hookups at the RV/trailer park and drove straight down Main Street, well aware of the stares his fifty-foot red-and-black motor home and the red Jeep Cherokee he was towing were getting.

But he was doing some staring of his own, surveying the damage the hurricane and subsequent flooding had done here. Watermarks were visible on the outside of buildings. A few were still boarded up and in various stages of repair. The police station was open for business, as was the drugstore. A beauty shop called the Curl Up and Dye was one addition to Main Street he didn't remember, but the Piggly Wiggly grocery store and Granny's Country Kitchen were very familiar. At least he knew where he was going to eat tonight.

By the time he got to the park, he was more than ready to get out and stretch his legs but he still had to check in at the manager's office, then hook up to the facilities. He'd done this countless times in hundreds of places over the past few years, and after the business of checking in had been taken care of, he drove to the campsite, unhooked his SUV, and finished the setup.

A couple in a small fifth wheel were sitting outside their little camper grilling supper. They waved at Bowie when he got out, and he waved back. He was well-accustomed to the RV life and how friendly the people were who'd chosen that lifestyle, but he hadn't come here to make friends. He'd come to put Gran and Aunt Ella's world back together.

The recent hurricane that hit here had, according to the letter he'd received from Aunt Ella, flooded their house clear up to the windowsills. With nowhere else to go, they were residing in the local nursing home.

The timing of Aunt Ella's letter and the end of his last project couldn't have been better. His company built expensive homes in out-of-the-way locations all over the States, and he was just getting ready to move out when her letter came. He'd expected one of her usual newsy letters, but when he began to read, he was stunned by the message and horrified at what they must have lived through.

> Bowie, Mama and I hate to ask, but we are desperate. Hurricane Fanny put four feet of water in the house. In its present state, it is uninhabitable, and we are both in the nursing home here in Blessings. I wouldn't ask, but we know it's in your line of work, and Mama cries every night, afraid she's going to die in "this place" as she calls it.
>
> There is a charity house here in town called Hope House that we might be able to use for a bit, but Mama says she's never taken charity in her life and she won't start now. You know how she is.

*We know you're on the go all the time, so I
hope this letter reaches you, and that you are
in good health.
We need you.*

Love, Aunt Ella

But for them, he would never have set foot back in
this town, and he knew, as well as he knew his own
name, that because of his presence an old feud was
likely to rear its ugly head once more. However, he was
here, and whatever happened, so be it.

As soon as he was satisfied that all was in order at
the campsite, he locked up, then got in the Cherokee
and headed for town. He hadn't had anything to eat
but snacks since breakfast, and if Granny's food was
as good as it used to be, he was going to bed a well-
fed man.

The couple with the fifth wheel waved at him again
as he drove out. He waved back, and took a left at the
entrance and kept driving.

It was just after 7:00 p.m. when he pulled into the
diner's parking lot and got out. He stretched, weary of
so much sitting, then fingercombed the too-long black
hair hanging halfway down the back of his neck, a side
effect of big projects in out-of-the-way places and little
sleep. Maybe he'd find the time to get a haircut here, he
thought, and headed for the entrance.

He met a couple coming out and held the door for
them, nodded when they told him thank you, and then
noticed their double take.

Shit.

It was hard to deny your heritage when the family looks ran deep through the blood.

A strikingly beautiful woman smiled as he entered. "Welcome to Granny's. A seat for one?" she asked.

"Yes, ma'am." He noticed the little badge on her blouse said her name was Mercy, but out of curiosity, he asked. "Does Lovey still run Granny's?"

"Yes, sir, she does. But she was injured during the hurricane and is recovering at a friend's house while her home is being repaired. My name is Mercy Pittman. I'm just filling in."

"I'm sorry to hear that," Bowie said.

Mercy nodded. "We all are. This way, please," she said, and led him through the dining room to a smaller booth. "Your waitress will be here shortly. Enjoy your meal."

Bowie glanced once around the room as he sat down. Grateful he didn't see any familiar faces, he picked up the menu just as his waitress appeared.

"Evening, sir. My name is Wendy, and I'll be your server tonight. What can I get you to drink?"

"The biggest glass of sweet tea you have on the menu," he said.

Wendy giggled. "It only comes in one size, but I think it'll hold you for a bit."

She left as abruptly as she'd arrived. Bowie was still reading the menu when she came back with a small basket of biscuits and his tea.

"You'll want to dig into these while they're still hot," she said. "Do you know what you want to order, or do you need a few minutes?"

"I haven't had good barbecue in a while. How about the ribs?"

Wendy rolled her eyes and giggled again. "Everything is good at Granny's. You want the four-rib or the six-rib dinner?"

"I think four, with fries and coleslaw," Bowie said.

"Coming up," Wendy said, and pointed again at the biscuits. "Those things are amazing. I recommend one with butter and honey first."

Bowie eyed the biscuits, wondering what all the fuss was about. Granted they were a perfect golden brown on top, and he couldn't remember when he'd seen biscuits rise like that, but it was all about taste. He took one from the basket, put it on his bread plate and split it open, buttering both sides. He took a bite while he was digging through the little containers of jams and jellies, and then paused midchew.

Whoa, Nellie! That might be the best biscuit I ever ate.

He chewed, swallowed, then put the last half of the biscuit in his mouth while he was buttering the second. He ate one half with honey, and the other half with strawberry preserves.

Wendy came flying past his table on the way to deliver another order and grinned at him. "Told you they were good, didn't I?"

He grinned. "My compliments to the chef."

Wendy pointed back at Mercy Pittman. "We've all had to switch jobs up a bit after the hurricane, but that lady up front is the one with the now-famous recipe. She trained a couple of subs to help us out, but she is pure magic in the kitchen," Wendy said.

"A woman that beautiful, and she can cook? I have to ask, is she married?" Bowie asked.

Wendy laughed out loud. "Yes, sir, to the police chief."

"Then my compliments to the chief as well," Bowie said.

He made himself stop at two biscuits, but if he'd known how good they were, he could have skipped the ribs and just ordered a bowl of gravy to go with them. Now he was going to have to come back for that in the morning.

He was answering a text from one of his crew chiefs when his food arrived. He finished sending the orders, then put down the phone to eat his meal. For just a few minutes, he'd forgotten where he was and was simply enjoying the food, when two men walked into the dining room and stopped to look around.

Bowie just happened to look up as they began scanning the room, and silently cursed. He might not have recognized anyone in here, but he'd lay odds someone had recognized him and felt obliged to share the news.

He put down his fork, wiped his hands, and stood up. The moment he did, they locked gazes. He saw the shock come and go on their faces, and had a few moments of satisfaction. He wasn't the skinny fifteen-year-old he'd been when they last saw him. He was bigger and taller than either one of them and, from the sizes of their bellies, in much better shape.

He took a step forward, and when he did, they turned around and bolted out of Granny's.

All Wendy saw was the man at her table standing up, and she hurried over to refill his tea.

"I'm sorry. I should have been here sooner. We're extra busy tonight."

She topped off his tea as he sat back down.

"You're fine," Bowie said. "But I have a little business to attend to. Do I pay you or—"

"No, sir. You pay at the register as you go out." She pulled his tab from her order pad. "Would you like for me to box up your leftovers?"

"Not this time, but I'll probably be back for biscuits and gravy in the morning," he said.

"Then, thank you, and enjoy the rest of your evening," she said, her eyes widening as he tossed a twenty-dollar bill on the table for her tip and headed for the exit.

Bowie was right in guessing that he'd been recognized, but the people who'd seen him come in, and then subversively watched him throughout his meal, hadn't meant to stare. They just thought they were looking at a ghost.

Bowie didn't look anything like the kid he'd been when he and his mother left Blessings in the middle of the night. The fact that he'd grown into the spitting image of his grandfather, Judson Boone, must have been as startling to his sons as it was to Bowie every time he looked in a mirror.

Once outside the restaurant, Bowie stopped and scanned the parking lot, waiting. He knew they were there and called out. "What are you waiting for?"

They came out of the shadows, one from his right, the other from his left.

Emmitt Boone had a baseball bat.

Melvin Boone was brandishing his brass knuckles, gleaming beneath the lights on his short, fat fingers.

Melvin was a couple of steps closer and ran at Bowie with a fistful of brass.

Bowie waited until Melvin was about to swing a fist,

then stepped aside and gave Melvin a quick karate chop to the throat.

Melvin squawked, grabbed his throat, and fell flat on his face.

Bowie heard Emmitt coming up behind him and spun, took out the bat in Emmitt's hand with one kick, and followed up with a fist to his nose.

Emmitt yelped as blood spurted and dropped flat on his back.

Bowie stood over both of them, staring. "Where's Randall? Is he hiding out there in the dark, or are you two all there is?" he asked.

Emmitt moaned. "Randall is dead."

"That's fair enough," Bowie muttered.

"You broke my nose," Emmitt cried.

"No, you ran into my fist," Bowie said. "I did not start this. I came here to fix my gran's house, and then I'll be leaving, so you've been warned. While I'm here, stay away from me. Because if you don't, I will take all of you through court and bare every shameful secret you've been hiding in the process. Now you crawl back to your daddy and remind the old bastard that the sooner I'm gone, the sooner my obvious resemblance to him will be forgotten."

Melvin had rolled over onto his back, still gasping for air, still unable to do more than squawk.

Emmitt had a handkerchief jammed up both nostrils, but the blood was still running between his fingers.

"Daddy's not gonna like this," Emmitt whined. "He told you and your mama he would see you both dead if you came back."

Bowie bent over them, his voice barely above a

whisper. "My mother killed herself the day after my eighteenth birthday. In my eyes, you're all responsible. So. Don't. Piss. Me. Off. Understand?"

The shock of what he'd done to them—and without breaking a sweat—was beginning to set in. And the threat in his voice was too real to ignore. They nodded.

Bowie left them sitting in the dirt as he drove away, but the rage inside him was so strong that instead of driving straight back, he swung by his old high school, only to find out there was a football game in progress.

Curiosity won out as he parked, got out, and walked across the parking lot to pay at the gate, then went all the way up to the bleachers before he stopped. The crowd was loud. Someone had just completed a pass that took the home team all the way to the five-yard line.

A man in the stands glanced his way, then stared. Bowie shifted his position and moved beneath the bleachers until he could see the field from between the seats.

Once this had been his biggest dream, to be good enough to make the Blessings High School football team. Only back then he wasn't very tall, and he'd been skinny—not exactly football material.

He watched the quarterback receive another snap, then pull a quarterback sneak and dash across the goal line before the opposing team saw what was happening.

The crowd erupted into screams and cheers of delight. Bowie thought about sitting on the bleachers to watch, but he'd already pushed his luck for the night. If it hadn't been for that damn hurricane, he wouldn't even be here, and it was time to get some rest.

He drove back to the trailer park without incident, set

the alarm on the car as he got out, and then went inside. He turned on all the motion-detector lights affixed to the front and back, then set the security alarm inside the motor home as well. Without hesitation, he walked straight back to his bedroom, opened the safe, and removed both a Taser and his loaded handgun. He put the gun beside his bed and took the Taser to the living room with him.

He was tired. He'd planned on going to bed early, but now he was too wound up. Instead, he closed all the shades, turning off the lights as he went and turning on the TV as he passed it on his way to the wet bar. He poured himself two fingers of bourbon, neat, then returned to his easy chair and scanned the stations with the sound on Mute.

Finally, he settled on a show on HGTV and began watching a team renovating a home in Maine that had been built in the early eighteen hundreds. He slowly sipped on the bourbon, while working on his laptop, until he began to relax.

He thought about Gran and Aunt Ella. They didn't even know he was coming, but they were going to get a surprise tomorrow morning. Not only had he come back to Blessings to fix their house, but he was rescuing them from the nursing home and bringing them back here to stay during the renovation. They could have his bedroom and private bath, and he'd bunk out here for the duration. There were two pieces of furniture in the living area that turned into beds, as well as another, smaller bath, and the motor home was huge by motor home standards.

The kitchen was state of the art, so Aunt Ella would

have no trouble making their meals while he was at work during the day. Whatever discomfort he experienced by giving up his space was worth it to know they were happy and safe.

After a couple of hours, he shut down his laptop, turned off the television, and went to take a shower. He emerged a short while later wearing an old pair of gym shorts that he slept in, then put his cell phone on the charger and the Taser next to the handgun before crawling into bed. He thought about setting the alarm clock, and then fell asleep before he did it.

But as it turned out, a different alarm, the car alarm, went off just before daylight. Bowie swung his long legs out of bed, grabbing the Taser as he raced to the front door. The moment he opened it, the security alarm inside his home began going off, too, but he didn't stop to disarm it.

Motion-detector lights were already on as he ran out, highlighting the fact that his Cherokee had just been keyed, and then he caught sight of a teenage boy running away.

"Stop!" he yelled, but the kid didn't slow down.

Bowie had the advantage with longer legs, and as soon as he got close enough, he fired the Taser. The prongs hit the middle of the boy's back, and seconds later, he was on the ground, writhing in pain.

The couple in the fifth wheel came out, looking wild-eyed and scared.

"Everything's okay!" Bowie said. "But I need you to call the police. I just caught someone vandalizing my car."

The older man waved to indicate he'd heard and

darted back inside their trailer, while the woman just stood there, staring.

It occurred to Bowie, a little too late, that the old gym shorts he slept in were seriously small, and he was close enough to naked that the possibility of being arrested for indecent exposure might exist. Nothing like bringing down the house his first morning here.

He knelt down beside the kid and pulled the barbs out of his back, then grabbed him by the arm and yanked him upright.

"What name do you go by besides Dumbass?" Bowie asked.

The kid just shook his head. Either he was still reeling from the shocks, or he wasn't willing to talk.

"Fine. Dumbass works for me," Bowie said, and dragged him back to the car, shut off the alarm, and then opened the hatch. He pulled out a roll of duct tape and taped the kid's wrists together behind his back, then sat him down and taped his legs together at the ankles.

"That hurts," the kid muttered.

Bowie looked up. "No, it doesn't, and we both know it."

The kid started to respond, and then the look on Bowie's face changed his mind.

By now, lights were coming on all over the trailer park and men were coming out carrying everything from hunting rifles to baseball bats. Bowie watched one big redheaded man stomping toward them, waving a bat and yelling.

"What the hell's going on?"

Bowie pointed at his prisoner. "Damned kid keyed my car and set off the security alarm. Don't let him move. I need to shut off the alarm inside."

The man glared down at the kid, who persisted in staring at his own feet.

Bowie bolted through the doorway, turned off the alarm, then ran toward his bedroom, grabbed the jeans he'd taken off last night, put them on, and was back outside within less than a minute.

"Thanks," Bowie said. "I'm Bowie James. I appreciate the help."

"I'm Yancy Scott, but most everybody calls me Red. That's some rig you have there. You must have come in last night."

Bowie nodded. He could hear sirens. "Sorry about all the noise. It wouldn't have happened except for the dumbass who refuses to identify himself."

Red grinned. "I don't know his name, but I do know he's Emmitt Boone's boy."

Bowie turned around and stared. "Is that so?" he said. "Did your daddy send you, or was this all your bright idea?"

The kid looked up, and the hate on his face was easy for Bowie to read. "You broke my daddy's nose last night," he said.

"Why, yes, I did. I don't suppose he mentioned that he and your uncle, Melvin, ganged up on me in the parking lot at Granny's. Mel had brass knuckles, and your daddy had a baseball bat. If they had minded their own damn business, none of this would have happened. And now you have done the very thing I warned them not to do."

The boy looked stunned by the news and then frowned. "What did you warn them not to do?"

"Oh, you'll find out soon enough," Bowie said, and looked up just as the first of two police cruisers came flying into the trailer park, lights flashing and sirens screaming.

Chief Lon Pittman was the first out of the vehicle, and his deputy, Ralph Herman, pulled up behind him and got out on the run.

Lon quickly scanned the scene and saw only one person he didn't know.

"I'm Chief Pittman. What's going on here?" he asked.

"My name's Bowie James. I arrived here last night and was still asleep this morning when my car alarm began going off. I ran outside with my Taser, saw the key marks on my vehicle and this dumbass running away. I chased him, tasered him, and dragged him back here so I could shut off the alarms."

"Woke us all up," Red said.

The neighbors from the fifth wheel had joined the crowd.

"He's telling the truth," the man said. "Me and Jewel saw the boy running away and this fella chasing him down."

"I assume you want to press charges," the chief said.

Bowie nodded. "Yes. The damage to my Cherokee is going to cost enough to make this a felony, too."

The boy's eyes widened. "I'm a juvenile. I'm only fifteen."

"Being stupid and underage still gets you arrested," Bowie said.

The kid was bordering on tears. "But Chief, he broke my daddy's nose last night."

"Tell him the rest of the story," Bowie said.

"But I didn't know that at the time," the boy muttered.

Bowie shrugged. "You can ask Emmitt and Melvin

what happened last night in Granny's parking lot and see if they want me to file charges against them, too… for assault."

Lon frowned. "Obviously there's something going on here I don't understand."

"Nothing but an old feud," Bowie said.

Lon's frown deepened. "Between who?"

Bowie shrugged. "You're new to Blessings since I lived here. It was common knowledge then. My mother was raped by Randall Boone. She reported it. He denied it, and that was the end. Then she found out she was pregnant, and I am the result. They don't like me being here. I am proof of everything they denied. Pearl James is my grandmother. Gran and Ella James are all of the family I have left. They wrote asking me to help repair what the hurricane did to their home, which is what I came to do, and then I'm leaving."

"I'm missing something here," Lon said. "What's the grudge, if no one was arrested?"

Bowie pointed at the boy. "By the time I was his age, I was beginning to look so much like them that their denials that a rape never happened no longer held water. So they nearly beat me to death and told me to get out of Blessings. Afraid they would follow through on their promise, Mama packed up our stuff, and we ran in the middle of that same night. I haven't been back since, until now."

Lon frowned, thinking of all the complications that could still arise.

"Did your mother come with you?"

Bowie's expression went flat. "She committed suicide the day after my eighteenth birthday."

Lon didn't like hearing this. It sounded like a mess that wasn't likely to go away anytime soon. But, first things first. He looked down at the boy.

"What's your name, boy?"

"Emmitt Lee, named after my daddy," he mumbled.

Lon reached down and pulled him to his feet, eyed the duct tape, and then glanced up at Bowie. "Car alarms, duct tape, Tasers… What else don't I know about you?"

"I have a Luger, a hunting rifle, and a license to carry. My motor home also has a security system and motion-detection lights. Life has taught me to be wary, if you know what I mean. I'll get dressed and go to the police station to sign the complaint."

Lon nodded, then motioned to his deputy. "Hey, Ralph, come help me get him in the cruiser."

A few minutes later, both police cruisers were exiting the trailer park, leaving Bowie to meet his neighbors. He turned around and managed a brief smile.

"This is a poor way to meet, and I'm sorry for all the noise. My name is Bowie James. Ella James is my aunt, and her mother, Pearl, is my grandmother. They'll be staying with me during the renovation, so I hope you don't hold any hard feelings toward them that you might have for me."

Red grinned and slapped him on the shoulder. "No hard feelings at all, dude. The Boones are a little wild and hard-nosed for my liking. I'm pleased to meet you."

And just like that, the crowd around him began to echo similar feelings, vowing to make sure no one bothered the ladies while they were in his care.

"Much appreciated, and thank you," Bowie said. "But I need to get dressed."

The people began drifting away, talking among themselves about the incident and feeling bad for the ladies and their flooded house. More than one woman commented about what a good-looking man that Bowie James was, but it was Jewel, the lady from the fifth wheel, who brought the conversation to a halt.

"He's even more good-looking without them jeans he's wearing," she said, and grinned.

The women giggled.

"And how do you know?" one asked.

"Me and Frank saw him just as he came running out of his rig. I reckon he don't sleep in much."

Giggles erupted again.

"I might set off that car alarm again just to see that," the woman said.

"I wouldn't," Jewel added. "The Taser he used on that Boone boy looked like it caused a world of hurt."

Chapter 2

BOWIE WAS AT THE FRONT DESK SIGNING THE VANDALISM complaint when Emmitt Boone burst into the station. Even though the doctor had put a brace over Emmitt's nose to keep it from being bumped and dislocated again, it was too swollen to ignore.

Emmitt took one look at Bowie and turned white as a sheet. "What's he doing here?"

The chief looked up. "Signing a complaint against your son."

Emmitt gasped. "But you said when you called that he'd been arrested for vandalism. What does *he* have to do with it?"

Bowie kept writing without looking up. "It was my vehicle he vandalized. Keyed the hell out of it, too. It will cost thousands to get that fixed."

Emmitt groaned.

Bowie slid the complaint across the desk toward the chief. "If that's all, I'll be leaving now."

"That's all," Lon said.

Emmitt started to grab Bowie's arm, then thought better of it. "Wait! Wait! Let's talk this out. I don't want my kid having an arrest record."

"You're the one who raised him," Bowie said. "Besides, he's getting off easy from me. When I was his age, you and your brothers beat the hell out of me, and I didn't do anything to any of you. I told you what would happen if you didn't leave me alone. I'll see you in court."

Emmitt cursed beneath his breath as Bowie walked out of the precinct, then turned to the chief. "Can I talk to my boy?"

"I suppose, after I pat you down," Lon said, and confiscated a large pocketknife. "You can have that back when you leave."

"Hell, Chief! You're treating us like common criminals," Emmitt muttered.

Lon shrugged. "Unfortunately, your son is a criminal now. And the cost of the repairs on Mr. James's vehicle will turn this arrest into a felony."

Emmitt's lips parted, but then he thought better of arguing.

While Lon took Emmitt back to see his son, Bowie was on his way back to his motor home. He didn't have any sympathy whatsoever for the kid, or for Emmitt. He hadn't been here even twenty-four hours, and he'd been assaulted and his car vandalized. He could only imagine how the rest of his time here would play out. And, it was already daylight. Time to begin another day.

He hurried inside and changed the sheets on his bed for his girls' arrival, cleaned up the bathroom, and moved most of what he used daily into the other bathroom.

Closet space was limited, so they'd have to manage with what he had, and hopefully the renovation would go smoothly and wouldn't take too long. A half-dozen men from one of his work crews were on their way to Blessings. He'd made reservations for them at a local bed-and-breakfast and paid two weeks in advance. After that, he'd pay week by week until they were done.

Once he had everything neat, clean, and put away, Bowie headed to Granny's for breakfast. It wasn't yet eight o'clock, too early to go visiting at a nursing home. He set the security alarm again, then locked up as he left.

Frank and Jewel were sitting at a little table outside, having their morning coffee, and waved at him from the front yard.

He grinned and waved back. Sometimes that was the extent of being neighbors in the life he led.

By the time he got to Granny's, the parking lot was nearly full. He hoped they didn't run out of biscuits before he got his share. They were the best he'd ever eaten. And then it dawned on him that he'd already met the police chief, the man who was married to the baker.

Bowie was thinking about biscuits and gravy when he walked inside. The dining room was packed, but there were a couple of vacant tables and one empty booth.

Mercy welcomed him back as she took him to a small table.

"Enjoy," she said, and left the menu with him, only Bowie didn't bother picking it up. He already knew what he wanted.

A different waitress showed up with a coffeepot and filled the empty cup in front of him.

"Good morning, I'm Lila. Do you know what you want, or do you need a few minutes?"

"I want sausage, biscuits, and gravy," he said.

"No eggs to go with them?" Lila asked.

"No eggs," Bowie said.

She smiled. "Coming right up."

Bowie leaned back and took a quick sip of the coffee, then set it aside to cool a bit as he glanced around the room. This morning, the other diners were staring without apology.

He stared back until they looked away. The news was probably already spreading about the teenager who keyed his car. For the people who knew Bowie when he was growing up, the fact that the boy in jail was Emmitt Boone's son only made the news juicier.

His phone signaled a text. He read it and grinned. His crew was less than an hour out of Blessings. He sent back a text telling them about Granny's, and to go ahead and get settled in the bed-and-breakfast before they ate. He'd get in touch with them later.

When his food came, Bowie looked at the plate of browned sausage patties, the basket of hot biscuits, and a bowl of white gravy, and couldn't wait to dig in. The first bite did not disappoint, and he ate two plates full before he stopped. He was finishing up his coffee when Lila stopped by and left his bill on the table.

Bowie left a tip and headed up front to pay. It was almost nine o'clock now, and he was anxious to go to the nursing home.

He and the girls had stayed in touch for the past twenty years by phone calls, letters, the occasional postcard he would send, and as technology changed, now by FaceTiming on their phones. And then it occurred to him that their phone must have fallen victim to the flood, since they hadn't called him about the house, but had written the letter instead. He'd find out details soon enough.

He was pulling out money to pay when the entrance door opened behind him. He heard the heavy footsteps, the angry growl of a man's voice, then saw what amounted to panic on Mercy's face.

"Turn around and face me like a man!" the man yelled.

Bowie ignored him and kept talking to Mercy. "Breakfast was great. Do me a favor, and please call the police. Oh, and keep the change," he said, and handed her cash.

The man behind him was obviously impatient, but Bowie already knew who it was, and when Judson Boone grabbed him by the shoulder and tried to yank him around, he didn't yield.

Bowie shrugged off the hand, turned to face the nemesis from his childhood dreams, and took satisfaction in the shock he saw on Jud's face.

"Like looking in a mirror, and seeing a vision of your younger self, isn't it? Outside," Bowie said quietly, and pointed to the door.

"Like hell! You don't tell me what to do!" Jud shouted, and took a swing at Bowie.

Bowie calmly grabbed his wrist in midair and tightened his hold until the old man grimaced.

"I said outside," Bowie said softly, and took off for the exit, dragging Jud with him.

Once they were in the parking lot, Bowie turned him loose.

"What's the matter with you, trying to start a fight in there? You truly don't give a shit about anything but yourself, do you?"

Jud was still trying to wrap his head around the fact that the family bastard was his doppelgänger, and didn't bother answering the questions. He'd come here to straighten out the mess his family was in, but was beginning to realize it might be harder than he'd expected.

Bowie James was a good four inches taller than him and bulked up big-time beneath his clothes. He should have brought backup. Instead, he pointed a finger in Bowie's face.

"You broke Emmitt's nose and—"

"Don't do that," Bowie said, and grabbed the finger and pushed it away. "Whatever happened to your little thugs they brought on themselves. They jumped me in the dark, and both had weapons. They should be ready to take what they were trying to dish out, don't you think?"

Jud didn't know how to respond to this quiet menace, but he was well aware it could go wrong at any moment, so he spat out the rest of what he'd come here to say.

"I want my grandson out of jail, and you're gonna drop charges. Understand?"

"Go home, old man," Bowie said. "I told your boys last night that I didn't want any trouble. I came here to fix my grandma's house, and then I'm leaving. I don't want anything to do with Blessings, and that includes anyone named Boone."

"You don't tell me no! No one tells me no!" Jud shouted.

Bowie could hear sirens coming up Main. "You want a cell next to your grandson?"

"I want him out!" Jud said, and swung at Bowie again. But Bowie dodged the blow, grabbed Jud's arm, and yanked it behind his back, then pinned him against a van just as a police cruiser pulled into the parking lot.

Jud was struggling and cursing and trying to get free.

Bowie recognized Deputy Ralph as he hurried toward them.

"You again?" Ralph said, eyeing the man Bowie James had pressed up against a van.

"I'm sorry to say, it's just more of the same," Bowie said.

"I'll kill you! I swear to God, I'll see you dead!" Jud screamed.

Bowie just pushed Jud's head a little firmer against the van and yanked his arm a little higher behind his back.

"Well, that was stupid," Bowie said. "You just threatened my life in front of a policeman."

Deputy Ralph cuffed Jud and then pulled him around. "You get the cell next to Junior. I think he'll be glad to see you. Jail isn't anything like home."

Jud was so shocked that he was actually in handcuffs that he began to stumble and stammer.

"Oh, well, y'all know I didn't mean it. I was just pissed off about Junior being in jail. How about we let bygones be bygones?"

Bowie's eyes narrowed. "Do you remember Mama begging you to stop your sons from beating me?"

Jud's face paled, but Bowie kept talking. "I remember. I couldn't see you because my eyes were swollen shut, but I heard you laugh and call her a whore."

A couple had come out of Granny's, saw what was happening, and stayed to watch. It was the beginning of the crowd that was gathering.

Jud was embarrassed to be seen in this situation and started shouting again. "So you're out for revenge?"

Bowie shook his head. "I already told you why I came. And when I'm done with Gran's house, I'll be gone. You started this again without taking one thing into consideration. I was only a kid when you ran me and Mama out of town. I'm not a kid anymore, and you bit off more than you can chew and swallow here, old man. You figure all this out with the judge. Maybe he'll give you and your grandson a bargain…like a two-for-one deal."

"I didn't touch you," Jud said. "You can't put someone in jail for arguing."

Then Mercy stepped out of the crowd. "Jud Boone tried to start a fight in Granny's, and this man stopped him and dragged him out without disturbing any of the diners. I was watching from the window after they left. Jud kept trying to fight, and this man just kept stopping him without fighting back."

Jud glared at her.

"I'll remember that. I can make you sorry you ever opened your mouth," he yelled.

"You just threatened Mr. James and the police chief's wife in my presence," Deputy Ralph said, and grabbed Jud by the elbow and opened the back door to his cruiser. "Watch your head," he added, then shut the door and drove off with his prisoner.

Bowie was beginning to doubt his ability to stay out of trouble long enough to finish what he'd come to do. And the crowd from inside Granny's was staring at him again. He'd had enough.

"Didn't your parents ever tell you it's rude to stare at people? How many of you are thinking about taking a swing at me when my back is turned again?"

Shock spread across their faces, and then they all began talking at once.

"No, never."

"Sorry for staring."

"No, we're sorry."

"It wasn't that!"

Then one old man spoke up. "I'm sorry, sir. I remember you and your mama…a real sweet girl. But you don't look the same. You look so much like Jud Boone looked when he was young that I thought I was seeing things."

Bowie shrugged, but at least now he got the reason for the stares. "Think what it's like to be me. I look in a mirror and see the devil."

Then he got in his car and drove out of the parking lot. It was time to get the girls.

Ella James was pinning up her mother's long braid into a little doughnut shape at the back of her head. Pearl's hair had turned completely white the year Billie Jo committed suicide, and she'd never been the same. This setback with the flood had taken her mother all the way down.

Twenty-five-year-old Rowan Harper, the girl kneeling at Pearl's feet, was also a hurricane refugee who'd lost everything. The county sheriff had picked her up on a road where she'd been walking, and when he heard her story, he called the director of the nursing home in Blessings to see if he had room for one more refugee. After he was assured there was a room for her, he'd taken her to Blessings and dropped her off where people were sent to die, arriving at her temporary lodgings with nothing but the clothes on her back.

Ella and Pearl had taken to her, and after a week together, they'd become each other's family. This morning, Rowan was tying the laces on Pearl's tennis shoes, while Ella was still working on her mama's hair. It took a village to get the old woman dressed these days. She'd sunk into a depression that no amount of distraction could change.

Rowan rocked back on her heels when she was finished and patted Pearl's leg. "Did I get them too tight, honey?"

"No, dear, they're just fine. Thank you," she said.

As Rowan went to make up Pearl's bed, she couldn't help but remember doing this for her father every day. The loss of him was still fresh and painful, and she kept blinking away tears. Hurricane Fanny had not only washed away their home, but taken her daddy with it.

When Pearl and Ella offered her a place to live with them, she cried from the relief. Only right now, everything was on hold, because they had nowhere else to go, either.

Rowan finished with the bed and was going into the bathroom to clean it when a man's deep voice interrupted the silence.

"There are my girls," he said.

She heard Ella gasp, and Pearl let out a cry of such joy and then begin to weep.

Rowan only got a glimpse of the giant of a man walking in before Ella was in his arms. He was laughing and hugging her so tight that he swung her off her feet.

For a moment, Rowan wondered what it would feel like to be loved like that, watching Pearl flying out of her chair crying and laughing. "You came, you came! Ella said you would."

Bowie held out one arm. "Come here, Gran. I need a hug from you, too."

Pearl fell into his arms.

So, he's Pearl's grandson.

Rowan could see that he mattered greatly to them and stood quietly, watching the reunion and their joy with only a brief flash of envy. Then, as if sensing he was being watched, the man looked up and saw her. She caught a flash of something beyond curiosity, and then it was gone.

Bowie was so happy to see his family that it took a bit for him to realize there was another woman in the room. He knew he was staring, but didn't look away.

She was young and leggy, like a colt, and with a lot of long hair as dark as her eyes, wearing a pair of worn-out shorts and a green T-shirt about two sizes too large. Her feet were bare, and there was sadness on her face, even though she smiled at him.

Bowie smiled back. "Hey, Aunt Ella, why don't you introduce me to your friend?"

Ella frowned. "Oh, where are my manners? Rowan, this is my nephew, Bowie James. His mother, Billie Jo, was my younger sister. Bowie, this is Rowan Harper. She's in the same predicament Mama and I are, only she lost her daddy *and* her home in the flood."

"A pleasure to meet you, Rowan Harper. My condolences on your losses. That hurricane was a bad one."

"Yes, it was," Rowan said. "Thank you for the sympathy. It is a pleasure to meet you, too."

Pearl patted Bowie's arm. "When we get our house fixed, Rowan is coming to live with us. She doesn't have anything or anybody left, and we have those two extra bedrooms."

Bowie blinked. This certainly added a hitch to his

plans, but what the heck. He had the extra sleeping space, and it wouldn't be for that long. He couldn't take the girls and leave her behind.

"That sounds like an answer to everyone's prayers," Bowie said. "So, Gran, I haven't seen the house yet. Is it locked?"

Ella nodded. "Yes, wait a second and I'll get the key."

She got her purse from the small closet, dug through the contents, and pulled out a key ring and handed it over.

"It's the gold one, and it's going to take you a while to fix the mess that house is in. Oh…you should also know that right after the floodwaters went down, some people from church came to the house and helped Mama and me pack up what hadn't been ruined. We got some clothing, our business papers, the pots and pans, of course, and also my granny's sideboard and the family silver. It's all in storage here in town. Whatever is still in the house is to be thrown away."

"Good to know. And it's not going to take as long as you think," Bowie said. "I brought one of my best work crews with me. They'll be staying in the local bed-and-breakfast while we're here, and I am taking all three of you to stay with me in my motor home until we're done. No more nursing home."

When Pearl's eyes welled, Bowie hugged her again. "Don't cry, Gran. I'll fix the house. But you all need to know that there may be some more trouble while I'm here."

Ella frowned. "What do you mean, more trouble?"

Bowie ran a hand through his hair in frustration. "I only arrived here last night, and in that short length of time, I have had three run-ins with the Boones, so be prepared. As long as I'm here, Jud isn't going to let anything rest, although he'll have to get out of jail to do it."

Ella gasped. "Jud Boone is in jail? What did he do to you?"

"Emmitt's oldest boy is in jail, too, Mel is probably drinking meals for a while, and Emmitt's nose is broken," Bowie said.

Rowan eyed the width of Bowie James's shoulders, the muscles visible beneath his shirt, and the size of his hands, and guessed the Boones, whoever they were, might have come off luckier than they knew.

Pearl wasn't amused. "I won't stand for any of this," she said. "It's Jud's fault Billie Jo took you and ran away in the middle of the night. I never saw her again. I'll be having something to say to him myself, if he starts this old feud up all over again."

"What feud?" Rowan asked.

Pearl threw up her hands in disgust. "Oh, it's so stupid, and it began three generations back. My father and Jud's father were sort of friends, but always in competition, and they loved the same girl. The animosity grew when the girl chose my father instead of Jud's father. And then even though Jud's father later married someone else, the hard feelings grew between them, and he passed it down to his children. Any chance Mr. Boone had to cause trouble for my daddy, he didn't hesitate to take it."

Bowie stopped her. "You can finish this ugly saga for Rowan later. How about I get you all out of here? How long will it take you to pack?"

"We have one suitcase between Mama and me," Ella said.

"I don't feel right intruding on you," Rowan said. "I accepted these sweet ladies' generosity, but it does not mean you should pick up the slack. I'm sure the director will let me stay until you repair the house."

"No, ma'am," Bowie said. "I came to rescue my girls, and the way I look at it, you're the bonus I didn't know was coming. Now I repeat… How long will it take you to pack?"

Rowan felt like Pearl. She wanted to cry from the joy and relief of not being left behind.

"Everything I have will fit in a grocery sack," she said.

"Then let's get crackin'," Bowie said. "I already met with the director and told him you all were leaving, so there's nothing left to do but take you away."

What had begun as just another day had turned into a rescue, and a family reunion for Ella and Gran.

But for Rowan, it was a whole other thing. It hadn't taken her long to go from curiosity about the stranger to having something of a crush. She'd always dreamed of the knight-in-shining-armor version of true love, and he was certainly a good example of that. Even though she'd known him less than fifteen minutes, and she'd turned out to be the unexpected guest at the shelter he was offering, she wasn't going to turn down the first ray of hope she'd had since before the storm.

Chapter 3

BOWIE FELT LIKE SANTA CLAUS AS HE CARRIED THEIR belongings to his Cherokee. The girls were behind him, chattering among themselves, obviously relieved that their lives had just taken a turn for the better. He was putting their things in the back when Pearl frowned and then pointed to the deep gouges on both sides of his car.

"Bowie! Your car! What happened here?"

"That's why Emmitt Boone's oldest boy is in jail. He keyed it this morning. It set off the car alarm, and he got caught."

"Why would he do something like this?" Pearl asked.

"Get in, and I'll tell you on the way," he said.

They all piled into the vehicle. Ella and Pearl got in the back seat so they could sit together, which left Rowan in the front seat beside Bowie.

"Now, tell me about those scratches," Pearl said.

"As I was leaving Granny's last night, Mel and Emmitt jumped me in the parking lot. I don't know how they found out that I was in town so fast, but there they were. One of them had a baseball bat. The other one, brass knuckles. Stuff happened. Mel went down face-first and most likely will be swallowing nothing but liquids for a while. Emmitt went home with a broken nose. I guess he raised enough hell about it after he got home…excuse my language…that it fired up his boy to enact his own little version of retribution."

Ella snorted. "Stuff happened. I'll bet it did, if you laid both of them out without suffering so much as a bruise. You haven't changed a lick. You never lied. Not once that I knew of when you were a kid, but you were the best at omitting details."

He grinned. "Buckle up," he said as he started the engine and drove away. "Oh…hey, Aunt Ella, I've been wondering what happened to your car. Was it a victim of the hurricane, too?"

"Yes, it floated away. They found it about a mile outside of town, caught beneath a bridge. Insurance company sent money. It's not enough to buy a new car, of course, but it's in the bank. We'll figure something out after we're home again."

Bowie was listening, but he was also looking for the vehicles his work crew would be in. When he saw all three of them parked at Granny's, one towing the trailer with the tools, he knew they'd already checked in at the bed-and-breakfast. He'd meet up with them shortly, and they'd go through the house together.

Ella was pointing out flood damage to her mother and bemoaning the loss of big trees and landscaping throughout Blessings. But Rowan was noticeably silent.

Bowie glanced at her once and thought he saw tears in her eyes. He felt true empathy for her situation. He knew what it felt like to lose your footing in the world. The farther he drove, the quieter all three of them became, until he drove into the trailer park and stopped at the red-and-black motor home.

"This is yours?" Rowan asked.

"Lordy be, Bowie," Gran said.

"This must have cost a fortune," Ella said.

"It's the only home I own," Bowie said. "I'm never in one place long enough, so I take my comfort with me."

"Ah...I don't think I knew that," Pearl said. "I know when we do that FaceTime thing on the phone, you're always on a jobsite. I just didn't think."

Bowie grinned. "If you think the outside is fancy, wait until you get inside. Now let's get in out of the heat."

They piled out of the car, excited and talking again as they walked up the little path to the door. Bowie turned off the security system, unlocked the door, then stepped aside to help them up the steps. Once they were in, he ran back to get their things.

All three of them were still standing in the middle of the living room, huddled together without moving, when he got back.

"What's wrong?" he asked, and set their things on the sofa.

Ella kept shaking her head in disbelief. "It's so grand...marble countertops, white cabinets, that gold-flecked backsplash."

"And the furniture," Gran said. "It all looks so, so—"

"Homey?" Bowie asked.

"Yes!" they echoed.

He grinned. "I told you this was my home. Gran, you and Aunt Ella will be sharing my bedroom and the private bath. Rowan, that sofa behind you turns into a full-size bed for you."

"But where will you sleep?" she asked.

"That bench seating on the far side of the dining table pulls out to a bed as well."

"Then that's the one I'm sleeping in," she said. "I appreciate your offer of the full-size bed, but I think we all agree that you aren't going to come close to fitting on that other one, and I will, with room to spare."

"We'll see," he said. "If you can prove to me that you won't fall out in the night, then okay."

Rowan put her hands on her hips in a sudden gesture of defiance. "I don't have to prove anything to you, mister. I'm sleeping in that bed or walking back to the nursing home."

Bowie blinked.

Ella grinned at the look on Bowie's face and guessed not very many people told him no. "Oh…didn't we mention our girl Rowan has a mind of her own?"

"No, ma'am, you did not," Bowie said, and then laughed. "Point taken, Miss Rowan."

Now that beds were sorted out, he left the suitcase and his girls exclaiming again at the elegant decor and gave Rowan the small sack she'd brought with her.

"Is that all you have?" Bowie asked.

She nodded. "It's enough. I'll be getting my daddy's retirement pension next month. It took a while for the paperwork to go through. I'll get some more things when I have a place to put them."

"Then let me show you where the pantry is. It's well stocked, but after I get the crew started at the house, I'll come back and take whoever wants to go shopping to the Piggly Wiggly. We'll stock up on what everybody needs."

Rowan nodded. "Thank you. I really appreciate your kindness."

"And I appreciate how you've obviously been helping Aunt Ella take care of my gran."

Rowan shrugged. "It was an easy choice. They are

both wonderful women, and I haven't seen Pearl this happy since I've known her. You are a really special grandson to be doing this for them."

"They helped raise me. They're all the family I have."

Before Rowan could respond, Pearl and Ella came back into the living room.

"This is the most wonderful day we've had in years," Pearl said. "You have grown into a fine man, Bowie James. Your mama would be proud."

"Thanks, Gran. While you three settle in, I'm going to get my crew and take them to the house to begin demo. Poke around to your hearts' content. I'll be back later."

"Do what you have to do," Gran said. "We'll be fine."

"One other thing, Aunt Ella. Did you lose your phone in the flood, too?" Bowie asked.

Ella nodded.

"Then we'll get you another. I need to be able to keep tabs on you two. Here you were, going through that hurricane, and I was up on a mountain in Tennessee, building my client a fifteen-thousand-square-foot mansion, hardly aware there was even a hurricane, let alone that Blessings was in its path."

Rowan's eyes widened. "Did you say 'fifteen thousand'?"

He grinned. "Yes. It was a monster of a house."

Then he gave them both a quick goodbye peck on the cheek and Rowan a thumbs-up. He was on the way out the door when he stopped.

"Someone come lock up behind me."

"I will," Rowan said.

He closed the door behind him, then drove away as Rowan turned the lock.

"Well now," Ella said. "I think our Bowie has certainly landed on his feet. I knew he was successful, but I did not know it was at this level."

"We have a job to do while he's gone," Rowan said. "We're going to the Piggly Wiggly for whatever we need when he comes back. I thought maybe we should make a list."

Bowie called his crew chief, Ray Tuttle, on the way and found out they were getting ready to leave.

"I'll meet up with you in the parking lot. You can follow me to the jobsite."

"Will do," Ray said, then disconnected.

"Was that Bowie?" Joe asked.

Ray nodded at his brother. "He's meeting us outside. Let's hustle."

Matt Roller took his last sip of coffee. Presley Smith left the tip. Samuel Hooper had a biscuit in his hand, reluctant to leave it behind, and Walter Adams took off to the restroom. As soon as he was back, the six-man crew trooped through the dining area and paid on the way out. Bowie was already waiting.

They loaded up and followed. He turned off Main Street a couple of blocks later and led them through a neighborhood of old homes, most of which were ranch-style brick or Craftsman style, although there were a few that would once have been considered quite grand.

The closer Bowie came to the turn, the more his heart began to pound. The last time he'd been in this place, his eyes were swollen shut and he'd needed stitches in both his head and his lip, but his mother was too afraid to stay in Blessings to take him to the doctor there and was going to stop in another town. He had two broken ribs and one broken finger from Randall Boone stomping his hand. He'd had so many wounds and contusions that the simple act of getting into the car that night had made him cry out in pain.

He'd heard his Aunt Ella and Gran crying and saying goodbye to him and his mom, but he couldn't see them, or her. All he knew was that she was sobbing as the car began to move.

When he drove up on the street and signaled a left turn, the hair rose on the back of his neck. Bowie hated that momentary memory of fear, and he reminded himself he was no longer helpless.

I am not that boy. I am a man. I have conquered mountains to do my job. No old man, or the people he bred, have any power over me.

Then he saw the white, single-story house with a big front porch. The last place he'd called home. A sudden spurt of tears blurred his vision, but he quickly blinked them away and began looking at the house from the standpoint of a builder.

She wasn't in the best of shape and, due to the flood, was wearing what looked like a rusty-red petticoat beneath a white, tattered dress. New siding would fix that. He pulled up to the curb, then jumped out and told his crew to leave the driveway open because he had a roll-off, one of the long, dumpster-style bins, being delivered today. He grabbed a mask from the console, waved it at them to do the same, and then led them to the house.

"So this is it? The house you grew up in?" Ray asked.

Bowie nodded. "Let's get inside and see what we're dealing with. The house is bigger than it looks from the street. Four bedrooms, a big kitchen and dining room, a big living room, and a decent-size utility room off the kitchen."

"How many bathrooms?" Joe asked.

"One. It was built in the late forties. At the time, indoor plumbing was still a luxury," Bowie said, and got the house key out of his pocket as he walked up onto the porch.

The boards sagged a little from his weight. Definitely needed new decking on the porch. The door stuck when he tried to open it. After he used a little shoulder action, the door broke free, and swung inward.

Bowie groaned. "Lord Almighty, I smell the mold from here. Mask up, guys. This isn't going to be pretty."

There was a good inch of Georgia silt on the floors, left behind by the receding flood, and white mold growing on anything made of wood.

"I ordered a roll-off. It should have been here already. Give me a sec to check."

He stepped back outside and made the call. "This is Bowie James. I'm on site waiting for the first of three roll-off containers to be delivered to an address in Blessings today. Can you give me a heads-up as to when I can expect it?"

He waited a few moments for the clerk to pull up the work order, and then he was back online. "It should already be there," he said.

"Well, it's—" Then they all heard a big vehicle shifting gears, and turned in unison. "Oh. Wait. Never mind. The driver is just pulling up," Bowie said, and disconnected.

After a discussion with the driver as to where Bowie wanted it, it took another fifteen minutes of some fancy driving for the trucker to get the long container backed up into the driveway and then unhooked.

Bowie signed for the delivery. "You're based out of Savannah, right?"

"Yes, sir," the driver said.

"Okay. I have two more of these on order, so do you do same-day pickup and delivery, or next-day?"

"Almost always same-day, unless we'd happen to have a truck down or be short a driver or two for the day."

"Good enough," Bowie said. "I'll probably be calling you soon to pick up and deliver another one, but I'll know more after we empty out the contents before we begin demo."

"Just give us a call," the driver added, and got in his truck and drove away.

"Okay, guys, get at it. And…if you find any secret stashes, do me a favor and save them for me."

Samuel grinned. "So, you're saying no finders, keepers here."

Bowie laughed. "That's exactly what I'm saying. Ray, you're the ramrod. Call me if you run into any kind of problems. If you find asbestos, or the roof appears to be falling in on top of you. You know the drill."

"Will do, Boss," Ray said.

"I have to make sure my family is settling in and pick up some more groceries. Call me if you have a question about anything, and I'll be back as soon as I can," Bowie said, and opened up the endgate on the roll-up before he left.

—ᴧᴧᴧ—

Peanut Butterman was in his law office working on a brief when the outer door to his office suddenly slammed. He sat there a moment, listening, and heard his secretary, Betty, trying to reason with someone.

"No, that's not happening," Peanut muttered, and strode out of his office.

"I'm sorry, Mr. Butterman," Betty said.

Peanut arched an eyebrow. "For what, Betty? I didn't hear you shouting." Then he shifted focus and stared the couple down without saying a word, taking note of the broken nose Emmitt was sporting.

Finally, Emmitt Boone spoke up. "Me and my wife, Tiny, need to hire you."

"It's a matter of life and death," Tiny said. She squeezed out a single tear, then dabbed it before it messed up her makeup.

"Who's in danger of dying?" Peanut asked.

Tiny continued the explanation. "Papa Boone! He's too old to be in jail. And my boy, Junior, is too young."

Both of Peanut's eyebrows arched. "They're both in jail?"

Now that they had his attention, Tiny turned on the waterworks.

"My little boy is in jail for hardly any reason at all, and Papa Boone didn't lay a hand on anyone, and he's in jail, too."

Peanut sighed. "Come into my office to discuss this."

Satisfied they'd gotten what they wanted, Tiny smirked at Betty as they passed her desk.

"Please sit down," Peanut said, and waited for them

to be seated. But instead of sitting in his chair on the other side of his desk, he stood between them and the desk, then leaned against it and crossed his arms.

"First, I want to know why your son is in jail."

Emmitt shrugged. "He keyed someone's car."

"Why would he do that? Didn't you tell him damaging or destroying other people's property is against the law?"

"The man broke my poor Emmitt's nose!" Tiny screeched. "My boy was just upset and felt obliged to seek retribution on his father's behalf. It says in the Bible, an eye for an eye!"

"Who broke your nose, Emmitt?"

Emmitt shifted nervously. "A man named Bowie James, that's who."

Peanut frowned. "Why do I know that name? It seems very familiar," he said.

Tiny glanced nervously at Emmitt.

"Hang on a second. I'm going to ask Betty. She remembers names better than I do."

He strode to the door, and then opened it. "Hey, Betty. Does the name Bowie James mean anything to you?"

Betty rolled her eyes. "Well, yes. That's Pearl James's grandson. You remember Billie Jo, right?"

And just like that, Peanut got it. "Oh, yes…right. Thank you," he said, and closed the door before resuming his post. The look he gave both of the Boones was expressionless.

"Regardless of what happened, I am sorry to inform you that I will not be able to represent you regarding either one of your family members. Pearl and Ella James are two of my clients, so that would be a conflict of interest. I'm sure you understand."

Tiny started to cry, but not genteel tears this time. She turned loose the ugly cry. "My son is going to have to spend the night in jail! I can't bear it!"

"He's just paying the price for his crime," Peanut said. He strode back to the door and opened it wide.

"Get up, Tiny!" Emmett muttered. "You heard him." Then he grabbed her by the arm and hauled her to her feet. He took off out the door without waiting for her, leaving Tiny to pass by Betty's desk once more, a chastened and weepy mess.

As soon as they were out of the office, Betty unloaded.

"I heard all about it at Granny's this morning. I don't know what happened between Emmitt and the James man, but I do know Emmitt wasn't alone. Everyone is saying he and Mel jumped Bowie when he came out of Granny's last night. And my friend Julie, who lives out in the trailer park where Bowie James parked his motor home, says Junior Boone keyed Bowie's car something awful, just before daylight. The car had an alarm, and Bowie heard it and ran Junior down. Tasered him and called the cops. Julie also said it was gonna take thousands of dollars to fix it.

"Then Jud Boone caught Bowie at Granny's this morning where he'd gone to eat breakfast, and tried to pick a fight with him inside Granny's. They said Bowie asked Mercy Pittman to call the police, then took Jud by the arm and led him out into the parking lot to keep him from tearing up the place. Only everyone in Granny's came out to see what was going on. Bowie had Jud subdued, and he was furious. He kept saying he was going to kill Bowie and kept trying to swing at him, but Bowie held him down. The cops came, and when Mercy spoke up for Bowie, Jud subtly threatened her life, too. Deputy Ralph cuffed him, reminded Jud that he'd threatened to kill Bowie, and threatened the police chief's wife in front of a sworn officer of the law, and that he was going to jail, too. That's what is going on."

"All of this happened in less than twenty-four hours?" Peanut asked.

"Yes. And all because Bowie came back to renovate Pearl's home. It was one of the ones that flooded bad."

"Good lord," Peanut muttered. "Looks like I might wind up in the middle of this after all, if they continue to harass the James family."

Betty sniffed. "At least you'd be on the right side."

Peanut sighed. "I'll have that brief ready for you shortly."

"Yes, sir," Betty said, and went back to work.

Peanut shut himself in his office.

And Emmitt and Tiny were on their way to Savannah to find a lawyer, with the day fading fast.

Bowie pulled up at his motor home and got out. He was almost at the steps when he heard a laugh that cut to his core. He knew it was Rowan. He didn't know what had made her laugh like that, but it was such a joyful belly laugh that he was already grinning when he unlocked the door and walked in.

The trio was sitting at the dining table, playing cards. Ella looked up and waved.

"You're back! Thank God. We're playing strip poker, and I'm losing."

He grinned. His aunt Ella was missing both shoes and her skirt. Luckily for all of them, she still favored slips.

But it was Rowan who startled him most. The quiet, dark-eyed beauty was doubled over with laughter, and every time she looked up at Pearl, she started laughing all over again.

Pearl was blushing. "It's not funny, missy. Just because you're still wearing all of your underwear doesn't mean you shouldn't worry."

Rowan couldn't even look up. She just rolled out of her chair onto the floor, laughing until tears were running down her face.

Pearl slapped the cards she was holding facedown on the table and pointed at Rowan.

"Bowie, take this snippet with you to Piggly Wiggly so we can put our clothes back on. I've never played such a game in my life."

Ella laughed. "Mama, don't lie. I remember you and Daddy playing this after you put me to bed."

Pearl gasped and then blushed again. "Well, never mind."

Rowan groaned. "Oh my God…somebody help me up. I can't breathe," she said, and then covered her face.

Bowie couldn't take his eyes off her…flat on her back on his floor, so gloriously sexy he could hardly think.

"Well, get her up and out of here," Pearl said, and then hid a grin. Even she was entranced by the unexpected delight.

Bowie moved toward Rowan. When she held up her hand, he grasped her by the wrist, her hand engulfed within his fist, and pulled her upright.

"Thank you," Rowan said, and then turned loose of him and ran around the table to hug Pearl. "I'm sorry, sweetie, but thank you for the first joy I've felt since before the storm."

Pearl kissed the side of Rowan's cheek and hugged her back. "I'm happy to have been of service."

Rowan started giggling again. "I need my shoes. I think I left them in the master bedroom. I'll be right back," she said, and bolted toward the back of the motor home.

Bowie was a dedicated bachelor with an image to protect, but they had yet to pass one night under the same roof, and he was already feeling a complication in his life that he didn't need.

"I'm back," Rowan said, and snagged their grocery list from the table.

"Then I guess we're off," Bowie said. "You sure you two don't want to come with us?"

Ella shook her head. "I guess we'll pass. I'm not dressed, and Mama isn't wearing underwear, so there's that."

Rowan was still giggling when she got in the front seat with Bowie and buckled up.

"Oh my word...I didn't know I could still laugh. That was the best medicine ever," she said, and then burst into tears and started apologizing.

Bowie handed her a pack of tissues from the console. "Honey, don't apologize. I grew up with three women. There's little I haven't already seen or heard about." Then he grinned. "I can't believe you got Gran to play strip poker."

"It was Ella's suggestion, and then she kept losing. Pearl is the one who made me laugh, though. I guess she figured if she shed her drawers, she could still maintain her dignity…unlike Ella, who just peeled stuff off as she went."

Now Bowie was chuckling, imagining Gran getting up and taking off her panties.

"What did she do with them?" he asked.

"She heard you drive up and sat on them," Rowan said. "That's when I burst out laughing."

That image was too priceless to ignore. Bowie laughed all the way to the Piggly Wiggly.

Right before they got out, Bowie paused. "I don't know what's on the list, but if you have things you need that you might be embarrassed about, I can easily wait up front and just pay when you're finished."

Rowan shrugged. "Mama died when I was ten. Daddy raised me. He's the one who told me about the birds and the bees and all the girl stuff. I'm used to shopping for all that with a man, so I'm fine if you are."

"Then we're good," Bowie said. "Remember…three women and me."

Rowan grinned. "We're quite a pair, aren't we?" she said, and jumped out. He got out and followed her into the store, trying not to think about what it would be like to be part of her world.

Chapter 4

Bowie grabbed the shopping cart. "You have the list, so I'll just follow you."

Rowan nodded, then looked up at him with such delight. "I haven't done this since before the storm."

"You mean, buy groceries?" Bowie asked as she started down the produce aisle.

"No, just being out in the world doing normal stuff. It is an empowering feeling not to feel helpless anymore. Pearl offering me a home again was huge, but the chance of it being fixed was slim to none, so all three of us were in a kind of limbo, you know?"

"I can only imagine," he said, absently watching the way her hands moved over the apples, then the pears, as if there were an inner radar to choosing the right ones. Then he cued back in to the fact she was still talking.

"Then you showed up, and the promise of a home became a fact. You are a wonderful grandson to do this," she said, then pointed to a display of peaches. "Oh, look. Nothing better than Georgia peaches. Do you like cobblers?" she asked.

"Do dogs have fleas? Yes, ma'am, I like cobblers."

Rowan grinned. "They aren't on the list, but I'd make a cobbler for dinner one night, if you have bakeware for that."

Bowie grabbed a plastic bag from the dispenser and

opened it. "I have bakeware I've never used. How many peaches do you need?"

She picked one up and lifted it to her nose. "Umm, just smell that. You can always tell when peaches are going to taste good by the way they smell. The peachier the smell, the sweeter the peach."

"I didn't know that," Bowie said.

Rowan nodded. "Stick with me, dude. I know all kinds of useless information. You might not be able to use it to build one of your big, fancy houses, but next time you'll know what kind of peaches make the best pies."

Bowie was in trouble, and he knew it. She was oblivious to her beauty and uninhibited to a fault. Enchanting? Yes, that was the word. A dark-eyed enchantress who was tempting him with peaches, like Eve tempted Adam with that apple.

He shook off the thought and tried to focus on the task at hand. "How many peaches do you need to make a cobbler?"

"Mmmm, about ten of those, I think, and pick the ones that are verging on overripe because—"

He interrupted. "Let me guess. Because they cook up better than the ones that are still firm?"

She looked up, then grinned. "Don't give me that poker-face look. You're a ringer, aren't you? You already knew all this stuff, and you're just letting me rattle. That's okay. At least now I know not to play cards with you."

"Not even strip poker?" he asked.

Her eyes narrowed. "Do you have oatmeal in your pantry?"

He blinked. That conversation had ended abruptly. Maybe it was something he said.

"No, should I?"

"Your gran loves her breakfast oatmeal."

He stopped, thinking back to the years of growing up in that house, and suddenly remembered. "With raisins cooked in it, right?"

"That's what she asked for every morning at the nursing home."

"Then we not only need oatmeal, but we need to get raisins, too," Bowie said.

"Okay, then we go this way," Rowan said, and took off down an aisle, leaving him to follow her with the cart.

She shopped. Bowie tried to follow but was stopped often by people he barely remembered but who had known his mother and had watched him grow up. He'd forgotten how swiftly news traveled in small towns, especially when the news was bad. They had already heard about his run-ins with the Boones, expressed their dismay that the incidents had happened, and praised him for coming to fix his grandma's home.

Finally, Rowan slipped the cart out of his hands and took off down another aisle, leaving him caught between the cereal aisle and a woman he'd gone to school with. At the point she pulled out her phone and started showing him pictures of her kids, he made the appropriate comments and excused himself to go look for Rowan.

When he found her in the dairy section at the back of the store, he walked up behind her and tugged on the back of her hair.

"Don't ever do that again," he muttered.

She turned around, and she was grinning. "Do what?"

"You know," Bowie said.

"They're your friends, Bowie. They're glad to see you, so be nice."

He sighed. "You're right. I guess I've been alone too long, and it sure beats the welcome I got from the Boones. So what are we buying here?"

"I don't know. I'm just looking, trying to remember what was in your refrigerator."

"About half a quart of milk with a week-old expiration date, some longnecks, and the usual condiments. I know I'm out of eggs. Not much cheese, if any, and no lunch meat. And no meat. But I don't expect you guys to cook meals for me. Just buy what you like to feed yourselves, and when I'm home in time, we can always go to Granny's."

"Don't take away Ella and Pearl's right to baby their boy," she said. "I've never seen them so happy."

Bowie frowned. "I didn't think about that."

Rowan patted his arm. "Don't feel bad. You wouldn't be expected to. Most women like to do things for the people they love. It's part of who we are. In their eyes, you have saved them from a fate worse than death. You are the hero putting their world back together. Let them cook for you."

"How did you get so wise?" he asked.

Her dark eyes filled with tears. "It's the way of a woman to know things...and I remember the special things I used to do for Dad."

Bowie saw the tears. The brief elation she'd experienced was gone. The girl he'd first met was back. The quiet one with the sad eyes.

"I'm sorry," he said.

Rowan nodded. "Me, too."

There was an uneasy moment of silence, and then she chose a couple of items from the dairy case. Bowie added three quarts of different flavors of ice cream, and then they moved to the meat department.

"We need a couple pounds of hamburger meat for sure, and then you choose the meat you like, and we'll cook it."

Bowie started putting in packages of chicken pieces, pork chops, steaks, and sausage.

Rowan eyed the assortment, remembered the large two-drawer freezer at the bottom of his refrigerator, and decided there was room for all that and more. At that point, the shopping was finished in relative silence.

They were on their way across the parking lot when a car pulled up behind them, then honked.

Bowie glanced over his shoulder. "Damn it," he muttered, and pushed the cart aside, hoping the driver would pass.

But she didn't. She put the car in Park and got out.

Bowie remembered her as really pretty, but the years of being married to Judson Boone appeared to have been hard on Cora. Her hair was gray and thinning, and the world-weary look in her eyes told the rest.

"Mrs. Boone," Bowie said.

Cora walked to the front of her car, then stopped. She opened her mouth to speak, then stopped. She had to take a breath and start over before words would come out.

"Bowie James?"

"Yes, ma'am?"

"They said you looked like my Jud, but I didn't

believe it. And yet here you stand, looking at me like the ghost of the man I married—not the way he is now. I need to apologize for so much. Will you allow me that much?"

"I'm listening," he said.

Cora was shaking. She needed to get this said before she passed out.

"Back when that terrible thing happened to your mother, I saw her poor face and the wounds on her body when she was still in the hospital. I went home and asked Randall if it was true. Did he really hurt her like that? He swore on his deathbed that it was a lie. I told myself Randall wouldn't lie to me." A single tear rolled down her cheek. "But now I know he did, and he went to his death with that lie on his conscience. You can't wear that face and not be my grandson, which leads me to what I have yet to process. I can't wrap my head around what Judson and my sons did to you. You were just a boy, innocent of the hate between both families. They all knew the truth about your mama and still did that, didn't they?"

Bowie felt sorry for her. "I can't speak for them or what they were thinking, other than knowing they hated me for being born and wanted me gone."

Rowan walked up behind him, then held out her hand. Bowie dropped the keys in her palm and relinquished the cart, leaving her to get the groceries loaded.

Cora couldn't quit staring. "They said you came back to fix up Pearl's house."

"Yes, ma'am. That's true."

Cora looked at the red Cherokee a few yards away, wincing when she saw the huge gouges in the paint and metal.

"I don't believe it's right for people to get away with crimes they commit. My grandson should have known better. And I know why Jud's sitting in jail and won't argue with that, either. But I can promise you now, at this moment, neither me nor mine will bother you again."

The relief of hearing that was huge. He'd been concerned on the girls' behalf, afraid they'd wind up in the middle of some confrontation.

"I thank you for that," Bowie said.

Cora was struggling not to cry. "You're all I have left of Randall, and I don't even know who you are. That's the worst crime of all. Denying blood kin. God forgive me for being so blind."

Then she ducked her head and got back into the car.

Bowie saw her wiping tears, and then she put the car in gear and drove away.

"Damn," he muttered, and turned around. Rowan was already in the Jeep.

He loped across the parking lot and jumped inside, grateful that she'd started the car, because it was already cool.

"Sorry I didn't help you load," he said.

"Are you okay?" she asked.

He nodded, then put the car in gear and took off. He was all the way down Main and getting ready to take the turn to the trailer park before he spoke.

"If she can keep them under her thumb, she promised none of them would be bothering me again."

Rowan tried to read his face, but couldn't. "That's good news for you."

Bowie thought about that a moment and then nodded. "You're right. That *is* good. Good news, indeed."

Rowan leaned back against the seat, letting the cool air blast her in the face. He was a complicated man with a very kind heart.

When Bowie pulled up to the motor home again and killed the engine, he handed her the keys. "If you'll unlock the door, I'll carry in the groceries."

"Deal," she said, and hopped out, while he went to the back seat and began grabbing sacks

He walked in carrying two handfuls of sacks, set them down on the counter, and then jogged back out to get the rest. The girls were already putting things away when he set the last sacks down.

"Are you guys good to go for a while?" he asked.

"Yes, we're not only fine, we're wonderful. You're wonderful," Pearl said.

Bowie smiled. "Thanks, Gran. I'm going to go back to the house and help with demo. I'll be home around five thirty or six, okay?"

They nodded.

He watched Rowan making herself scarce and said nothing. She'd gone back into her shell again.

"Aunt Ella, I'll get you a new phone tomorrow. You guys rest, watch TV, whatever you want to do, and if you play any more strip poker, make sure the blinds are down."

They were still giggling as he walked out the door.

The heat was already bearing down, and it wasn't yet noon. Bowie stopped at a bait and beer shack to pick up some ice for the cooler in the back of the Cherokee, along with some cartons of bottled water. As soon as he had some of the bottles iced down, he shut the hatch and jumped back inside, anxious to get to the jobsite.

He kept thinking about the changes Gran wanted done to the house and was reminding himself of all the details that would need to be addressed to rearrange the layout.

Bowie rarely took renovation jobs. Nearly all of them were new builds, but this was different. This was home, and the fact that they were tearing out what had been familiar was something he would have to face.

He parked at the curb, grabbed a mask and his work gloves, and took the cooler to beside the house, leaving it in the shade beneath a tree.

Joe and Ray were carrying out a moldy mattress from one of the bedrooms as Bowie masked up again. One glance at the debris piling up in the big bin, and he could already see how hard they'd been working.

The brothers had walked back up onto the porch as he was about to go inside.

"Did you get your family settled?" Ray asked.

Bowie nodded. "They're a little more than I expected. One extra woman, not related, and pretty to boot. I walked in on the three of them playing strip poker. It was a sight to behold."

They burst out laughing, just as Samuel came out carrying an armful of moldy bath towels.

"What's so funny?" he asked.

"They're just laughing at a joke on me," Bowie said as he was pulling on his gloves. "I'm going in."

He stepped across the threshold, then stopped in his tracks. The front room was empty of furniture. Even the mud-stained and moldy drapes had been pulled down. He'd never seen the room bare. Three generations of furniture and the energy of the people who'd lived here were gone.

"It's a mess, Boss," Ray said.

Bowie shuddered. That was an understatement. The pain of loss was brief but sharp, and then they moved on through the house.

Gran's room had already been emptied, and they were all working on Ella's room when he walked in. Matt and Presley were taking down a bed so they could get it through the door and up the hall, and Samuel was pulling a dresser away from the wall. Bowie grabbed one end of the dresser and Samuel the other. And so it began.

Lon Pittman was talking to Avery, his dispatcher, when Cora Boone walked into the station. She didn't look any better than Lon felt about having her husband and grandson in jail.

"Mrs. Boone."

Cora nodded. "Chief Pittman. Might I have a word with you?"

"Absolutely, ma'am. Avery, no calls."

The dispatcher gave him a thumbs-up.

"This way," Lon said, and escorted her down the hall and into his office.

After he seated her, she leaned back in the chair and momentarily closed her eyes.

Lon feared she was about to pass out and quickly offered a drink. "May I offer you a cup of coffee…or maybe water?"

"No, sir, but I thank you for the offer," Cora said.

As Lon sat down, he noticed Cora's shaky fingers curling around the arms, as if needing the familiar to anchor herself in the chair, and then she looked up.

"Chief Pittman, I thank you for seeing me on short notice. I didn't know how these things work regarding prisoners and visitors, but I want you to know that I am humiliated by what my family has done to Bowie James. I have spoken to Bowie and assured him that there will be no more trouble from the Boones, leaving him free to do what he came to do…to put Pearl's house back in order."

"That's good news," Lon said.

"I also want to know when Jud and Junior will be available for bail."

"Court is in session at two this afternoon, so they'll be arraigned then, and charges, if any, will be filed."

Cora took a tissue out of her pocket and mopped the sweat beads on her upper lip.

"If that offer of water is still good, I think I'll take it."

"Yes, ma'am," Lon said. He jumped up and got a cold bottle of water from the mini-fridge behind his desk, and then got a little red plastic cup from the stack on top of the fridge and filled it with cold water.

"Thank you," Cora said, and took several sips before setting it aside. "Okay, so the judge will set bail?"

"Yes, ma'am."

"And when we post bail, they will be released to come home?"

"That's the process," Lon said.

Cora reached for the water and took a few more sips, then surprised Lon by chugging the rest down like a shot of whiskey.

"Now, my last question. Am I allowed to see them?"

"Yes, ma'am. I can take you back."

"Will you stay there while I'm talking to them?"

"I can give you a bit of privacy if—"

"No! You misunderstand. I'm asking you to stay."

"Then I will," Lon said.

"Good. I have a few things to say to them, and I want a witness."

"Yes, ma'am," Lon said, and got up. When he offered his arm, she clutched it like a lifeline as he walked her back to the jail.

Cora's nose wrinkled as they entered. The scent of disinfectant wasn't quite strong enough to mask the old mattresses and open toilets in the cells. She turned loose of the chief, lifted her chin, and strode past the empty cells to the prisoners occupying the last two.

It was the sharp, staccato sound of the little square heels on her sensible shoes that got the two inmates' attention.

Cora saw Junior duck his head, obviously ashamed to be seen in such a state.

But Judson's reaction was just the opposite. He stood up, his hands curled into fists.

"It's about damn time!" Jud shouted.

Cora gasped, as if he had suddenly revealed himself as the monster he was.

"Don't raise your voice to me!" she snapped. "I saw Bowie James today. I know now that Randall lied to me. Mel and Emmitt lied to me. And you lied to me! I am struggling to understand how you thought any part of beating a kid to within an inch of his life absolved your son's guilt."

Jud moved to the front of the cell and grabbed onto the bars. "I never did any—"

"Shut up!" Cora said. "You did, and you know it.

That man is as much my grandson as the little hoodlum in the cell beside you. Today, I told Bowie James no one from this family will be bothering him again."

Jud's face turned a dark, angry red. "You don't speak for—"

The urge to back up from him was strong, but her anger was stronger.

"I won't say this again, so listen closely…both of you. You cause that man even one more minute of grief, and none of you will ever be welcome in my house again."

"It's our house," Jud said.

"No! It's mine! Daddy willed it to me. My name, and my name only, is on the deed. I'm not afraid to be an old divorcée, and I'll be fine giving up my place in this world as wife, mother, and grandmother to every Boone within a hundred-mile radius just to be rid of this shame."

Cora watched the blood draining from her husband's face, and for a few moments, she thought he was going to pass out.

"Cora. Don't do this," Jud said.

"I'm not through talking. I heard the stories of why you are here. You made a pure ass of yourself at Granny's. You threatened Bowie's life this morning. He's our grandson, and you are an abomination in the eyes of God. When I found out that you even threatened the wife of the chief of police, I knew you'd lost your mind."

Lon reeled as if he'd been punched and then walked all the way up to the cell. "You threatened my wife?"

Jud groaned. "I was just mad. I didn't mean it."

Lon took a deep breath. "You actually threatened her life?"

"I popped off," Jud said. "I'm sorry."

"Then let me add a bit of advice to your wife's warning. You don't want to do that again. There are serious consequences to messing with my wife in any way, shape, or form. Do you understand what I'm saying?"

Jud's head was bobbing up and down like a bobblehead doll riding shotgun in a demolition derby.

"I swear, I would never hurt your wife."

"Don't take his word for anything," Cora said. "Our whole marriage is a lie." She shifted her focus back to Jud. "I'll make sure the money is there to bail you both out of jail, but I will never forgive you for what you've done." She turned her back on the cells. "Chief, thank you for your time. I'd like to leave now."

Lon pointed a finger at Jud, then escorted Cora out of the jail, letting the door slam shut on his way out.

Chapter 5

COURT BEGAN AT 2:00 P.M.

Cora was in the courtroom with her purse clutched to her chest, a shield against the curious looks she was getting from everyone in the courtroom.

They called her grandson first and led him up to the judge in handcuffs. Her son, Emmitt, was sitting in front of her, and she could tell by the red flush spreading up the back of his neck that he was scared.

Emmitt, Jr. was shaking as he stood before the judge, listening to the charges against him. When he pled guilty, his bail was set at a thousand dollars.

The tic in her right eye was the only sign of Cora's emotions as they led him away.

The court clerk read the next name aloud. "The court calls Judson Boone to the stand."

Cora didn't even flinch as she watched her husband led up in handcuffs. The judge read off the offenses. Disturbing the peace, and two charges of harassment. He pled guilty, and bail was set at five hundred dollars. They led him out as well.

She had heard enough. Now she knew how much money to draw from their bank account, so she left the courtroom. She'd bail them out, and then she was done.

—⁂—

Later that afternoon, Junior was released on bail into the custody of his parents. It was a silent reunion and an equally silent exit as they left the station.

Mel was in the lobby, waiting to get his daddy and take him back to Granny's to get his car.

When Jud came out and saw his son instead of his wife, he frowned. "Where's your mother?"

"I don't know, Daddy. She put up the bail money and left. I'm taking you to get your car."

Jud retrieved his personal belongings and left the police station, leaving Mel to follow. The ride to Granny's was equally silent, and he got out without thanking his son, got in his car, and headed home. He had a world of talking to do to get off of Cora's hit list.

But when he drove into the yard, there were three suitcases sitting on the porch, along with his three hunting rifles, all of his hunting gear, and a large box.

Jud's gut knotted. She was serious.

He got out of the car with bravado he didn't feel and stomped up on the porch. He glanced down into the box, saw all of his shaving gear and the bottles of medicine he took, and grabbed the doorknob, only to find the door was locked.

He used his key, only to realize she had the chain on the door, too.

He began pounding on the door, shouting, "Cora May, open the damn door."

"No!" she shouted. "You get your stuff off my porch, and get off my property and out of my life. You will be hearing from my lawyer."

A shiver of fear ran up his back. This couldn't be happening.

"You don't have a lawyer," he yelled.

"I do now. Peanut Butterman is representing me."

He tried whining. "But Cora, honey! All these years of marriage? You're just gonna throw them away like they never mattered?"

"You threw our grandson away, and he mattered. You did it. Not me. You broke my heart, Jud Boone. I don't know you anymore. You turned into a monster... or maybe you were always a monster, and I just didn't know. Stay away from me. I don't ever want to look at your face again."

Jud flinched. Rage rose in him like a fire in his belly, and before he thought about what he was doing, he kicked in the door.

Cora was standing in the middle of the room, and it was obvious she'd been crying. Her eyes were puffy, and her face was blotchy red. She gasped when the chain broke, and then they were staring, face-to-face.

"What are you going to do? Beat me like you beat Randall's son? If you do, everyone will know it was you. That's why I talked to you in front of Chief Pittman. If you mess with Bowie and his family, or if you hurt me, you will be right back in jail. And if you're going to hurt me, then just finish the job and kill me, because I will not live one more hour under the same roof with you."

Jud was in shock. The sight of the fear on her face was enough to put him on his knees.

"I would never hurt you, honey. I swear."

"But you did, Jud. You broke something between us that will never be fixed. I won't love a man I can't trust. Either get out, or put an end to me now."

Jud kept shaking his head. "I can't believe you think I

would do you physical harm. I have never raised a hand to you in my life."

"There are far worse pains than a physical blow. I'll say this one last time. Get. Out. Of. My. House."

Jud turned and lurched back out over the threshold. He heard the door lock behind him and then began carrying the suitcases to his car. It took several trips to get all of them in the car.

He drove all the way to Savannah, bought a fifth of whiskey, then headed to a motel to spend the night. He couldn't face his sons and admit Cora had kicked him out, and he didn't want anyone in town to know, either. Granted, they'd find out soon enough, but not yet.

The motel he stopped at was clean and decent enough, but it wasn't home. And as soon as he thought that, he knew nothing was ever going to be home again. He wanted to be pissed. But he had no recourse without serious consequences. If anything happened to Bowie James now, even if Jud had nothing to do with it, they'd come after him. He didn't know what to do next. Should he just cut his losses and leave Georgia, or did he dare go back and fight for Cora?

Then he remembered the shattered look on her face. He'd done a lot of things wrong in his life, and he'd always gotten away with them. Until now. It appeared that his luck had finally run out. He was old—a man used to being in control—yet somehow, he'd let a bastard and a woman get the best of him.

The irony did not escape him.

Bloody hell.

He crawled in bed with his whiskey and proceeded to drink himself unconscious.

—~~~—

Bowie and his crew had emptied the house of debris and were moving on to the removal of silt and dried mud on the floors, scooping it up with shovels and taking it out in wheelbarrows. They'd just finished with the first two rooms when Bowie called it a day.

"It's almost six o'clock. Let's round up our tools. Have a good evening, and get some sleep. We'll start up in the morning at eight, okay?"

"Sounds good to me," Matt said.

They began carrying out tools and putting them in the trailer. After having all of his tools stolen years ago, Bowie had put a security alarm on it, too. Ray was towing the trailer on this job, so at night it was parked at the bed-and-breakfast where they were staying.

"Here's the door key, Boss," Ray said, and tossed it to Bowie so he could lock up. "Enjoy your family tonight. See you in the morning."

"Thanks," Bowie said, and caught the key in midair. Then he stood on the porch watching them drive away before going back inside for one last look.

What they'd done today had stripped away every reference point he had. He was thinking about opening up the wall between the kitchen and living room, then taking the bedroom next to Granny's room and turning it into a nice roomy bathroom and walk-in closet. He'd talk to her tonight to see what she thought about that. It was her house, after all.

He went through the rooms, shutting and locking windows, then locked the back door off the kitchen, and then the front door as he went out. He paused, then flattened the palm of his hand on the old door, feeling the rough surface and peeling paint.

"I'll be back," he said softly. "I won't leave until you're beautiful again."

Then he got in his Cherokee and drove home.

It was habit for him to think back over the jobsite after they'd ended work for the day, reminding himself what permits to pull and to check into local suppliers. He'd momentarily forgotten he was no longer living alone, until he pulled up to the motor home and parked.

The aroma of frying chicken hit him first. His mouth began watering just thinking about it. He set the alarm on his car and was walking up the steps with his house key at the ready when the door opened abruptly.

"Welcome home!" Rowan said.

The smile on her face knocked Bowie for a loop. He had a momentary fantasy about what coming home to her would be like.

"That's the best welcome ever," he said, and stepped over the threshold and went to greet the girls.

Ella turned to greet him when he stopped her.

"Don't hug me. I'm filthy, but something sure does smell good in here," he said, and kissed her on the cheek. "I have to take a shower before I can sit anywhere. Today was all about cleanup."

"Was it bad?" Gran asked.

Bowie nodded. "Yes, ma'am, but we're going to fix it. I'll fill you in while we eat. Give me about ten minutes, and I'll be back."

Rowan was blinking back tears, a witness to the love between them. She didn't know her face reflected her emotions so easily, but it did, and Bowie saw them.

Determined to change her mood, he reached toward her, pretending he was going to put his dirty hand on her face.

When she squealed and jumped back, he grinned and kept moving toward the bathroom.

He shed his dirty clothes just inside the door and turned on the shower, then grabbed a washcloth and stepped inside. The water was cold at first, but he was hot, so he didn't really care. He just stood beneath the spray, letting the water sluice off the initial dirt as he shampooed his hair, then scrubbed himself clean. Normally, he shaved every morning, so as was his habit, he left the day's worth of beard on its own.

Thinking about the meal awaiting him, he dressed in a pair of clean sweats and a T-shirt and came out barefoot, carrying his dirty clothes. He dropped them in a plastic laundry basket in front of the stackable washer and dryer to deal with later.

"You have just about everything in this trailer that you could ever want," Ella said as he snitched a hot, crunchy crumb from the edge of the platter of chicken.

"It was built to my specifications. I had to wait almost a year for it to be finished, but it's been worth it."

"Everything is ready," Gran said. "Take a seat, and I'll pour your iced tea."

"Are you sure I can't help?" he asked.

"I'm positive," she said. "Go. Sit."

And just like that, the memories came flooding back. This was supper. Every single night of his young life, it had played out this way. Granny telling everyone to sit, and his mom and Ella carrying dishes to the table. Only his mom was missing. The rest was just the same.

Then he caught Rowan watching him and amended that thought. It wasn't the same. Dark Eyes was here.

He held up his hands. "Better?"

She grinned. "Much."

He sat, watched the women carrying food to the table, unprepared for the wash of emotions running through him. Finally everything was on the table, and the girls were seated.

"Bowie, we still say grace before a meal," Ella said.

"Then bless this food and me, because tonight I feel like the luckiest man in the world," he said.

Rowan was the first to reach for his hand, and one by one, they linked themselves in a circle, as Ella bowed her head in prayer.

The knot in Bowie's throat tightened. Rowan's skin was soft, but he felt little calluses on her palms, a sign of growing up on a farm. Gran's grip was surprisingly strong—as if she was holding on tight for fear she'd lose him again. Then Ella said, "Amen," and he blinked. He hadn't heard a word she'd said, and he'd lost the connection to both women when they let go of his hands. The scene before him was so surreal that for a moment, it almost seemed like a dream.

"This is the first time I have eaten with family since the night of my eighteenth birthday, and the first time I've had a real meal at this table. I just wanted you all to know how special this is to me," he said.

"We're just as glad to have you home as you are to see us," Gran said, and passed him the platter of chicken. "Help yourself, and pass it to the left."

Bowie grinned. "Yes, ma'am," he said, and forked a piece onto his plate and passed the platter to Rowan.

And so the meal progressed. Bowie talked about the day of demolition, and that they'd had to take it all down to the studs because of the mold and water damage. Then he broached the subject of opening up the space between the kitchen and dining room and making Gran's room a true master with a bath en suite and a walk-in closet.

Pearl's eyes widened in delight. "Oh, Ella…just like I talked about."

"That's great, Mama," Ella said, then patted Bowie's hand. "Once Mama knew what your chosen profession became, she began watching all of the remodel shows on HGTV. Every time they'd go in to renovate a house, her favorite thing to watch was them opening up the spaces from little enclosed rooms to one big one."

Bowie loved hearing that. "Gran, do you want the living room opened up, too?"

Pearl beamed. "You can do that?"

"Yes, ma'am. I can do that," Bowie said.

"I'm so excited," Pearl said.

Bowie grinned. "Well, I'm excited about this meal, and I think I'd like one more piece of chicken."

"That'll make three, but who's counting?" Rowan said.

Bowie burst out laughing. "Guilty," he said, and finished off his meal with that last piece of chicken.

"You bought ice cream. Do you want dessert?" Ella asked.

"Not for me," Bowie said. "At least not right now. I want to savor what I've already eaten."

When they began cleaning up, he got up and helped. Even when they were claiming they'd do it, he ignored them.

"I've taken care of myself too long to let that happen," he said. "And now you have to mind me, Gran. You come sit. Put your feet up, and find something you like to watch on TV."

Pearl fussed a little, but Bowie could tell it was just for show. She looked tired. Today had been a big day for everyone. He turned on the television, then handed her the remote. She was already surfing channels when he got back to the sink.

Ella had the dishwasher loaded and was looking for the detergent.

"I've got this, Aunt Ella. You go join Gran. Rowan and I will wash up the stuff that didn't fit."

"I won't argue," she said, and dried her hands.

Rowan was already running hot water into the sink and adding some liquid dish detergent.

"I'll wash. You dry and put away, okay?" she said.

"Okay," Bowie said, and got a clean dishtowel from the drawer.

They worked together in comfortable silence, grinning at each other once when Pearl began complaining about what she called "those spoiled women" who were negating every aspect of the houses they were touring.

"Sounds like they're watching *House Hunters*," Rowan said. "It was one of her favorite shows at the nursing home."

Bowie glanced over his shoulder. Ella was dozing, and Gran was shaking her head in disgust. The age on their faces was a painful reminder of how long he'd been gone.

A few minutes later, Bowie was drying the last skillet, and Rowan was wiping off the table. As soon as they were finished, he put his dirty clothes in the washer.

"I do this every night," he said when Rowan followed him back to see if she could help. "My work clothes always get so dirty that it's easier to wash them the same day than to have them lying around stinking up the place."

She leaned against the wall with her arms folded across her chest, watching, remembering.

"I did the same thing when Daddy started cutting wood for the winter. We always had some deadfall curing in the woods. All it needed was to be cut up and hauled to the house. His clothes always smelled like chain-saw oil, which stinks to high heaven."

Bowie grinned. "I haven't heard that phrase since I left Blessings."

Rowan had never been out of Georgia and envied him the places he'd seen.

"I guess since you've worked all over, you've heard and seen far more than the little world of Blessings, Georgia."

"Yes, I guess I have," he said. He poured in the soap, then adjusted the washer settings, and turned it on. "That's that. So, what do you like to do in the evenings? Do you have favorite shows on TV that you like to watch?"

"Daddy always did. I'm not much for watching TV, even though it was always on if he was in the house."

"Then what do you like to do?" he asked.

"I read a lot. My favorites are romance books, because they have happily-ever-after endings. And I knit, but my books and knitting things are gone. Once I move in with Pearl and Ella, I'll be looking for a job. Even though I will be getting Daddy's retirement income soon, I don't intend to live off their kindness. I'll be wanting to pay my way."

Bowie thought about her living in his old room, which was where she'd wind up when he used the other empty bedroom to enlarge Granny's room.

"There's a full moon tonight. Want to go outside for a bit?" he asked.

"Oh yes! I miss night in the hills."

"I'm usually far away from cities on a jobsite. I like quiet nights, too. Hey, Gran, we're going to sit outside for a bit. Do you want to join us?"

"No, no, I'll just watch a couple more shows and then go to bed. Looks like Ella already needs to be in bed," she said, eyeing her sleeping daughter. "She always did sleep with her mouth open. I told her time and time again that's what her nose was for, but she still does this."

Ella frowned with her eyes closed. "I'm sitting right here, Mama. I can hear you."

"Then close your mouth," Pearl said.

"I will if you will," Ella said.

Bowie burst out laughing. "Here's where we make an exit."

Rowan let him help her down the steps, and then they moved to the picnic table nearby. She climbed up one of the bench seats and sat down on the tabletop. Bowie sat down beside her.

Frank and Jewel were sitting outside beneath the glow of their porch light. They waved. Bowie waved back.

"That's Frank and Jewel. Don't know their last names, but they seem really nice," he said softly.

Rowan looked up, situating herself within the heavens, and sighed. It felt good to be out. Even if she didn't hear coyotes this close to town, she could still smell the dampness of night air and still find her place in the sky.

The full moon cast lighter-blue shadows within the darkness, as it painted the ground with moon glow. She inhaled deeply. Someone had mowed their yard this evening. The scent of freshly cut grass was prevalent and familiar. After the month of hell she'd had, it was grounding to be beneath the stars.

Without thinking, she pointed up. "There's the North Star...and the Big Dipper, and the Little Dipper. They were the first things Daddy taught me about the stars. They are in the Sagittarius constellation."

Bowie looked up at the night sky, then turned his head and looked at her. Her profile was bathed in moonlight, giving her dark hair a midnight-blue hue. He'd never wanted to kiss a woman more than he did right now. But that wasn't going to happen. She was his guest, not a future conquest.

He looked away.

"I have a book about constellations on the shelf in my bedroom. I'll get it for you when we go back in, if you'd like."

Rowan smiled. "So you like the stars, too? That would be awesome."

He nodded. "You should see them from flat on your back at the top of a mountain. If you stare at the sky long enough, the stars come down to you."

"You have done that?"

"Yes. I've done that," Bowie said, then noticed his neighbors across the way were coming to say hello.

"Hey, y'all," Frank said. "Just checking in to see if you got everything ironed out about your car."

"Yes, I think so. I'll still have to see about a good body shop to get it fixed. Frank, Jewel, this is Rowan Harper. She's staying with Gran and Aunt Ella. I'm sorry, Frank, but I don't know your last name."

"Crockett. Nice to meet you, Rowan."

Jewel nodded. "Nice to meet you."

"Thank you. It's a pleasure to meet you two as well."

"Are you kin to Davy?" Bowie asked.

Frank laughed. "That's what everybody asks…and the answer is yes. He's like an uncle six times removed, or something like that, but we're not as daring. This fifth wheel is as close to pioneering as we get."

Rowan liked them and their easy manner.

"Do you live here, or are you travelers?" she asked.

Jewel was the one who answered. "Oh, we used to be on the road all the time. We came through Blessings about four years back and liked it so much that we stayed. Now we're too comfortable here to think about leaving."

Rowan smiled. "Blessings is a special place."

"That it is," Frank said. "We'll be getting back to the house and leaving you two to your visit. Just wanted to check out the dude here. He's a dang good shot with that there laser gun."

They were walking away when Rowan asked, "Who did you shoot with a laser gun?"

"It was a Taser, which I used to stop the kid who keyed the Jeep," Bowie said, watching the expression on her face to see if that horrified her in any way.

"It's better than a backside full of buckshot, which was probably what Daddy would have done."

Bowie laughed.

Rowan grinned.

And there they sat.

They had a long, comfortable moment of silence, and then Bowie grasped her arm and pointed.

"Look! Just across the way at the trailer next to Frank's."

"Oh, a raccoon," Rowan said. "Wait! There are two more! Babies! Oh wow…how cute!"

"They're probably looking for trash cans to get into. They are notorious little bandits."

"We always saw their tracks around the pond back at the farm, but rarely saw them," Rowan said.

"Night prowlers," Bowie said.

She nodded, then took a deep breath and closed her eyes.

"What are you thinking?" Bowie asked.

"How fast life can change," she said.

"That's for sure," Bowie said, watching the raccoons disappearing into the shadows.

Rowan glanced at the man beside her when he wasn't looking. She was almost five feet seven inches, a good portion of which was legs, and Bowie James was much taller. The plus side of that was that he didn't feel threatening in any way. She'd only met him this morning, and it seemed like she'd always known him. A strange feeling for her, because she wasn't the kind to make friends easily.

Then Bowie suddenly grasped her hand.

"Look! A shooting star!"

"I see it!" she said as she looked up. "Oh wow…that one lasted a long time before it burned out."

"You have to make a wish," Bowie said.

"You saw it first. It's your wish to make," she said.

Bowie looked back at the sky, then closed his eyes and made his wish.

"I hope it comes true," Rowan said.

The hair crawled on the back of Bowie's neck as he glanced down at her.

"I hope so, too," he said, then felt a little sting and slapped his arm. "Mosquitoes found us. We better go in."

Rowan jumped down from the picnic table without hesitation, and then waited so they could walk back together.

"Thank you for this," she said. "It felt good…almost as if I had my life back."

Bowie frowned. "What do you mean?"

"The doors at the nursing home were locked during supper. I haven't been able to do this since the night before the hurricane hit."

He thought of Gran and Aunt Ella. No wonder Gran thought she'd die in that place. It must have felt like jail.

"Damn, I never thought of that. I'm sorry. That had to be a defeated feeling."

She smiled shyly. "But you rescued us today, so you are officially my hero."

Chapter 6

THE PRAISE RODE HEAVILY ON HIS SHOULDERS AS THEY walked back. That wish he'd made was anything but heroic. He wanted to make love to her, and she had just given him a halo to hold instead.

The television was off, and the door to the master bedroom was closed when they walked in, but they could still hear the girls talking.

"I guess they're getting ready for bed," Rowan said.

"I'm going to do the same," Bowie said. "We worked our butts off doing demo today, and we're back at it tomorrow at 8:00 a.m. I've already had my shower, so why don't you take the bathroom first while I make up your bed."

"Okay, but no funny business with the beds. You take the bigger one."

He grinned. "I remember. Go do your thing. I'll have the bed ready for you shortly."

He was pulling out the bed as she dug through her little bag of clothing, took what he assumed was her nightgown, and went into the bathroom. Bowie pulled out a set of clean sheets, and a blanket, then made up the bed. He pulled a pillow out of a drawer, slid it into a clean pillowcase, and then turned the covers back neatly, making it easy for her to get in.

He heard the shower come on as he was making up his bed. Now he had a mental image of her wet and naked.

Sweet merciful God.

After the beds were done, he put the clothes he'd washed into the dryer, tossed in a dryer sheet, and hit Start. He was so used to falling asleep to the sound that he hoped it didn't bother his guests.

Ella opened the door.

"I thought that might be you," she said, and gave him a quick good-night kiss on the cheek. "Oh, honey, thank you for coming. Mama is already asleep and is as happy as I've seen her in years. Love you, and sleep well."

Bowie grinned. "You're welcome. I love you, too. Let me know if you need anything. I'm a light sleeper."

"We're fine. You have such a grand home. This is like being on an amazing vacation," Ella said, then slipped back into the bedroom and closed the door.

Bowie pulled the T-shirt he was wearing over his head and tossed it onto the back of a chair as he went to the kitchen. That ice cream he didn't eat earlier suddenly sounded good.

He got out two spoons and sat down at the table. The first bite was in his mouth, and he was scooping up the next when Rowan came out of the bathroom. She wasn't wearing a nightgown. It was a huge, oversize T-shirt, as decent as any nightgown, but he was struggling not to stare.

Oh my lord. Those legs. Longer than the law allows. Just shoot me now.

Rowan laid her clothes on a chair near her bed. Bowie was no longer wearing a shirt, and the muscles in his arms and the breadth and width of those shoulders were something to see.

He held up the pint of ice cream.

"Nightcap? It's Bourbon Caramel. I have an extra spoon."

"Maybe just a taste," she said as she slid into the chair beside him and picked up the spoon.

She aimed for the swirl of caramel, digging into the little frozen river of sweetness for her first taste.

She closed her eyes and sighed.

"This is so good."

"Want another bite?" he asked.

She didn't need any urging. "Yes, please."

Quiet descended upon them as they scooped and ate, until the container was empty. The only evidence of what had been in it was the tiny smear of caramel at the edge of Rowan's lower lip, and it was driving Bowie crazy.

Rowan cleared the table and dropped the carton in the trash and the spoons in the sink. When she came back, the smear of caramel was gone.

He sighed, then put his cell phone on the charger by his bed.

"I'll take my turn in the bathroom, but I won't be long. Turn out all the lights that you want. I'm used to finding my way about in the dark."

"Okay, and thank you again for letting me stay."

"I wouldn't have had it any other way," he said.

Rowan turned out the kitchen light as he closed the bathroom door, and then the living room light as well. But the moment the room went dark, little built-in night-lights began to glow.

"How cool is that?" she said, and then climbed into bed. The sheets were soft against her skin, and the light-weight blanket just right.

Bowie heard a slight, nasal snore as he emerged from the bathroom. That would be Aunt Ella, breathing with her mouth open, and Gran likely sleeping through it.

Then he glanced toward the twin bed on the opposite side of the room. Rowan was asleep on her side, curled up like a baby in a womb, but tightly clutching the covers beneath her neck.

He frowned. It made him think she was afraid, and that was the last thing he would have wanted her to feel. He thought again about how alone she was in the world. That's how he'd felt after his mother was gone.

Seeing Rowan in such a vulnerable manner was the cold shower he needed. So he took his guilt to bed, certain he wouldn't sleep a wink, and didn't wake up until the alarm on his cell phone began to beep. He quickly silenced it before it woke the others.

It was time to begin a new day.

Jud's head was pounding, and his cell phone was ringing. Even worse, he'd forgotten to close the curtains last night, and the sunlight coming through the slats in the blinds was adding pain to his hangover headache. When he saw caller ID, he passed on his misery by yelling at the caller.

"What the hell do you want?"

"Good morning to you, too, Daddy," Emmitt said. "I just went by the house. Your car was gone, and Mama wouldn't let me in. What's going on?"

"I'll tell you what's going on. Your mother saw that damn bastard and lost it. She's divesting herself of Boones, so consider yourself no longer welcome in her house. Not just me, not just you, but all of us."

Emmitt laughed nervously. "Oh, she'll get over it… won't she? I mean…she can't just kick you out. You guys have been married for almost fifty years."

Jud glanced at the empty whiskey bottle. What he wouldn't give for a little "hair of the dog."

"Those years mean nothing to her now. She made that clear yesterday. The house is hers. Willed to her by her daddy the year before we married. She grew up in it. I moved in with her. The money in the bank and the money from the sale of our sporting goods store belongs to both of us, and that's it."

The silence that ensued was telling. It took Jud a few moments to realize Emmitt was crying.

"Suck it up, boy! Face the facts. She knows everything we did, and most of Blessings is figuring it out, too. She knows Randall lied about what he did, and she knows we backed him. She also knows it's why we ran Billie James and her kid out of Blessings. I'm not gonna stay here and be judged by people for doing what I thought was right. My pa drilled the hate into all of us. It is what it is."

"But Daddy—"

"You and Mel figure it out on your own. Stay or move. I'll be satisfied if I never see another member of the James family."

Emmitt couldn't believe what he was hearing. He and Mel hadn't been able to buy a bottle of beer without their dad telling them what kind to drink. Now their mother had disowned them, and their dad was basically abandoning them. When he heard the connection suddenly end, Emmitt frowned. His dad had hung up. This was serious. He needed to go talk to Mel.

Bowie was moving as quietly as he could when he headed to the bathroom. He needed to shave and shower before the girls woke up and started trying to feed him. It wasn't that he didn't want their food, but he didn't have the time. He got his clean clothes out of the dryer and took them with him into the bathroom.

Because this was so routine, he had shaved, showered, and dressed in just over fifteen minutes. He came out of the bathroom with droplets of water still clinging to his hair.

He still needed that haircut. Maybe he'd take time to stop by that salon down on Main when he went to get Aunt Ella a new phone.

He was barefoot and carrying his socks when he saw Rowan sitting at the table with a box of cereal and a carton of milk. And he smelled fresh coffee.

"Morning," she said, and pointed at the extra bowl and spoon. "Have a seat if you're interested."

He grinned. It was pretty much what he'd said to her last night about the ice cream. He glanced at the time.

"I'm interested," he said. He poured himself a cup of coffee, then sat down and started pouring presweetened cereal into the bowl. "Did you sleep okay?"

She rolled her eyes. "Like a baby. That mattress is so comfortable."

"I'm glad you were able to rest," Bowie said as he reached for the milk and poured some in his bowl. "I won't be in at lunch, but sometime today I'm going to get Gran and Ella a new phone. We can replace yours, too, if you'd like."

"I don't have the money to pay you yet. I can wait."

"Android or iPhone?"

"Daddy had an iPhone. I didn't have one of my own and don't know anyone to call, so it doesn't matter whether I have one or not."

"You know me," Bowie said, then grinned. "I'll take your calls."

She laughed.

He took a quick sip of the coffee. "Hey, this is really good coffee."

"Thanks. I made it for Daddy all the time."

"You don't drink it?"

She shook her head. "I love the smell of it, but I never could enjoy the taste, so I finally quit trying."

Bowie nodded, then started eating, while keeping an eye on the time. He didn't want to be late. He was the one with the key to the house.

"What are you going to do today?" he asked.

"I thought I might make that peach cobbler. We can have it for dessert tonight."

"Now that's something to look forward to," Bowie said, and finished off the cereal. "I hate to eat and run, but the job is waiting."

"Have a good day," she said as he grabbed his coffee to take with him.

"Come lock me out," he said, and Rowan got up and followed him to the door.

He walked out, then paused at the bottom of the steps and turned around. She looked beautiful in the morning sunlight.

"You have a good day, too," he said, and then he was heading toward the Cherokee, unlocking the door and turning off the alarm system as he went.

He started the car and turned around. He looked back. She was still standing in the doorway.

She waved.

He waved back.

She was smiling as she backed up and shut the door. He was still smiling.

He stopped on the way to get fresh ice to cool down a twenty-four-pack carton of bottled water.

By the time he got to the house, it was ten minutes to eight. He carried the ice chest back to the shade tree, then unlocked the front door. The house smelled of mold and all of the dust they'd stirred yesterday.

He went through the rooms opening windows, and by the time he was through, the crew was pulling up and unloading wheelbarrows and shovels. They were talking among themselves as they neared the house, and when Bowie came out onto the porch, they all started talking at once.

"That bed-and-breakfast lady sure can cook," Ray said.

"She had a little breakfast buffet set up in the dining room and kept refilling our cups with the best dang coffee I've had in years."

"Awesome," Bowie said.

"What did you have for breakfast?" Samuel asked.

"A bowl of Frosted Flakes and a cup of coffee…and the prettiest breakfast partner I've ever had."

"Well, hell," Samuel said. "I sat between Matt and Joe, and I can't say as how I'd call either of them pretty."

They all whooped and laughed, and so the day began.

Cora Boone hadn't slept much last night. She'd feared Jud would wait until he thought she was asleep and come back anyway. He still had a key, and he'd broken the chain, so she knew it was a possibility. And even when she did manage to fall asleep, she dreamed Jud was kicking in the door. No one had ever been more relieved to see daybreak.

She got up and dressed with purpose. She had things to do today, and she didn't want to look as terrible as she felt. She was sitting at the table having buttered toast with her coffee when she heard a truck pull up in the yard. She listened to the footsteps coming up the steps, then crossing the porch to where they stopped at the door.

She didn't have to get up and look to know who it was. Emmitt always dragged his feet when he walked. He'd done it all his life, and no amount of fussing at him when he was growing up had changed him.

He knocked.

She didn't move.

He knocked again and then yelled, "Hey, Mama!"

She gritted her teeth. There was no way she was going to the door. What she felt about her sons was nothing short of disgust. It wasn't until she heard him driving away that she breathed easy again.

As she carried her plate and cup to the sink, she thought about the years she'd cooked for Jud and washed his clothes, slept with him, tended him, even when she was sick with all three pregnancies. What did he think of her? She had given him plenty of leeway to assume she was malleable and oblivious to all that they'd done. She believed now that she had ignored what she didn't want to face and blindly believed what she'd been told. And look what had happened. She had to take as much blame for her refusal to see what was happening as the men had for what they'd done.

It was a few minutes after 9:00 a.m. when she left the house. Her first appointment was with Peanut Butterman, and then the unplanned trip to the locksmith

———

Emmitt called his brother. His sister-in-law, Nell, answered.

"Morning, Emmitt."

"Morning, Nell. I need to talk to Mel."

"He's in the john. I'll have him call you."

"Just tell him to meet me at Granny's. It's important."

"Y'all aren't about to get into trouble again, are you?"

Emmitt frowned. "No, but there's trouble in the family. You tell him to meet me."

"Yeah, yeah, okay," Nell said.

"I'll be waiting," Emmitt said, and disconnected, then got in his car and headed to Granny's.

He parked and went in as he'd done a thousand times before.

"Table for two. My brother's joining me," Emmitt said.

Mercy eyed him without comment as she picked up two menus and seated him at an empty table.

"Wendy will be your waitress. Enjoy your meal," she said, and went back to the front.

As promised, Wendy came by and filled up the coffee cup at Jud's place setting.

"Are you ready to order?" she asked.

He shook his head. "I'm waiting for my brother."

She moved on to the next table.

As Emmitt reached for a couple of sugar packets, he glanced up. At least half of the diners were watching him. He shrugged it off and stirred the sugar in his coffee while waiting for it to cool.

Mel showed up a few minutes later and strode straight to where Emmitt was sitting. He pulled out a chair and plopped down.

"Well, I'm here. What's the big deal?"

Emmitt lowered his voice and leaned forward. "Mama kicked Daddy out of the house and, according to Daddy, has disowned us all."

Mel blinked. "You're not serious."

"Yes, I am. I went over to the house this morning. Daddy's car was gone, and Mama wouldn't open the door, so I called him. I think he's in Savannah, but not sure where, and he's not coming back to Blessings," Emmitt said, and watched his brother turn pale.

Wendy came back, poured coffee in Mel's cup, and asked the same question again.

"Y'all decide what you want to eat?"

"I already ate," Mel said.

Emmitt shrugged. "Then I'll have pancakes and sausage."

"Comin' up," Wendy said, and went to turn in the order.

Mel leaned forward. "Why would she do that?"

"According to Daddy, she saw Bowie James yesterday and lost her mind. She knows Randall lied. She knows we all lied."

"But why won't Daddy stay and fight for her?" Mel asked.

Emmitt shrugged. "Said he wasn't going to stay here

and be judged for how he was raised, or something to that effect. He also told me we are on our own."

Mel wiped a shaky hand across his face. "So what do we do?"

"I don't know," Emmitt muttered. "We've lived here our whole lives. I don't see why we need to do anything."

Wendy came back with his breakfast and refilled his coffee. "Enjoy," she said, and left again.

Emmitt began buttering the pancakes while they were hot, then doused them with syrup and took his first bite.

"I wish Tiny could cook like this," he said, talking around the mouthful he was chewing, then forking a piece of sausage and popping it in his mouth.

Mel was in shock. He reached for his coffee and took a quick sip, then glanced up. Everyone was staring at them. He frowned. Some of them looked away, but some did not.

"What's going on?" Mel muttered.

Emmitt paused. "What do you mean?"

"Everybody is staring at us, and some of them don't look very friendly."

Emmitt laid down his fork and looked up. It appeared he and Mel were the center of attention, but he didn't know—

And then it hit him. This was exactly what Daddy had said would happen. Their dirty little secrets were coming to light.

"I guess this is what life in Blessings is going to be like now."

"And all of this is happening because Bowie James came back to town," Mel muttered.

Emmitt sighed. "No. It's happening because Daddy

stirred up the old feud again, and this time, we all got caught."

"I'm going to talk to Mama," Mel said.

"And explain what? That we didn't mean to beat the hell out of a kid just because he was starting to look like us?"

Mel shivered suddenly. "I gotta go talk to Nell."

"About what?" Emmitt asked.

"Moving near her parents." He laid down some money for his coffee and walked out without looking up.

It was bravado that got Emmitt through the rest of his meal, and then he picked up the ticket Wendy laid on the table and paid on his way out. The food in his belly felt like lead by the time he got home.

He and Tiny didn't have the option of leaving Blessings. Junior was out on bail, with a pending court date for sentencing. Emmitt couldn't believe that had happened and took full blame for the way he'd come home carrying on about Bowie James breaking his nose.

Every action has a reaction, and this one had ricocheted from Emmitt to his son. He and Mel had taken the easy way out in life and let their father pay their way from the income off the fish and tackle shop their dad had inherited from his parents. Over the years, it had grown into a large sporting goods business in Savannah. About the time he and Mel were old enough to start working there, Jud decided to sell it to a big chain store, so they had become his flunkies. After Billie James and her kid left town, Jud had calmed down.

And then Bowie James came back to Blessings. Enraged that his order never to come back had been ignored, Jud had refused to let the old feud die—and look what had happened.

Emmitt was sick at heart. His son might be sent to some juvenile detention center. His parents' marriage was on the rocks. His mother had disowned them.

And where the hell was the man who'd caused all this?

Gone.

He took off, leaving his family and his troubles behind.

It was a hard thing to accept, but it was painfully obvious to Emmitt now.

Judson Boone wasn't only a bully—he was also a coward.

Chapter 7

CORA LOOKED AT HERSELF IN THE MIRROR AS SHE ADJUSTED the tie at the collar of her blue dress, then frowned.

When she was young, everyone had told her she looked like Shirley Temple, the old-time child star from the glamour days of Hollywood. Back then, it was fun being cute. But as she aged, her little turned-up nose and baby-blue eyes were disappearing within the wrinkles.

The once-blond, curly hair that had been her crowning glory was gray and thinning, and the last time she'd worn this dress had been to a funeral. Going to file for a divorce was the death of a marriage. It was oddly fitting.

Satisfied that she'd done the best she could with what she had left, she got her things and left the house, taking care to lock up behind her.

First stop was Peanut Butterman's office. She parked in the shade of a large elm and then couldn't bring herself to move. She was sick with nerves and felt like crying, but she wasn't about to let on how awful this was to her, or that she felt like a disgrace. But feeling sorry for herself would get her nowhere, so she got out of the car and entered the building, then found Peanut's office down one of the hallways.

Betty Purejoy was Peanut's secretary. Cora had gone to school with Betty and was embarrassed to show her face, but when she walked into the office, Betty looked up and smiled.

"Good morning, Cora."

"Hi, Betty. You're looking good. I guess you've recovered completely from that horrible wreck you had some time back."

"Yes, I have, and I'm grateful that it wasn't worse. Just a moment and I'll let Mr. Butterman know you're here."

Betty got up and knocked on the door to Peanut's office, then opened it.

"Cora Boone is here," she said.

Peanut stood. "Oh, good. Have her come in," he said, and when Cora entered his office, he went to meet her. "Good morning, Cora. Would you care for a cup of coffee?"

Cora shook her head. "No, thank you."

"Then have a seat," he said, indicating the two chairs on the other side of his desk.

Cora put her purse in one chair and sat down in the other.

Peanut knew why she was there and gave her an encouraging smile.

"I understand you want to have a will drawn up," he said.

"Yes, and I'll be needing you to draw up some divorce papers, too."

Although Peanut was surprised, he didn't blink an eye.

"Of course. Let me get Betty in here so she can make notes as we discuss the details, and then she'll have all of these papers typed up and ready to sign later today."

Cora nodded.

Betty was all business as she sat down at a table behind them and gave Peanut a nod.

And so began the unraveling of Cora Boone's world.

By the time she left the office an hour and a half later, she felt like there was a hole in her heart where family had been.

It had been difficult to come to terms with the facts last night, but once the layers of lies had been revealed, she had accepted that there had been two versions of her world.

One where she lived happily unaware of the ugliness behind the facades of the people she'd loved—and the other the reality of her ignorance.

The sun was bright, and the sky was cloudless as she got back to the car. She started it up to cool off and then took a deep breath. One task down. Two to go.

Her next stop was at the bank. She could count the number of times on one hand that she had been in it this year. Jud had always done the banking. It was how he liked it.

Their social security checks went into the joint checking account and the money Cora got from a trust fund left to her by her father was all hers. And since the sporting goods store they'd owned began with the fish and tackle shop Jud inherited from his father, she'd make no claim on that money. It would be a simple division of a small savings account and the money in their joint checking. As for the house, the property was already hers.

She got out of the car with her head up. This wasn't exactly a firing squad, but it was another step in ending a marriage, so in the door she went and straight up to the secretary sitting outside the offices of the bank officials.

The secretary smiled. "Hello, Mrs. Boone. How may I help you?"

"I need to speak to someone about opening a new account and transferring some money."

"Certainly. Have a seat," the secretary said, and then glanced into the offices to her left to see who was free and buzzed their phone.

A couple of minutes later, Cora was sitting with one of the loan officers, explaining what she needed to do. Her requests were greeted with calm courtesy, and after a few other questions and signing a couple of papers, she had two new accounts. One for her checking, and one for her savings.

The officer told her what she needed to do to get her direct-deposit income sent to her new account, and she left with a pad of counter checks with her new account number on them and the promise of a new debit card and personalized checks, both of which should arrive within the next ten days.

Cora felt a little different as she was leaving the bank. The hole in her heart wasn't any bigger, but the distance between her and Jud continued to lengthen.

Her next stop was Mills Locks, next door to Bloomer's Hardware, so she drove back up Main, then parked in front of the shop.

Cecil Mills was making a new key for a customer when Cora entered the shop.

"Morning, Cora. I'll be right with you," Cecil said.

Cora nodded, then stood aside to wait her turn. A few minutes later, the customer was gone, and Cecil slapped his hands on the counter and smiled.

"Good to see you, girl! What can I do for you?"

Cora lifted her chin. "I need you to come put new locks on all my doors."

"Sure thing. When do you need this done?" he asked.

"As soon as possible, please."

Cecil glanced up at the clock. "Let me call my wife to come watch the shop for me, and I'll be there within the next thirty minutes or so, okay?"

"Yes, perfect," Cora said. "I'm on the way home now."

"Then I'll see you soon," Cecil said, and was already on the phone as Cora walked out.

Once more, she was back in her car. She drove away, the sense of loss for what she was doing becoming real. Her eyes filled with tears she tried to blink away, but this time they were stronger than her intent to ignore.

By the time they were running down her face, she was trembling. She made it all the way home and got into the house before she came undone. Tears turned into sobs, and the trembling sent her to her knees.

And the only thing going through her mind was wondering if this was how Billie Jo James felt when she gave up all ties to home and family for the love of her son.

The irony of what was happening now was not lost on Cora. That same boy had become a man and had returned out of love for the family they'd left behind. Only this time, the family falling apart was Cora's own.

She covered her face with her hands, remembering something her mother used to say: *That which you give out in life will come back to you a hundredfold.*

And then her phone began to ring. She crawled to her feet to get the phone and was so upset she didn't think to look at caller ID.

"Hello."

"Cora, it's me, Jud. Don't hang up. We need to talk."

"About what?"

"Us."

"There is no more us. I filed for divorce today and divided up the money in our checking account and savings account. I didn't touch the money from when we sold the store. I have my own account now, and the rest is yours."

Jud was sitting on the corner of the bed, staring down at the floor, listening to his life falling apart.

"So there's nothing I can say?" he asked.

"Not to me. Your sons might have something different to say about the yellow stripe running up your back."

Jud inhaled sharply. "What the hell are you talking about?"

"Well, you're the one who wouldn't let that stupid feud die. You're the one who raised our sons to hate the James family. You got them and a grandson in trouble, and then you took off out of Blessings like a scalded cat. You're a fake, Jud Boone. You're all about family honor, yet you have none. Don't call me ever again."

She disconnected, then went to wash her face. Cecil Mills would be here any minute, and she didn't want him to know she'd been crying.

Her phone rang again, but she ignored it. Then it rang again just as Cecil was pulling up to the house. Maybe she needed a new phone number.

Cecil knocked on her door. She heard it from the bathroom and went to let him in.

"Come in, Cecil. I sure appreciate you doing this on such short notice."

"My jobs are always short notice, Cora. Nobody calls me unless they're locked out of their house or their car."

She smiled. "Oh. Well, of course. I never thought of it like that. So what I need are new locks put on both doors. The front one here, and the one in the kitchen that goes out to the backyard."

"Will do. How many keys do you want made?" he asked.

"Two for each door. One to carry. One to hide."

Cecil had heard the Boones were having trouble, but it appeared to be more than trouble if Cora was, for all intents and purposes, locking her husband out of the house.

"Okay. It won't take long, and I make the keys right out in my truck."

"Good," Cora said. "I have to go downtown again this afternoon to get some papers signed. I'll be in the kitchen if you need me. I want to start a pot of beans cooking."

———

Bowie had just overseen the delivery of a port-a-potty and had it set up behind the house to accommodate the neighbors' sensibilities. He had just walked in through the back door when Matt met him in the hall.

"Uh, Boss, you need to come see this."

"What's wrong?" Bowie asked as he followed Matt into one of the bedrooms.

"I was tearing out the rest of that lathe and plaster wall and found this," he said, handing Bowie a pink leather-bound book. "Wasn't your mama's name Billie?"

The hair crawled on the back of Bowie's neck when he saw his mother's name embossed in faded gold lettering.

"Yes. You said it was behind the wall?"

"Right here," Matt said, pointing.

Bowie stood there a moment, then walked out and into the bathroom next door and opened the linen closet. It didn't take long for him to find a loose board at the back of a shelf, and when he pulled it out, he could see straight into the bedroom.

"She put it in from here," Bowie said.

"Well, I'll be. I didn't think about that."

Bowie shrugged. "I had the advantage, since I grew up here. Thanks for this. I better put it in the car."

He went out and unlocked the car door, dropped the journal in the driver's seat, and locked his car on the way back to the house.

For the next hour, Bowie, Samuel, and Matt tore out lathe and plaster walls, while Ray, Joe, and Presley pulled down drywall from the ceilings.

With every piece of the old house that came down, Bowie was removing another piece of the past.

It was beginning to feel like a good thing.

It was almost noon when he glanced at the time and went to look for his notebook. He tore out a blank page and called the crew together.

"We're all too dirty to go eat anywhere, but I'll gladly spring for lunch *from* Granny's if you'll write down what you want to eat. I'll call it in, then go pick it up when I stop by to check on my girls."

"That's a deal I won't turn down," Ray said. "And the front porch is shady now. If someone would just turn up the volume on that stingy-ass breeze, we'd be good to go."

They laughed, agreeing they'd all appreciate a stiff breeze, as they wrote down their orders. They went back to work, and Bowie headed for the car.

He picked up the pink journal so he could sit down and then started the car so the air conditioner could begin cooling off the sweltering interior.

The journal was an unexpected find. He flipped through a couple of pages but didn't read them. From the date on the first page, it was obvious she'd had this since before he was born. He laid it aside, called in the orders, then headed to the trailer park.

When he pulled up to his home and parked, he noticed Frank and Jewel were noticeably absent from the front yard, and their truck was gone.

He grabbed the pink journal as he got out, hoping this discovery wasn't going to upset Gran. He had the door key in his hand when the door swung inward.

"I thought I heard your car!" Ella said. "What a nice surprise. Are you going to eat lunch with us?"

A wave of cool air washed over him as he stepped over the threshold. Rowan was at the stove frying bacon, and from the looks of the sliced tomatoes and lettuce, he guessed it was for BLTs.

"No, I'm going to pick up lunch for the guys, but I wanted to come by and show you something we found in the house."

Rowan flashed a smile. "Are you sure you can't stay? It wouldn't take long to fry a few more strips for you."

"I wish," Bowie said. "It all smells great. Where's Gran?"

"I'm right here," Pearl said as she came out of the bedroom.

Bowie gave her a quick kiss on the cheek. "Come sit down with me," he said, and led the way to the sofa.

Gran frowned. "What's wrong?"

"Nothing's wrong, but I have a surprise. We were taking down the lathe and plaster walls in the bedroom that used to belong to Mom, and we found this in the wall. I haven't looked in it. Not sure I even want to."

He laid the journal in Pearl's lap, and when he saw tears roll down her cheeks, he hugged her. "I'm sorry. I didn't want to make you cry."

"How on earth did she get this in the wall?" Pearl asked.

"I figured that out. It was from the bathroom side. I found a loose board all the way in the back of one shelf in the linen closet. She was hiding it in there, but when we took out the wall on the other side, it fell out."

Ella sat down on the sofa with her mother. "Oh, Mama. Don't be sad. It'll almost be like getting to talk to Billie again."

Rowan had taken the last of the bacon out of the skillet and turned off the burner. She was wearing an old pair of shorts from Goodwill and yet another oversize T-shirt. Her hair was up in a ponytail, and when she dropped onto the floor at Pearl's feet, Pearl reached out and patted her head.

"Sweet girl. What would Ella and I do without you," Pearl said, and then clutched the journal to her breast.

"Aren't you going to open it, Mama?" Ella asked.

"Not this instant," Pearl said. "We're gonna go make our sandwiches, pour up some of that good sweet tea, and relax. We can look at this later."

Bowie was relieved. Granted she hadn't had a chance to pass judgment on what was inside, but at least it hadn't thrown her into a tailspin.

"Okay, then. I'm going back to work. You'll have to catch me up on it tonight at supper. Love you, Gran."

Pearl smiled. "I love you, too, honey. You're all we

have left of our sweet Billie, and we are so blessed to
have you home."

Bowie was about to leave, but Rowan was too close
to ignore. When he got up, he reached down and pulled
her ponytail before heading out the door.

She shook her head. "He's a big tease, isn't he? He's
also really handsome, but you guys already know that.
So, if you're ready to eat, I'll get all the food on the
table," she said, and jumped up.

Ella and Pearl looked at each other and grinned.

"Wouldn't it be wonderful if something started
between them?" Ella whispered.

Pearl nodded. "He's thirty-five years old, and I'm
not getting any younger. I'd like to know he had found
the woman of his dreams before I go…and Rowan is so
sweet and loving. What a wonderful granddaughter she
would make."

"Lunch is ready!" Rowan called.

"Coming," Ella said.

Bowie caught a glimpse of himself in the rearview mirror
as he started the car, then grabbed a handful of wet wipes
to clean his face and hands before heading back to town.
He knew Granny's was likely to be busy since it was so
close to the noon hour, and he was right. The parking lot
was nearly full when he stopped to pick up lunch.

Frank and Jewel, his missing neighbors, were sitting
in a booth eating lunch when he walked in. They waved.

Bowie waved back and then smiled. So far, most of
their interaction was waving at each other. That was just
about perfect for him.

Mercy was counting back change to a customer, and as soon as the man left, Bowie gave her a quick smile.

"I came to pick up an order to go."

"I'll get it for you," she said, and headed for the kitchen. Moments later, she came back with two large bags and totaled up the tab.

"If it tastes as good as it smells, we're in for a treat," Bowie said, then signed the credit card receipt and left.

He swung by the quick stop to pick up a dozen cold bottles of Coke, which he iced down in another Styrofoam cooler he kept behind his seat, and headed back to work.

The men were outside when he arrived, washing up from one of the big water cans Ray hauled around on the job.

Joe saw him and came running. "What do you need me to carry?"

"The cooler in the back seat. It's full of cold bottles of Coke."

"You rock," Joe said, then picked up the cooler and followed Bowie to the porch.

They sorted out the orders, grabbed a Coke apiece, and sat down in the shade on the porch to eat.

Bowie thought about the BLT he'd turned down as he bit into his burger.

Beef was good.

Bacon was better.

Lunch was over for the girls. Rowan had cleaned up, leaving Pearl and Ella to retire to the bedroom. When they closed the door, she knew they were reading Billie's journal, and there was nothing left for her to do but stay out of their way. So she unfolded the lightweight blanket from the back of a recliner, wrapped it around herself, and stretched out on the sofa.

She could hear the faint murmur of the girls' voices and wondered what, if any, revelations they might be discovering. She was wondering how the journal would affect Bowie when she drifted off to sleep, and as she did, she began to dream.

"Rowan, wake up, girl! The water's rising! Get your clothes on, and take your purse with you. Get some snacks and water, and head to the barn loft."

"Come with me, Daddy!"

"I'm right behind you, just hurry."

She did as she was told and bolted out of the house. It was just after sunrise, light enough to see water was already on the porch. She jumped into the water and started trying to run, but it was halfway to her knees and moving fast, and she was moving against the current. The creek had never been out like this. At least not in her lifetime, and she was scared.

About halfway to the barn, she turned and looked back. Her daddy was coming out the back door carrying two sacks, one in each hand. Oh my God! He'd gone back for a stash of food and water.

She started to go back to help, but he shouted for her to keep going, so she did. When she reached the barn, she headed straight for the ladder on the wall leading up to the loft, threw her purse strap over her shoulder, and began to climb. She was only a few steps up when she began hearing what sounded like a roar.

She looked back out of the breezeway. Her daddy was over halfway to the barn, but struggling. The water was up to his waist.

She screamed. "Daddy! Drop the sacks and run!"

She saw the terror on his face and then looked out the other side of the barn. There was a wall of water coming at them like a tidal wave. This wasn't just a creek out of its banks.

"Climb, Rowan, climb!" her daddy shouted.

And so she did, then crawled to the hay door in the loft and looked down. The water was up to her father's chest when the wave hit him. She saw him go under, and then he was gone.

She was screaming when the rising water washed through the breezeway in the barn. And it was still rising when she crawled back into the farthest corner of the loft and closed her eyes.

Either she would drown like Daddy, or she wouldn't. And at that point, she wasn't sure which would be worse.

All of a sudden, someone was shaking her awake. Rowan opened her eyes and saw Ella leaning over her.

"What's happening?" she said.

"You screamed, child. It scared the soup out of us."

"I'm so sorry. I was dreaming," Rowan said, and as she sat up, the blanket fell down around her waist.

Ella sat down beside her. "About the flood?"

Rowan nodded and burst into tears.

"I keep seeing it wash Daddy away, and I don't know how to make it stop."

"It's all still fresh in your mind," Ella said, and hugged her close. "Like all things, the longer you live with a truth, the more familiar it becomes. Like a scar, only one you can't see."

"Where's Pearl?" Rowan asked.

Ella sighed. "She's crying, too. It's been years since we lost Bowie's mother, but today, there are things we just learned that brought new pain to old wounds."

Rowan wiped the tears from her eyes. "Oh, I am so sorry."

"So are we. We know, but Bowie doesn't. At least, not yet. Mama and I are trying to decide the best way to tell him."

"Why don't you let him decide if he wants to read it for himself? Didn't he say he wasn't sure he wanted to read it?"

Ella nodded. "But if he does read it, it might change the way he feels about her, and he's already lost so much."

Rowan wondered what on earth he would read that might make him love his mother less.

"Then maybe…let his curiosity be the guide. It's not like you can keep the journal a secret, because he's the one who found it."

"That's what I told Mama," Ella said.

"Bowie strikes me as a very strong man, both in body and spirit, and no matter how hard it is to learn, if it's your truth, it's your truth," Rowan said.

Ella stroked the tangles of Rowan's hair away from her face, then tilted her chin so they were looking eye to eye.

"How did you get so wise at such a young age?"

Rowan sighed. "I don't even remember being a kid."

"Your mama died when you were young, didn't she?" Ella asked.

Rowan nodded as Ella hugged her again. "You and

Bowie are a pair. Both of you losing your mothers at a young age."

Then they heard the bedroom door open and turned to look. Pearl emerged, wiping her eyes and blowing her nose.

"Well, that's that," she said. "We need a project. I can't just sit here and do nothing. Not with all this on my mind."

"I promised Bowie I'd make a peach cobbler for tonight," Rowan said.

Pearl smiled. "That's a fine idea. Ella can peel the peaches, I'll cut them up, and you start on the crust."

Rowan threw the blanket aside and jumped up. "A pie party. We're going to have a pie party!"

Even as they set to work, laughing and talking about cooking disasters from the past, when the conversation lulled Pearl got pensive, and the look in Rowan's eyes still mirrored her sadness.

Bowie was tired to the bone when they called a halt to the day. He had a whole other list of supplies to order, not the least of which were two different structural headers needed to open up the space like his grandma wanted. As soon as they got those in place, they could start rewiring the house and putting in all the new plumbing they'd need for that second bathroom.

When they locked up for the night, the men headed to the bed-and-breakfast to clean up, and Bowie went home.

He thought about that journal all the way to the trailer park, wondering if it was just teenage-girl stuff or if his mother had revealed something Ella and Gran hadn't known. Either way, it would have been tough for them to see the posts in Billie's own handwriting, all of them unaware of how brief her life was going to turn out to be.

As he drove through the neighborhood, he saw kids on bikes and a woman on her knees, weeding a flower bed along the front of her house. A teenage boy on the opposite side of the street was washing a car. Blessings looked like any place in small-town America, but there were always secrets to be kept, no matter where people lived.

Finally, he entered the trailer park, saw a little red-headed girl on a bike, and then saw Yancy Scott out there beside her. Like father, like daughter.

As always, he set the car alarm as he headed to the door. This time, he let himself in. The only person in sight was Rowan. She was setting places at the table, pattering around it in her bare feet and as unconcerned with her state of being as he'd seen her.

"Welcome home," she said.

Bowie made himself focus on her smile instead of her long legs and bare feet. "It's nice to have someone to come home to," he said. "When all this is over, I'm going to miss it."

Rowan paused. "If this is too personal, then just tell me to mind my own business…but I have to ask… Why in heaven's name do you live alone?"

He shrugged. "I don't stay in one place long enough to connect with anyone like that. And the locations I'm on for months at a time are nearly always isolated."

Rowan nodded and went back to placing cutlery at the place settings.

"What about you?" Bowie asked. "You are a beautiful woman."

She stopped, then laughed. "That is pure flattery. We both know that's not the truth."

Bowie blinked. "Who told you that?"

"Daddy. He was just being honest. He always told me I was as sweet as could be, and that it was okay being a little homely. He didn't want me disappointed by having no boyfriends."

Bowie was in shock. "Your daddy...told you that?"

She nodded.

"And you didn't have any boys ever wanting to take you out on a date?"

"Oh...a couple of boys called, I think, but then they never called back," she said.

"Then they were blind as bats," he muttered. "I'm going to shower off this dirt. I won't be long."

"There's time," she said. "We're having meatloaf, and it needs another fifteen minutes or so to be ready."

"I love meatloaf," he said, and pulled his work shirt over his head as he headed for the shower.

Comfortably unobserved, Rowan looked her fill at the muscles rippling across his back. It wasn't until he shut the bathroom door that she came back to her senses enough to go finish supper.

Chapter 8

COMPLETELY UNAWARE OF ROWAN'S INTEREST, OR THE girls secreted in the bedroom trying to decide what to do about him and his mother's journal, Bowie went through the ritual of shampooing his hair, which reminded him of how badly he needed that haircut, then scrubbing himself clean.

He put on the pair of sweats again, with a clean T-shirt, then carried the dirty clothes to the washer and started the load, just like the night before.

Pearl was already sitting at the dining table, watching Rowan and Ella. When Bowie emerged, he winked at her and grinned.

And in that moment, realization dawned. She no longer saw Judson Boone when she looked at Bowie. She saw him for the man he was.

He came to the table, kissed the top of her head, and then helped Ella fill glasses with iced tea. That's when he saw the peach cobbler sitting on the wet bar to cool.

"You guys made peach cobbler! It's my favorite dessert! Good thing I saw it before I sat down to eat. I'll be wanting to save room for that."

"Rowan made it," Ella said. "I only peeled the peaches for her. She made the crust and the filling. She sure knows her way around a kitchen."

Rowan's cheeks turned pink from the praise, which only reminded Bowie of her believing she was homely.

He suspected her father had been responsible for chasing the young men away. If this was true, it was a selfish thing to do, and likely so he wouldn't have to spend his aging years alone.

Once everyone was seated, Pearl said a blessing, and then they began passing food around the table and playing catch-up on their days. Bowie filled his gran in on their progress at her house, while Rowan listened as she ate.

"As soon as I get the men started in the morning, I'm coming back and we're going to get you some phones to replace the ones you lost," Bowie said.

Rowan immediately looked up. "Oh, I don't need—"

"You're getting one, too," Bowie said. "You probably have family somewhere trying to get in touch with you, making sure you're okay after all that happened."

"No, there's no one," Rowan said. "Daddy was an only child. His immediate family is deceased, and my mother was on her own when they met. I'm about as rootless as I could possibly be."

"Not anymore," Ella said. "Mama and I have already decided, so it's settled. You belong with us."

Rowan's dark eyes widened. She tried to smile, but tears were welling.

"That's the best thing that's ever happened to me," she said, then glanced at Bowie. "That almost makes us kin."

Bowie's eyes narrowed. "I can't be kin to you."

Pearl frowned. "Why not?"

"What if I wanted to take you on a date sometime? How the hell would that look…dating family?"

Rowan's lips parted, but for the life of her, she couldn't find the words to respond.

Pearl grinned.

"Oh lord," Ella said, and burst out laughing.

"Would someone please pass me the corn?" Bowie asked.

Rowan picked up the bowl and handed it to him.

"Thank you," he said, and served himself a second helping. "I don't know what you did to this can of corn, but it sure tastes better than when I heat one up."

"Add a bit of sugar, no salt, and a little pat of butter," Rowan said. "Takes away that canned taste and makes it taste more like fresh corn."

Bowie gave her a thumbs-up. "Sugar. I'm going to remember that."

A few minutes later, Rowan got up to get the cobbler, so Bowie went to get bowls out of the cabinet and then got ice cream from the freezer.

"You scoop cobbler, and I'll do the 'à la mode,'" Bowie said, then looked at the girls. "Ice cream, or straight cobbler?"

"Ice cream for both of us," Pearl said. "But just one scoop on mine or I'll be miserable."

Rowan had all the bowls filled with cobbler, except for Bowie's serving. She dipped one big spoonful and then the second, then glanced up at him. "Hey, you, is this enough?"

"Maybe one more," Bowie said. "One more *big* scoop."

Rowan grinned. "They're all big scoops. Now is *this* enough?"

Bowie eyed the bowl and then her. "Sometimes you can't get enough of a good thing to ever satisfy you."

Rowan's heart skipped a beat. "Is it enough pie?"

"Oh! Right... Yes, that's plenty." He added a couple

of scoops of ice cream, then put the carton back in the freezer while Rowan carried the bowls to the table.

He was still grinning when he sat down.

Rowan ignored him. She wasn't wise enough in the ways of men to know what to do with Bowie James and wasn't daring enough to think about what he might do with her.

Bowie lifted a spoonful of cobbler. "A toast to the pie maker tonight!"

The girls lifted spoons as well.

Rowan played along and nodded. "Thank you. Thank you. I owe it all to my amazing sous chefs, Pearl and Ella."

They finished dessert and were getting ready to clean up when Pearl left the table.

"Bowie, could you come here a moment, honey?"

He looked up. She was standing at the door to his bedroom.

"Yes, ma'am," he said. "What do you need?"

Gran pointed to the pink journal lying on the bed.

"It's yours to read, if you want."

Bowie felt a little tug of panic. "You've already read it?"

"Ella and I read it together," she said. "I didn't know whether we should let you read it or not, but Rowan said you were a very strong man, and whatever was in it was always going to be your truth, whether you knew it or not."

"She did, huh?" Bowie said, and looked back toward the kitchen, watching her measured movements and quick smiles.

Gran nodded. "Yes, but it is, of course, totally your call."

He walked into his bedroom and closed the door.

Pearl sighed. For better or for worse, the journal was a revelation.

Bowie crawled up on the bed, made a backrest of the pillows, and then picked up the journal, thinking of what his grandmother had just said. It sounded suspiciously like a warning.

Whatever is in this is always going to be my truth. So, I guess I'm about to find that out. A little nervous about what he might learn, he opened the book to the first page.

It began with a cover page for the new owner to fill out.

This book belongs to: *Billie Jo James*.

He ran his finger over the writing, and saw the date and counted backward. It was a Christmas gift from her mother, and she was nearly fifteen years old. He smiled to himself, wondering what kind of a girl she'd been before…

At first, the entries were just about girl stuff. Who had a boyfriend, and notes about going to an upcoming party, then a mention about the party afterward. Some of them even made him chuckle. She sounded like Gran. Kind of sassy, with a slap-you-in-the-face attitude about being honest.

There was a whole page on her fifteenth birthday, and then more of the same girl stuff for two months more. Then one entry about going to a slumber party, and that she was going to walk there because her sister, Ella, had just been released from the hospital after an appendectomy and Mama needed to stay close.

The whole rest of that page was blank, and the next entry was on a whole separate page and nearly three months later.

And it was gutting. Bowie read the words through a veil of tears.

> *I never made it to the slumber party. Randall*
> *Boone beat me up and raped me. I told my*
> *mama. I told the law. I told the judge in court.*
> *They did nothing to him. I am going to have*
> *a baby.*

Bowie wasn't stupid. He'd wondered all his life how his mother must have felt about him, and on three lines of the journal, he felt her horror and her fear.

His tears made him angry, and he used the hem of his T-shirt to wipe his eyes.

The next entry was a couple of weeks later.

> *I told my best friend, Haley. She won't talk to*
> *me anymore. The principal at school told Mama*
> *I couldn't come to school pregnant. They put*
> *me on homeschooling. I am in jail.*

And then the entries continued…each more heart-wrenching than the last. And all of them full of disgust for what was growing inside her.

Bowie was long past tears and numb with shock. He empathized with every emotion she had and understood exactly why she had them. She hadn't asked for any of this. Not the rape. Not the injustice afterward. And not the child.

The next one was a month later.

> *I just found out Randall's father offered Mama five thousand dollars to take me to have an abortion. This happened almost two months ago. It made me mad, but of course Mama told him to leave and never set foot on her property again. It was the first time I let myself think that the baby wasn't all about Randall. The baby was also part of me. It was the first time I thought of myself as the mother, and not the victim. It's time for me to grow up.*

There weren't any more entries until months later, and it was a single sentence.

> *I have a baby boy named Bowie and he is beautiful.*

Bowie read the sentence over and over, trying to come to grips with the poignancy of his arrival in her world. Then after that, the entries were intermittent, but all endearing. Entries about his growth, and what he was learning to do, and that the first word he said was *Mama*.

During the ensuing two years, there was also a mention of her getting her GED, the equivalent of a high school diploma, and talking about the available jobs in Blessings once he started school.

He turned a page, only to find an old Polaroid picture

of him sitting on Santa's lap in some store. In the picture he was screaming bloody murder. Below it, Billie had written *We do not like Santa*. He grinned.

He flipped through pages, quickly scanning the others, which were beginning to sound alike. As the only male in the house, he appeared to be running the show.

And then toward the last of the journal, they became dark again.

> *Jud Boone saw Bowie playing baseball and told me to take my bastard and leave town. I know why. The older my son becomes, the more he looks like them. I don't know what to do. I can't tell Mama or Ella. I already feel like a burden because I can't make enough money to move us out on our own. They don't begrudge us being here…but now, even our presence in Blessings is unwanted.*

Bowie didn't realize this had happened. She'd kept everything from him, thinking she was protecting him, when in fact it was his ignorance of the ongoing dispute that had left him open to attack. He knew the story of how he'd come to be, but he'd been raised among such loving people that it had never mattered. He hadn't wanted anything to do with that family. In his mind, they didn't exist.

Until they nearly killed him.

The last entry in the book was the night he and his mama ran away. Her rage for what they'd done to him was alive within the words, and the heartbreak for the solution she'd chosen was there as well.

Bowie was working in a booth at the Halloween Festival at school. I drove my car up to get him when it was over. The only people left at the gym were the high school kids who'd worked the booths and their sponsors. I went inside to let him know I was there, and we were walking out together when the Boone brothers grabbed us and dragged us into the shadows.

Jud was there, just watching. They cursed us. Randall slapped me, and then Bowie jumped all three men. They turned on him like the dogs they are. Despite me begging and screaming for them to stop, they kept beating him.

They didn't stop until they saw a police car cruise by. Then they said they'd be back to finish the job and ran away.

Bowie was hurt so bad. Mama and Ella were horrified when we got home. They wanted me to take him to the ER. Instead, I made them doctor him as best they could and ran to pack our bags. This is the last entry I'll make in this book. It belongs to our world in Blessings, and I'll never be back.

A part of me wishes I'd never been born, and the other part of me wishes the same of Bowie. God help the both of us. I don't know what's going to happen, but whatever comes, it will not be at the hands of the Boones.

May they rot in hell.

Bowie closed the journal and laid it aside.
Wished he'd never been born.

He rolled off the bed and left the room without comment.

Wished he'd never been born.

The girls were sitting at the table playing cards. Pearl looked up as the door opened. His face was devoid of emotion.

"Honey, are you okay?" she asked.

Bowie moved toward the front door without looking at any of them.

Ella saw his intent and called out. "Don't go outside in the dark barefoot."

He was out before any of them could stop him. The door swung shut on its own.

"His shoes! He needs shoes. Snakes abound at night," Pearl cried.

Rowan was out of her chair and running. She slid into her own tennis shoes, then ran to get a pair of his tennis shoes from the closet in his master bedroom and was out the door in seconds.

"Take a flashlight!" Pearl called.

Ella stopped her. "Let her be, Mama. He'll take help from her easier than he will from either of us."

Pearl shook her head and started to cry. "I was afraid something like this would happen."

Ella frowned. "He's in shock right now, like we were. He's stronger than this. And he knows stuff about their lives during the three years they were alone that we'll never know."

Bowie went straight to the picnic table and climbed up. He didn't think about his bare feet until he was already out, and he wouldn't go back because he wasn't ready to talk.

Then he heard the door open and close behind him and sighed. Only it wasn't Aunt Ella. It was Rowan. She stopped in front of where he was sitting and without saying a word put the shoes on his feet.

He was unprepared for this...for her, and when she bent over and quietly tied them on his feet so he wouldn't trip, her image blurred. He was crying again. She straightened up, then touched his knee.

"You helped me. I help you," Rowan said, and was starting to go back inside when he grasped her by the wrist.

"Please...stay," he said, and then he turned her loose, leaving the decision completely up to her.

Rowan climbed up onto the table beside him, like they'd done before, and let the night engulf them.

Bowie scrubbed the tears from his eyes with the heels of his hands, then took a deep breath and slowly exhaled, repeating the process several more times, just as he'd done to calm the panic attacks he'd had the year after his mother's death.

This emotion was nothing like panic, but it had been a shock, and he was having to weigh it against the fact that only three years later she committed suicide. She hadn't been able to change her past, but she'd damn sure given up on her future.

He'd felt sorry for her before, but right now he was gutted, thinking of how sad and desperate she must have been, when all that time he thought they were doing okay.

He glanced at Rowan. She was looking up...looking for her celestial signs.

"What do you see?" he asked.

"Proof."

He looked up, following her line of sight but not getting what she meant.

"Proof of what?"

She turned to face him, searching his features in the moonlight and realizing she was becoming far more attached than was probably good for her heart.

"Proof that as often as things change, they also stay the same. We aren't unique in our troubles, are we? As much as we've been hurt, so have other people, looking at the same stars and in so many lifetimes, long before we were so much as a flicker of light."

"I never took much stock in the phrase 'old soul' until I met you. Do you ever doubt this inner wisdom that seems to come when you most need it?" he asked.

Rowan shrugged. "I never thought about myself like that. Whatever I know did not come from books. It's just what I know. I came this way."

Bowie held his hand out to her, palm up.

Rowan didn't hesitate as she reached for him. His fingers closed around her hand, and there they sat, linked by their losses and the unexpected emotions of mutual attraction.

They sat without speaking, watching the lights in the trailers around them going off, one by one. The last to go was the little fifth-wheel trailer in the lot across the way.

Bowie glanced over his shoulder. The lights were still on in the kitchen area, but the rest of his home was dark.

"I'll go in, if you want to be outside on your own now," Rowan said.

Bowie shook his head. "What I want to do is kiss you.

But somehow that feels like I'd be taking advantage of your need for shelter."

Rowan froze. This was a moment she'd never known before, and something told her the chance might never come again. In her need to be loved, she forgot about everything she'd believed about herself and took a chance on believing in him.

"If I kissed you first, would that remove your guilt?" she whispered.

Bowie slid a hand beneath her hair, cupping her neck as he pulled her to him. He heard her sigh, then felt every muscle in her body acquiesce to his touch.

"We could try," he said. "But we might need to run more than one test kiss to be sure."

She leaned toward him and then made contact with his mouth right before the earth shifted, rocking them where they sat. His lips were smooth, and the kiss was gentle. She moved away.

"I think the guilt is still here," Bowie said.

She kissed him again, but this time he kissed her back, and it was soon apparent that second kiss wasn't going to be enough for her.

"I'm still uncertain," she said.

"Yeah, so am I," Bowie countered. "Maybe it's time I kissed you."

She scooted closer. He lifted her from the table into his lap, and when her arms went around his neck, he pulled her as close as breath would allow and put them both in orbit.

Rowan was feeling things she didn't know her body could feel, and there were aches and yearnings washing through her she didn't know how to control. It was the first time in her life that she regretted her inexperience with the opposite sex, because instinct was telling her they could light matches from the heat they would create between them.

And this time, Bowie was the one to pull away. But he didn't go far. He cupped her face, looking into her eyes and seeing the reflections of starlight.

"One of us has to stop now or we're both going to be too far gone to care."

Rowan sighed. It had been a beautiful moment between them, and she was sorry it was over.

"However," Bowie said, "I would gladly repeat the exercise. All you have to do is let me know."

Rowan shivered. "How would I do that?" she asked.

Bowie grinned, then gave her a quick kiss on the lips. "You'll figure it out. Are you ready to go inside?"

She nodded and slipped out of his lap.

He got off the table, then grabbed her around the waist and lifted her down as if she didn't weigh a thing.

"Thank you for sitting with me," he said.

"You're welcome, and I'm very glad I did or I would have missed all this…with you."

Bowie put an arm around her shoulder as they headed for the door.

"Just remember, there's more where that came from. And one other thing you need to know…if you begin to doubt me. This is not a thing I do. I don't let people get close. Just know that for me, you are one special woman."

When they reached the steps to go in, Rowan paused.

"I only ever had that one boyfriend in high school, and then only for a little while. After I graduated, there was no one, and as I told you, I assumed it was because I wasn't enough. Now I'm glad life kept me in such a suspended state of emotional growth. I think I would have been too trusting. I think I would have been very easy to hurt."

"I won't ever hurt you. I swear. If you feel as if life kept you waiting, I'd like to think it was because you were waiting for me."

Rowan sighed as he lowered his head for one last, very brief kiss.

Then he opened the door and they went inside. Just like the night before, Rowan went to shower while Bowie set the security alarm and made out the beds.

Then when he went in to get ready, she turned out the lights and crawled into bed.

Bowie emerged a short while later, saw her curled up in the same little ball with the covers held down around her neck, and then got into bed. He stretched out, then rolled over, and was on the verge of slumber when Rowan called out from across the room.

"Good night, Bowie."

He smiled. "Good night, Rowan."

And he slept without a single thought of the journal or that last entry of his mother's despair.

Chapter 9

IT WAS A LITTLE AFTER MIDNIGHT WHEN NELLIE BOONE rolled over in bed and, like always, reached out to touch her husband's arm just to know he was there. But she didn't feel him, so she turned on the light and saw Mel's side of the bed was empty.

She raised up on one elbow, saw the bathroom light was out, and he was nowhere in sight. This was so out of the norm for Mel that she got up to go check on him and found him sitting in the living room in the dark. He was leaning forward, his elbows on his knees, and looking down at the floor.

"Mel? Are you all right?"

Mel looked up. "I couldn't sleep."

Nellie sat down on the sofa beside him and patted him on the back.

"What's wrong?"

"Mama is divorcing Daddy. He left town. She's disowned all of us."

Nellie gasped. "You aren't serious! Why?"

Mel wiped a shaky hand across his face. "She saw Bowie James. The fact that he's the spitting image of Daddy when he was young made her realize Randall had lied to her about what happened to Billie James, and then it dawned on her that we must have known, which would explain the gossip about him getting beat up and why Billie took him and ran. She hates us all for denying our own blood."

Nellie sat without talking, trying to absorb what he was saying, until she finally had to ask.

"You mean that story I heard about you all was true? The boy was beaten up and his life was threatened?"

Mel shrugged. "Daddy wanted them gone."

Her voice rose a whole octave. "You beat up a kid?"

"Not just me. It was all of us, and Daddy was right there, egging us on."

Nellie's voice began to shake. "Randall knew that was his own child, and he still hurt him?"

Mel was beginning to notice the confession wasn't gaining him any sympathy.

"I don't know what Randall thought, and don't go carrying on like you didn't suspect anything. We've been married fifteen years, and you know how this goes. We work for Daddy. Only he's gone now, and it appears Emmitt and I are out of a job. I don't have a skill I can fall back on."

Nell stood up. "You could always go to work for a bill collector. If they needed any knees capped, you have the skill set for that."

Mel was so shocked he couldn't speak and let Nellie get all the way out of the room before he thought to respond.

Then he jumped up and followed her into their bedroom. She was sitting on the side of the bed, blowing her nose and crying.

He sat down beside her. "Don't cry, Nellie. I'm sorry. We'll figure it out."

"I'm not the one you should be apologizing to, so don't talk to me right now. I need to think."

"Think about what?" Mel asked.

Nellie turned and looked him straight in the eyes. "Whether I go home to Kentucky on my own, or whether I let you come with me."

Mel was like his father, quick to anger, and he unintentionally clenched his hands into fists as he stood.

"Let me? Let me? Are you saying you're divorcing me, like Mama is doing to Daddy?"

"If you'd been listening, I told you I need to think. Your best bet is to shut your mouth and go sleep on the sofa tonight."

Mel stormed out of their bedroom without uttering another word. He was so mad he felt like he might explode. He didn't know who he was maddest at—his daddy for teaching them to hate...or himself for not being man enough to stand up to him years ago and say no.

A similar conversation was still ongoing in Emmitt and Tiny's house. It began at the dinner table and carried on throughout the meal and all the way up to bedtime.

Tiny was furious that her easy way of life with no money worries was coming to an end. She was mad at Cora. She was mad at Emmitt. And she was mad at Judson for running away.

She'd sent Junior to his bedroom to watch TV, and now here it was almost midnight and neither she nor Emmitt had been to bed.

Emmitt was emotionally exhausted and worrying about his son and what he was facing.

Tiny was ablaze with misplaced indignation.

"I can't believe Judson just took himself out of Blessings like this. I never took him as a man who would roll over and quit all easy-like. Why, he even went off and left us to deal with Junior's situation on our own," she cried.

Emmitt shrugged. "He's our son, not Daddy's, which makes Junior our responsibility."

Tiny wouldn't listen. "Junior was only defending your honor."

And that's when Emmitt lost it. "Honor? What's honorable about what Mel and I did to an unarmed man? Tell me that!"

"Well, you were only doing what—"

"Exactly!" Emmitt shouted. "What Daddy told us to do. I don't like who I've become, and now I've poisoned my son with it to the point he might be facing juvenile detention."

Tiny threw up her hands and wailed. "I will not let my son go to jail."

"Oh, shut up, Tiny. He broke the law. You go raise hell about it and they'll slap you in jail, too."

The mere notion of being arrested was enough to shift her focus, but not the rant. She turned on her husband, enraged by the debacle they were facing.

"Then do something!" she demanded.

Emmitt turned around and got his car keys from the dresser and started out of the room.

"Emmitt Lee! Where are you going?" Tiny shrieked.

"Somewhere quiet. It's not like I have to get up and go to work in the morning," he snapped, and walked out of the house with her traipsing behind him, shrieking and bawling every step of the way.

Down the hall, Junior was lying in bed, staring at the ceiling. In his mind, everything that was happening was all his fault. He couldn't believe his grandparents were getting a divorce. And the fight he had been listening to between his parents had been just as eye-opening.

He rolled over onto his side and started to cry. If only he hadn't messed up that man's car, none of this would be happening. The last thing he was thinking as he finally fell asleep was—if he caused this, then it was up to him to fix it.

Bowie had just finished shaving, but instead of getting dressed, he was looking at himself in the mirror and thinking back over what his life had become.

He'd become used to work filling his every waking hour without thinking about how fast the years were passing. He was thinking that hurricane had done him a great big favor by giving him a reason to come back even if it was temporary. It had reminded him what being a part of a family meant.

Meeting Rowan had only added to the unsettled feeling, and last night had been a revelation. Just two short days, and she was no longer a stranger. He'd seen her laughing hysterically. He'd seen her cry. He'd seen fire flash in her dark eyes, and he'd seen an endless sorrow. Kissing her had only made him want more, but it was the innocence in her that filled him with an overwhelming need to protect.

Then he glanced at the time and reached for his clothes. When he emerged a couple of minutes later and saw Rowan sitting at the table eating toast with peanut butter and jelly, he grinned.

"No cereal today?"

She looked up at him and smiled. "It just felt like a PB&J morning…you know?" Then she pointed at the cabinet. "I made one for you, too, but you don't have to eat it if you don't want to. It won't hurt my feelings."

He leaned down and kissed the top of her head. "It will hurt my feelings if I don't," he said. He poured himself a cup of coffee and sat down with her and the sandwich, then began to eat.

"I'll be back at noon. We need to get phones replaced. Did you have an iPhone or an Android?"

"I didn't have anything, remember? Daddy got one, then did away with the landline to save money."

Bowie frowned as he took a sip of coffee, but to him, it sounded like another way for her dad to isolate her. He glanced at the time again and quickly finished off the sandwich.

"Want another one?" Rowan asked.

"No thanks, honey, but thank you for being my breakfast partner."

"My pleasure, too," she said.

"See you guys at noon. I'll take you to Granny's first, and then we're getting phones."

Rowan sighed, and Bowie heard it.

"Hey…what's wrong? I don't mean to be bulldozing you into something you don't want. It's totally fine if—"

"It's not that. It's this," Rowan said, pointing at her clothes. "I have three outfits, none of which look like going-out-to-eat clothes. I would rather stay here and you take your girls."

Bowie backtracked and then cupped the side of her cheek.

"If you're with them, then you're with me, you know."

She blushed and then finally smiled. "I know, but—"

"We'll talk about it later," he said. "Gotta go." He gave her a thumbs-up.

Rowan followed him to the door, and then stood in the doorway until he looked back. Then she waved. The smile on his face made her heart skip. She backed up and then locked the door. Bowie James *was* the bulldozer. He didn't waste time doing anything, including making known what he wanted.

She wrapped her arms around her waist and shivered with a sudden longing for more. Of everything. Then she began putting their cups and plates in the dishwasher, thinking this man would have made Daddy nervous. This man didn't think she was homely. And she was beginning to wonder how other people saw her, too.

———

The demo crew had been at work nearly an hour. They had taken down all the walls that weren't load-bearing. Bowie had ordered two long headers yesterday to shore up the walls that were load-bearing, and once those were in place, the studs could come down, too.

He was looking over an idea for the kitchen layout—he'd roughed it out, but needed to run it by the people who'd be cooking in it before final decisions were made—when Ray yelled at him from the front porch.

"Hey, Bowie! Someone here to see you."

"Be right there!" he shouted, and rolled up the plans as he headed for the front of the house.

Recognizing his visitor as the kid who'd keyed his car, Bowie frowned and went out to talk to him.

"Please don't be mad at me, Mr. James. No one knows I'm here, but I need to talk to you."

Bowie frowned. The fact that the teen had come all this way on his own made him curious.

"You have five minutes," he said.

Junior Boone let out a big sigh of relief. At least Bowie was going to let him talk, which was more than he deserved.

"First off, I'm sorry I was such an ass. From what I've learned in the past twenty-four hours, it runs in the family."

Bowie blinked. The kid was actually talking like he had a little sense.

"I'm still listening," he said.

"I have come to ask if you would let me work off some of what I owe you on your car. I know it won't clear the debt, but I caused a whole lot of trouble in my family…" Junior stopped, trying to regain his composure so he didn't cry.

Bowie saw him struggling with tears and wondered where the hell he was going with this, but then the kid picked up where he left off.

"…and I'd give anything to take it back. My grandma ran Grandpa off and filed for divorce. My mom and dad fought all night, and I found out this morning that my aunt Nellie is moving back to Kentucky, with or without my uncle Mel." His eyes welled with tears again, and now his voice was trembling. "I thought maybe if I didn't cost everyone so much money, it would fix some of this. I'm fifteen. I'm strong and I play football at school, so I'm in good shape for hard work. I don't care how dirty or hard it is. I'll do it…if you let me."

Bowie was impressed with the plea. He knew it was genuine, but what he felt worse about was that the kid thought he'd caused all the uproar.

"Junior? That's what they call you, right?" he asked. Junior nodded.

"Do you know who I am?"

"Yes, sir. Your name is Bowie James, you're kin to my family, and you all don't get along."

Bowie sighed. "That's probably the biggest understatement ever made, and I see you weren't paying attention the day we met when I told the chief who I was. See those folding chairs over there by that ice chest? Follow me and take a seat."

Junior sat down in the shade while Bowie opened the ice chest and got out a couple of bottles of water, then handed one to the kid.

He sat down in the other chair and took a drink, and then looked the boy in the eyes. "If you want to work off some of your debt, then you need to know who you'll be working for."

Junior was so excited he could only nod. It sounded like Bowie James was going to let him work.

"Yes, my last name is James, but I'm Randall Boone's son. You don't need the details, but what you do need to know is that you are responsible for none of the chaos within your family. That's all because of me. Your grandma is likely upset because her husband and all three of her sons lied to her about me, and my coming back to Blessings to fix my grandma's house has opened up a whole lot of old wounds."

Junior couldn't quit staring. "I never knew Uncle Randall. He died before I was born."

Bowie shrugged. "I can't say I'm sorry, because my mother is dead, too. She killed herself right after my eighteenth birthday, and it's all because of the trauma she suffered at the hands of your family. I've been on my own ever since, and if it hadn't been for that hurricane, I'd still be on the move. But you know how it is with family... When they send out a call for help, you come."

"Yes, sir," Junior whispered, but he kept looking at Bowie. He couldn't wrap his head around how that would feel. He'd be the same age in three years, and the thought of being on his own in the world then was horrifying. And then it hit him.

"Oh! Wait! Oh wow! We're cousins."

Bowie nodded. "First cousins."

"And my grandma is your grandma, too."

Bowie nodded again. "The only difference between us is that you were wanted and I wasn't. Now, if you can deal with all that and still want to work, I say yes, and I only have one question. Do your parents know where you are?"

Junior sighed. "No, sir."

"You have to clear it with them, or it will only cause more trouble. Go home, and if they agree, we start work at eight every morning. Wear old clothes, boots, not tennis shoes, and bring a pair of gloves. I'll furnish the rest."

Junior jumped up, so elated he could hardly speak.

"Thank you, Mr. James. Thank you for giving me this chance."

Bowie shrugged. "If we're going to work together, then you need to call me Bowie, or Boss, like the other guys. No mister."

"Yes, sir. I mean, yes, Boss. I won't let you down."

Then he took off running, still carrying the unopened bottle of water. He was still running when he disappeared from sight.

"Lord," Bowie muttered, and shoved a hand through his hair. "What the hell did I just sign up for?"

He went back inside to look for Ray and found him tearing out subfloor beneath where the old tub used to stand.

"Floor is rotted here, Boss. There must have been a slow leak for a long time before it was fixed."

"Not a bit surprised," Bowie said. "And what wasn't already ruined, the flood finished off. Hey, I need to be gone for a while. You guys decide what you want to do about lunch. I have some business to take care of."

"Will do," Ray said. "And we proceed with tearing out the old plumbing?"

"Yes. If you need me, just call." With that, he was gone.

Junior Boone ran most of the way home, well aware he still had to face both parents. He'd left without telling them where he was going and they were probably already mad. So he was not surprised by the glare his daddy gave him when he came inside, all hot and sweaty.

Both of his daddy's eyes were black from the broken nose, and he still had packing up his nostrils, so when he frowned it made Junior think of an old boar raccoon.

"Where have you been?" Emmitt asked. "The school already called to tell us you were absent, and you didn't tell anyone where you were going."

"Nobody was awake when I left," Junior said.

Tiny came in from the kitchen, drying her hands as she paused behind Emmitt's chair.

"Did you forget how to write? A note would have been appreciated," she said.

"I got a job. I start at eight tomorrow morning."

"A job? Doing what? What about school?" Emmitt asked, and Tiny chimed in with a second question: "Who hired you?"

Junior braced himself. "I heard you guys fighting last night. I heard you say Grandma and Grandpa have split up, and that Aunt Nellie is moving back to Kentucky, and I know it's all because of me and all the money it's going to cost us to get Mr. James's car fixed. I'll turn in the work I miss at school. But this is something I need to do."

Tiny put a hand over her heart, sad at what he'd assumed yet touched by his gesture.

"Honey. None of that had anything to do with you."

Junior shook his head. "I know better. Grandma came to the jail to bail us out. She came back to our cells. I saw the look on her face when she saw me, and she called me a little hoodlum. And I heard the fight between her and Grandpa."

"I didn't know that," Emmitt said. "Why didn't you tell me?"

"What for?" Junior said. "It didn't change anything."

Tiny sighed. "Well, I admire you for the effort you're making. Where are you going to work?"

"I'll tell you, and it doesn't matter what you think about it, either. I made the mistake. I went straight to the man to fix it. I asked Bowie James if he would let me work off some of what I owe him while he and his crew are remodeling his grandma's house."

Emmitt all but leaped out of the chair. "You did no such thing!"

Junior braced himself. "I did, but it wasn't an easy task getting him to trust me, and don't expect me to go back on my word. I won't be doing any skilled labor, but I can carry, and load and unload supplies, and clean up, and maybe they'll even let me paint when they get to that point."

Emmitt was so stunned he couldn't respond, but Tiny did, and in a way Emmitt did not expect.

"Good for you," Tiny said. "It is an honorable thing to admit a mistake, and even more so to go straight to the source to fix it."

"I have to wear old clothes and boots, not tennis shoes. And I'll need to bring work gloves. The rest he'll furnish," Junior said, and then paused and looked straight at his dad. "Have you always known he was Uncle Randall's son?"

Emmitt hesitated.

"No more lies, Emmitt," Tiny said.

"Yes, I guess we have," Emmitt admitted.

"You knew he was family, and it didn't matter?"

Emmitt sighed. "You don't understand."

Junior swallowed past the lump in his throat. "Did he do anything to you and Uncle Mel before he broke your nose?"

Emmitt's face flushed a dark, angry red. "We were just doing what Daddy told us to do."

Junior stared at his parents as if he'd never seen them before.

"Just so you know, I like him. He was fair with me when he didn't have to be. And that's that. I didn't eat breakfast before I left and I'm hungry. Mama, is there any milk for the cereal?"

"Yes," Tiny said. "Come with me. I'll fix it for you."

"No need," Junior said. "I can pour milk on my own cereal," he said, and then walked past them into the kitchen.

Tiny sat down on the sofa beside Emmitt's recliner. The silence between them was telling. One parent had already sided with Junior's decision, and the other one had nothing to say.

The division between them grew a little bit wider.

It was too early to take the girls to lunch, and Bowie had business to tend to. His first stop was the police station.

Avery, the day dispatcher, was on duty when Bowie walked in.

"Morning," Bowie said. "Is Chief Pittman in? I need to talk to him."

"Yes, sir. Just a second and I'll let him know you're here."

A couple of minutes later, Lon entered the lobby. "Mr. James. You wanted to talk to me?"

"Yes," Bowie said.

"Then let's go to my office."

Bowie followed him down the hall, then took a seat in the chair that was offered.

"Now, what can I do for you?" Lon asked.

Bowie took a slow breath. "I want to withdraw the charges I made against Junior Boone."

Lon was surprised and it showed. "Really? Can I ask why?"

"The kid came to me this morning asking if I would let him work off some of his debt by helping with the renovation we're doing on my grandma's house. From what all he said, it appears the Boone presence in Blessings might soon be dwindling. He said Cora kicked Jud out of the house and filed for divorce. His parents are fighting, and his aunt Nellie is moving back to Kentucky. And the kid thinks it's all his fault for costing the family so much money. He thinks if he works off some of the debt, it might heal the rifts."

"Oh wow," Lon said.

Bowie shrugged. "Yeah...pretty much what I thought. And there is a chance, albeit a slim one, that Junior Boone might actually have the makings of a good man. I don't want to be the one who denies him the opportunity to make that happen."

Lon nodded. "I see where you're going, and I must say, considering all you and your family have been through, it is a very generous offer."

Bowie shrugged. "He doesn't know much about any of that. Maybe this stupidity will end with his generation. Just don't tell the Boones I dropped charges...at least for a while. They seem to behave better under threat of prison. Anyway, that's all I came to say, and thank you."

Lon shook Bowie's hand and walked him back up to the lobby. Bowie left, while Lon turned to the dispatcher.

"I'll be at the courthouse for a bit. Call if you need me."

"Yes sir," Avery said.

Lon went out the back to his cruiser and headed for the courthouse to let the judge know, while Bowie was on his way to the women's boutique he'd seen on the way in.

He had never bought a single piece of clothing for any woman, and the whole notion was kind of scary. However, he wanted Rowan to go with them, and if she needed different clothes to do it, he would make that happen.

He parked in front of the Unique Boutique, then took a deep breath and got out. No need getting nervous about anything. It was only clothes.

And then he walked inside, and the first display was lacy underwear.

"If I can build mansions on the sides of mountains, I can do this," he muttered.

A woman was smiling at him from the counter and then came up front to meet him.

"Good morning. I'm Kitty. Can I help you find something?"

"Yes, ma'am," Bowie said. "I have a friend who needs a couple of outfits to replace what she lost in the flood. Just casual stuff. Nothing fancy."

"Of course. What size?"

He frowned. He'd only seen her in oversize clothing, but he remembered how tiny her waist felt when he helped her down from the picnic table last night, and he knew how wide her shoulders were, and remembered those long legs.

"I'm not sure, but I can size up anything if I see it. She has shoulders about this wide, and the top of her head is about here on me," he said, measuring just beneath his chin. "And her waist is this big," he said, gesturing with his hands.

Kitty hid a smile. He might not know the clothing size, but she'd bet money the woman was just the right size for him.

"Let's look at a pair of jeans first. They go with everything."

And so they began to shop. It didn't take Bowie long to decide Rowan was probably about a size eight in the waist, the length would be long, and he'd debated with skinny jeans or straight legs. There was something about the skinny jeans that didn't strike him as Rowan's style, so he chose the straight-legged jeans and the same size in a pair of slacks. With Kitty's urging, he chose two tops to go with them. The white blouse had peekaboo cutouts at the shoulders and flared out around her hips like the slightly ruffled bloom of a morning glory. The other top was pale blue with a stretchy cross-stitched bodice that hung just below the waist.

"These are great," Bowie said, and then saw backless sandals on a display behind the counter. "Let me see that shoe."

She handed it to him, then watched the way he seemed to be measuring it in his mind. She didn't know he'd seen Rowan barefoot far more than he'd seen her in shoes.

"Do you have this shoe in any other colors besides tan, and maybe a halfsize larger?"

Kitty grinned. "You have a good eye," she said, and looked through the sizes for an eight and a half. "I have it in the size you wanted, but the brown is the only color."

"No matter," Bowie said. "I'll take them." Then he

watched as she scanned the tags and rang up the purchases. When she gave him the total, he handed her a credit card.

A few minutes later, he was back in the car and on his way home. The excitement of giving Rowan something was tempered with a slight worry that none of it would fit, or that she wouldn't like it. Worry ended as he was pulling up to his home. Too late to back out now.

Chapter 10

BOWIE GOT OUT WITH THE PURCHASES HE MADE AT UNIQUE Boutique and headed for the door. There wasn't a woman in sight when he let himself in, but he heard a lot of chatter coming from his bedroom.

"Lucy! I'm home!" he yelled.

There was a moment of silence. Then the door opened, and Ella came out, laughing.

"You sure got our attention with that greeting," she said.

Pearl and Rowan were right behind her. "Bowie, do you remember all those old *I Love Lucy* reruns we used to watch when you were little?" Pearl asked.

Bowie grinned. "I sure do."

"We're mostly ready," Ella said, then frowned. "Rowan doesn't want to go."

"I think she might change her mind," he said, and handed her the sack. "Go try them on."

Rowan's eyes widened when she saw the Unique Boutique sack and peeked inside, then clutched the clothes to her chest and ran back into the bedroom.

"I'm going to wash up and put on a clean shirt," Bowie said.

Pearl hugged his neck. "You are an old softie…getting your not-really-kin friend something new."

He shrugged. "I haven't spent a dime of my own money on anyone but myself in ages. It makes me happy to be able to do this, Gran…for all of you."

He headed for the bathroom to make a quick change and emerged only seconds ahead of Rowan, who came out wearing the jeans and the white blouse with the peek-a-boo shoulders. They fit perfectly, and she was teary but smiling.

The girls exclaimed over how pretty she looked, but she needed to see the truth in Bowie's eyes, and she would know if he was lying.

"What do you think?" she asked, and did a little pirouette so they could get the full front and back view.

"Is it improper for me to tell the not-really-kin girl how stunning she looks?"

Ella smirked. Gran waited. And then Rowan smiled.

"Not improper at all," Rowan said. "And the shoes fit, too. How did you figure out my sizes?"

He shrugged. "I build things. I guess I have a good eye. So, is everybody ready to go?"

"Yes!" they echoed.

"We're going to Granny's first, and then to the phone store. Aunt Ella, did you all get your phones here in town?"

"Yes."

"Good. Then they'll already have your plan in the computer. All we'll need to do is get you replacements. So off we go."

He went down the steps first so he could hold onto them as they came down, then loaded them up into the car again. The last thing he did was set the security system, and then he drove away.

Once again, Rowan was riding shotgun and Pearl and Ella were in the back seat, chattering away about paint colors and new flooring for the renovation.

Bowie glanced at Rowan. She seemed to be very taken with her new clothes and kept feeling the fabric and fussing with her hair.

"You look beautiful," he said.

"Thanks to you," she said.

"No, thanks go to good genetics. It's not the clothes. It's you."

She smiled and then glanced out the window as they were passing the Unique Boutique and imagined him picking out these clothes.

"Who's hungry?" Bowie asked.

"We all are," Ella said. "When you told Rowan you were coming back to take us out at noon, we only had toast and coffee for breakfast so we'd have plenty of room for the food at Granny's."

"Awesome," Bowie said. "I haven't taken a pretty girl out on a date in years, and now I have three of them."

"I haven't been to Granny's in a long time," Rowan added. "I'm looking forward to it."

He pulled into the parking lot, parked as close to the entrance as he could get, and escorted them inside.

To everyone's surprise, Lovey was sitting on a tall stool behind the front counter. She had a cast on one arm and a few small, pink scars on her face and arms from where stitches and staples had been, but she was smiling.

"Welcome to Granny's."

"Oh! Lovey! It's wonderful to see you here," Pearl said. "Do you remember my grandson, Bowie?"

Lovey eyed the big, good-looking man and grinned. "Yes, but he sure didn't look like this last time I saw him. Welcome home, Bowie, and welcome back to Granny's."

"Thanks," Bowie said.

Lovey eyed the pretty dark-eyed girl beside him. "You look familiar, honey. Do I know you?"

"Maybe. I'm Rowan Harper, but I haven't been here in a long time, and I'm looking forward to it."

Lovey's smile shifted. "Oh, I remember you now. And I did hear of your daddy's passing. I'm so very sorry."

"Thank you," Rowan said.

Lovey waved down one of the waitresses. "I'm here on a trial basis. I missed being here so much that the doctor finally okayed it. However, I had to promise not to overdo for a while, so the girls are seating customers for me."

Then Becky appeared and grabbed four menus. "This way, please," she said, and took them to one of the large booths. Pearl and Ella took one side, and Rowan and Bowie the other.

Keenly aware of the man beside her, it was all Rowan could do to focus on food.

Becky took their drink orders. "Be right back with some hot biscuits," she said.

"I won't turn those down," Bowie said.

"Nobody does," Pearl said. "And since Lovey is here, that means Mercy Pittman is back in the kitchen, baking up her usual magic."

Becky came back with their drinks, and another waitress followed her up with a basket of biscuits.

"Enjoy," Becky said. "I'll give you a few minutes to look at the menus, then I'll be back to take your orders."

"Thanks," Bowie said, and passed the bread basket around, then took one for himself and reached for the butter.

"These are amazing," Rowan said. "I'm a good cook and a decent baker, but not on this level."

"I'll disagree with that," Bowie said. "That peach cobbler you made last night was so good."

Rowan smiled. "Thanks. It was my daddy's favorite fruit."

"In Georgia, peaches are everyone's favorite," Ella said.

They read the menu as they ate their biscuits and were waiting for the waitress to come back and take their orders when a young man got up from his table and walked over to where they were sitting.

"Rowan Harper? It is you! I thought it was, but it's been about eight years since I've last seen you. You look amazing." Then he glanced around the table and smiled at Bowie. "You must be her husband. I'm going to give you props for finding a way around her dad. It didn't matter how many times we tried to call, he answered them all and told us to go about our business. By the way, I'm Louis Bennett. I graduated with Rowan. Really nice to meet you," he said, and offered his hand.

Bowie shook it. "I'm Bowie James, and Rowan and I just met a few days ago. But that doesn't mean I'm not trying to get her attention."

Rowan was so shocked by what Louis was saying that she couldn't think what to say.

Louis laughed. "Oh, well, good luck, then. Her father is a tough nut to crack."

Rowan looked up. "Daddy died in the aftermath of the hurricane. He drowned."

Shock was evident on Louis's face. "Oh, Rowan, I'm so sorry to hear that. My sympathies," he said, then pointed to his table. "I'd better get back. My wife and I are expecting our second child in a couple of months, so I'm treating her to lunch before we go to her doctor's appointment."

"Congratulations, and my best to your wife," Rowan said.

Louis gave her a thumbs-up and then hurried back to his table.

Bowie leaned toward her just enough that their shoulders touched, and he pointed to the lunch special.

"I'm getting the lunch special. Fried shrimp and hush puppies. Can't beat that," he said, then looked up at the girls. "What are you two going to eat?"

"I'm having shrimp, too," Ella said.

"I'm going for a cheeseburger and fries," Pearl said, then glanced across the table at Rowan, unaware of the undercurrents. "Rowan, what are you going to have?"

"Gumbo. I never make it, and I love it," she said, and then glanced across the room to the table where Louis Bennett was seated.

Bowie reached for her hand beneath the table and gave it a gentle squeeze, but when Rowan clutched his hand and held on much tighter, he could tell how deep the shock had gone.

Becky returned, took their orders, and retrieved the menus.

Rowan reached for one of the little butter packets and then smeared butter on both sides of her uneaten biscuit. If she was eating, then she wouldn't be expected to talk.

Bowie said I was beautiful. Louis said I looked amazing. Daddy said I was homely. Never in my life have I felt so betrayed.

And then to add one more layer of confirmation, a couple was on their way to be seated and when Rowan glanced up, she recognized the woman as another classmate.

And the woman recognized her and paused. "Rowan, we heard about your father's passing. I'm so sorry. You have my condolences."

Rowan nodded. "Thank you, Justine."

Justine nodded. "Of course, and I just have to say, you always were a pretty girl, but you have grown into a beautiful woman. My apologies for interrupting."

She hurried on to her table and sat down.

Bowie glanced at Rowan again. "I didn't think about this happening. Hope you're okay," he said.

Rowan let go of his hand. "No, it's okay. It's perfectly normal, and it doesn't upset me. It's just friends being kind, you know?"

"Good. I don't like to see you sad."

Finally, their food arrived, smoothing over the rocky patch, and Rowan slowly got past feeling numb and actually enjoyed her food while listening to Pearl and Ella talk about Bowie's youthful adventures.

Judson Boone was still smarting from the slap-down Cora had given him yesterday. Calling him a coward had been hard to hear. He'd wanted to be angry with her, but looking at everything from her viewpoint made the accusations make sense.

He *had* gone off and left his troubles behind. But there was no way in hell he'd ever live in Blessings again. Still, he should probably talk to his sons. He could only imagine what was happening with them. He'd kept them all under his thumb by paying rent on their homes and giving them monthly stipends. They'd never worked at regular jobs and were seriously unprepared to support their families.

And he had gone off and left Emmitt Junior hanging, too. He wouldn't even know what happened to him when he had to return to court for sentencing.

But what was eating at him the most was being taken down by Bowie James. He was either going to have to come to terms with it and forget the bastard ever existed, or take a chance and exact his own kind of retribution. However, the biggest drawback was that if anything happened to Bowie, everyone, including the law, would immediately suspect him. And he wasn't willing to go back to jail, no matter how much crow he had to eat.

He glanced at the empty liquor bottle in the waste basket, the empty pizza box, the sack full of trash from the burger and fries he'd ordered in, then scratched the growth of whiskers on his face as he took note of the time. It was almost noon. He hadn't showered or dressed once since he got here, but he didn't need his pants on to talk on the phone. The first call he made was to Mel.

But the phone rang and rang, then went to voicemail. Jud immediately assumed Mel just wasn't picking up and got up to go shower and shave.

Mel's morning hadn't been any better than the night before. Breakfast with Nellie had been silent and a little nerve-racking. The fact that she was actively pursuing the notion of moving home to live with her family was shocking. They didn't always see eye to eye, but he didn't want to lose her.

After he came in from mowing the grass, he checked his phone and saw he'd missed a call from his dad, and there was a note from Nellie lying beside it saying she had errands to run and would not be home for lunch.

"Well, great," Mel said and headed back to the bathroom to wash up and change clothes, hoping Emmitt would go to Granny's with him.

But then he remembered the cold shoulder they'd received there the other day and hesitated. Maybe he'd call Daddy first, and if he was still in Savannah, he and Emmitt could go there and have lunch with him.

He called Jud's cell phone, heard it ringing, and waited for him to pick up. But he didn't. He let it ring until it went to voicemail and disconnected without leaving a message, then went to clean up.

He stripped in the bathroom before raising his chin so he could look at his neck, eyeing the bruise from Bowie's karate chop. It was still purple and very sore.

"Nearly broke my neck," Mel muttered, then turned on the water and got in the shower, just as Jud was getting out of the shower in Savannah.

Jud saw he'd missed the call and immediately called back, only to have it go to voicemail again. He wasn't in the habit of playing phone tag with people, especially his own family, so he got dressed and went out to get some food and then drive around the city to see if there was any place where he might want to live.

Rowan had eaten all of the gumbo she could hold and was sitting quietly, listening to Bowie laughing with his girls. She loved that he called them his girls. And she was touched by his continuing intent to include her, too.

There was no denying she was attracted to him. But she feared he would lose interest once he found out she'd never made love, let alone made out, except for last night when he'd pulled her into his lap out on the picnic table and kissed her—a lot.

She didn't know if that constituted "making out," but it had made a mess of her emotions. It had taken a while for her to finally fall asleep because of thinking about how he made her feel.

As for the revelation about her father, she was past the shock of learning he had purposefully hidden the boys' calls from her and was disgusted with herself for being so naive. And she was hurt that he'd encouraged her to believe she wasn't pretty, thinking it would deter her from seeking boyfriends on her own.

Knowing that made her remember the times when he'd looked at her from across the kitchen table and remarked upon her continuing presence at home and how blessed he was to know he wouldn't grow old alone. It all made sense now. Instead of letting her live a normal life and make a family of her own, he'd selfishly chosen to manipulate her life in an effort to keep her with him. It didn't feel right to be mad at him, considering he hadn't been in the grave quite a month, but she was seriously ticked off.

Then Bowie said her name. "Rowan?"

"Yes?" she said.

"Do you want dessert?"

"Oh, I'm way too full for anything else, but thank you."

"Then we're good to go. Are you ready?"

"Yes," she said, and when he got out of the booth to help the girls get out, she slid out behind him and followed them up front to check out.

Lovey's cheeks were pink, and there was a faint sheen on her skin from the continual blasts of hot air as people came and went.

"How was your meal?" she asked as Bowie handed her his credit card.

"It was lovely," Pearl said. "And such a treat to have our boy home, too."

Bowie was signing the credit card slip when the door opened behind him. He slid the pen and slip of paper back toward Lovey.

"Have a nice day," she said.

"You, too," Bowie said, and when he turned around, he found himself face-to-face with Melvin Boone.

Mel frowned, but when Bowie's face remained expressionless, he stepped aside to let them pass and looked away.

Bowie slipped his hand beneath his gran's elbow and winked at Rowan, and out the door they all went. The car was hot, but he turned the air conditioner up on high and it quickly began to cool off.

They were on the way to the little phone shop just off Main when Pearl spoke up.

"Was that man behind us Melvin Boone?"

"Yes, ma'am," Bowie said.

"Did you put that bruise across his neck?"

"Yes, ma'am," Bowie said again.

Rowan glanced at Bowie, who seemed undisturbed by seeing the man again. Then she kept looking, trying to figure out why he seemed so calm in the face of the chaotic life he'd been born to.

Bowie caught her staring. "Everything okay?"

"Yes, everything's okay," Rowan said, surprised that she meant it. A little confidence was good for what ailed you, and maybe that's why Bowie didn't appear fazed by the unexpected. He oozed confidence...and sex appeal, but that was another thing altogether.

The next hour they spent at the phone store was something Bowie hoped he'd never have to endure again. By the time they had replacement phones added to the girls' phone plans and new phones picked out, and then Rowan added to their phone plan and a phone for her, they were all in something of a mood when they started home.

"I'm never going to figure this thing out," Gran muttered.

"I'll help you, Mama," Ella said.

Rowan was so happy to have one that she wasn't going to complain about anything.

"Is there anything else you ladies need before I take you home?" Bowie asked.

"I need a nap," Pearl muttered.

"Yes...yes, you do," Ella said.

"There's no need to be a smarty-pants, and that wasn't funny," Pearl snapped. "You're no Lucille Ball."

"If I dye my hair red, then will I be funny?" Ella asked.

Pearl snorted.

Ella grinned.

Rowan glanced at Bowie, who was trying not to laugh.

"They need to take that show on the road, don't they?" he said.

Rowan laughed out loud, and the sound sent shivers up Bowie's spine.

"You need to do that more often," he said.

"Do what?"

"Laugh. It makes everything better when you laugh," Bowie said.

Rowan smiled. "Well, as soon as I figure out how to record voices on this phone, I'll record a big belly laugh for you and then play it on command. How's that?"

He glanced at her, then shook his head. "Hey, Aunt Ella, I've got another comic up here in the front seat. If you and Gran go on the road with your comedy tour, she'd be a great opening act."

They laughed and were all still smiling when he pulled up at the motor home and parked.

Frank was mowing the grass, and Jewel was at the side of the house, hanging up laundry on the small clothesline. They waved as Bowie and the girls got out.

Bowie waved back and then made sure all of them had their stuff before following them inside.

"Oh, it's so good to be home," Pearl said.

"Pearl, would you and Ella like something cold to drink?" Rowan asked.

"Yes, please," Pearl said. "Just cold water, and then I'm going to nap a bit."

"Ella, what about you?" Rowan asked.

"If there's any sweet tea, I'd take a glass."

"Yes, ma'am, there's tea," Rowan said, and went straight to the kitchen to get the drinks.

Pearl and Ella sat down on the sofa and started comparing their new phones with the ones they'd had.

Bowie watched the scene playing out with a lump in his throat. They all fit. It was as if Rowan had been born into the family, and he was the one who'd come to visit. It wasn't anything he'd chosen. Life had taken him away, and it had truly taken a hurricane to get him back. He didn't know how the future was going to play out, but he knew one thing for sure. He'd be back here every chance he got, and the Boones be damned.

Rowan delivered their cold drinks, then turned to look for Bowie, who was getting a cold bottle of pop to take with him.

"Are you leaving now?" she asked as she walked into the kitchen area.

He nodded, then surprised himself by hugging her.

"Thank you," he said, and abruptly let go.

"I didn't do anything," she said.

"You love…better than anyone I ever knew. And you are doing, from the goodness of your heart, what I should have been doing. Thank you for taking such good care of my girls."

Then he left so abruptly that Rowan didn't get to the door to wave goodbye before he was gone. She locked the door, looked up, and saw Pearl and Ella watching her.

"Are you ready for that?" Ella asked.

"For what?" Rowan asked.

"I think he's falling for you, girl," Ella said.

Rowan sat down beside them. "And what would you think about that?"

"When two people love each other, there's nothing better," Pearl said, and reached for Rowan's hand.

Ella clasped the other one. "We love our Bowie. And we've grown to love you. If you can find your way to each other, then as far as we're concerned, it's a match made in heaven. But if you decide it's not right, it still won't change a thing about how we feel about you. Okay?"

Rowan squeezed their hands, trying not to cry. "I'm learning everything about relationships on Bowie, and at a heart-stopping rate, but if this is what loving feels like, then yes, I'm ready for him."

They both hugged her, then Pearl announced she was going to lie down and Ella went with her, leaving Rowan with the rest of the place on her own.

She didn't know whether to cry about what her father had done to her or dance for joy about what was happening in her life now. But there was a roller coaster of emotions racing through her.

On the other side of town, Bowie was pulling up to the remodel site. Still rattled by what he was feeling, he had to put his personal life aside and concentrate on what had to be done. But when he got out of the car, he could still feel the impression of her body against him and the scent of his shampoo in her hair.

He wasn't a hundred percent certain yet, but things were happening that left him with that can't-live-without-her feeling.

Chapter 11

Mel was in a bad mood as he waited on Emmitt and Tiny's arrival before he ordered. Not even the famous biscuits were tempting enough to get him past nibbling on one to pass the time.

Finally, they arrived, spotted him, and wound their way through the tables to join him.

Tiny chose the chair at the back of the wall facing the dining room and looked around to see who was here. She spotted Ruby Butterman and tried to catch her eye to wave, then gave up when Ruby never looked her way.

Lila, their waitress, came with menus and took drink orders, while Tiny was observing the diners. When she caught one of them staring, he quickly looked away. She reached for Emmitt's arm and lowered her voice.

"What in the world is going on in here?"

Emmitt looked up, noticed that every diner was purposefully ignoring them, and shrugged.

"Last time Mel and I were here, we got a whole room full of go-to-hell looks. It appears today they've chosen to pretend we do not exist."

"But why?" Tiny asked.

Mel frowned. "For the same reason Nellie is leaving me and Blessings behind. We're the bad guys now…the people who denied and assaulted our blood kin. Wait until they find out Mama is divorcing Daddy, and that he already made his getaway. We'll be lower than dirt."

Tiny leaned back in total dismay. She'd never been shunned or dismissed as a person of no importance—ever. She glared back at all of them, then grabbed Emmitt's hand.

"Emmitt, what are we going to do?"

"Deal with it," he said.

"No! We have to move. I can't live here like this," Tiny said.

Emmitt shrugged. "Except we can't, because of Junior and his legal troubles, so there's no more discussion."

Mel was silent. He'd already had this conversation with Nellie.

"Emmitt, give me the car keys," Tiny said.

Emmitt frowned. "Why? We haven't even ordered our food."

She stood up. "I've lost my appetite. Mel can bring you home."

As soon as Emmitt handed her the keys, she sailed out of the dining room with her head up and eyes blazing. They heard the door slam when she left, and Emmitt winced when he heard her peel out of the parking lot, imagining the gravel she was slinging as she went.

"She's pissed," Mel said.

Emmitt arched an eyebrow. "You think?"

Then Lila arrived. "Are y'all ready to order, or do you need a few more minutes?"

"We're good," Mel said. "I'll have the lunch special...chicken and dumplings."

"I'll have the same," Emmitt added.

Lila smiled. "Good choices," she said, and left to turn in the order.

Emmitt glanced back at his brother. "What are you gonna do?"

Mel shrugged. "I don't have a clue. It's not like we have any real trade to fall back on, and even if we did, no one in Blessings is going to hire us. I was thinking about driving up to Savannah and talking to Daddy but I don't know where he's staying. We've been playing phone tag this morning, and I haven't had a chance to see if he's interested in seeing us."

Emmitt was shocked by the whole idea. "Why wouldn't he be willing to talk to us?"

"Who knows? He left without a word, and I never thought that would happen."

Emmitt's shoulders slumped. "If I could take one thing back in my life right now, it would be that beating. He was just a kid, and we did it anyway because Daddy said to."

"Did you ever think about why Randall up and killed himself?" Mel asked.

Emmitt frowned. "Well, he took too many pills."

"Except he didn't do drugs until after the thing with Billie James."

"So what are you getting at?" Emmitt asked.

"Remember when Mama told us about Billie James committing suicide?"

"Well, yeah, but—"

"She also said she felt sorry for that boy and wondered what would happen to him. And a week later, Randall was dead."

Emmitt's eyes widened. "Are you saying it was Billie James's suicide that made him do that?"

Mel shrugged. "All I know is after we came back

from roughing up the kid, the next night I found Randall drunk and crying. I asked him what was wrong, and all he would say was that he heard the bones break in the kid's hand when he stomped it."

Emmitt's gut knotted. "I didn't know."

"There wasn't any need to tell," Mel said. "The damage had already been done when Daddy sent him out to hurt Billie. He kept saying it would be the perfect payback to the James family—leaving their pretty girl unwanted by any men. The rest has just been festering, waiting for someone to knock off that scab."

Their conversation ended with the arrival of their food. Later, Mel dropped Emmitt off at home. That's when he noticed his dad had called him, but he was in no mood to talk. Bringing up their ugly past was a reminder of what a negative impact Jud had had on their lives. If they were ever going to change their ways, the first thing needed was to distance themselves from Jud Boone.

The work crew was replacing the deck on the front porch, using their portable generator to run their power tools, and Bowie had gone to run down a local plumber and a local electrician. He and his men had the skills to do the work, but for it to be certified by a city inspector and qualify to be insured afterward it had to be done by people who were licensed in the area.

He had a plumber on board to come out tomorrow. He needed old plumbing replaced and then new plumbing added to the area where the second bathroom was going to be.

He'd googled electricians in Blessings, Georgia, and

was now on the hunt for the business. He thought he remembered all the streets in town, but had to resort to his GPS to find Ken's Electric. He finally found it in the alley behind the lumberyard.

A bell over the door jingled as he walked inside. The small, wiry man behind the counter looked up.

"Good afternoon. I'm Ken Abernathy. How can I help you?"

"Afternoon," Bowie said, then introduced himself and told him what he needed.

"Are you the guy working on the old James house?" Ken asked.

"Yes. Pearl is my grandmother."

Then Ken grinned. "Oh heck! You're Billie's boy, aren't you? I went to school with her."

Bowie smiled. It was a good feeling to know people who remembered her.

"Yes, I'm her son."

"Real nice to meet you," Ken said. "So, how about I follow you back to the house and take a look at what's going to be needed? I have a couple of guys who work with me on bigger jobs, so I need to see the scope of the project."

"Let's do it," Bowie said.

"My work van is out back. I know where the house is at. I'll be right behind you."

Bowie gave him a thumbs-up and left the building. He was on the way back when he glanced in the rear-view mirror and saw a big white work van about a block behind him. He parked at the curb then got out, waiting to escort the electrician inside.

Ken got out carrying an iPad. "Lead the way."

"We need to go in the back door for now. As you can see, my crew is laying down a new deck on the porch," Bowie said as they circled the house to get inside.

With all the walls down and nothing left but the studs to indicate where the rooms were laid out, they could see all the way through the house to the front door.

Bowie began leading Ken around the house and explaining where they were in the process. "The power is off, and so is the water. Besides rewiring the whole house to accommodate the new appliances, we're turning one of the bedrooms into a master bath and walk-in closet for my grandma's bedroom. We're removing the existing studs between those two rooms today, and I already have the floor area marked off with spray paint. You can see where the jetted tub will be, the shower, and the two-sink vanity as well. That should give you an idea of where to run wire."

Ken made notes on his iPad as they moved from room to room, and when they got into the kitchen, took note of where wiring was needed there, as well as the wiring need for outlets for the big island Bowie was adding.

"Are you adding any outdoor lighting beyond what's already here?" Ken asked.

Bowie shook his head. "No. She has a street light to the west of her house. I think what's already here is more than sufficient."

"Okay, then all I need from you is a phone number, and I can send you a quote."

"Will you be available to start within the week?" Bowie asked.

"You let me know when you're ready for us and we'll be here."

"Awesome," Bowie said. They shook hands, and then Ken was gone.

Bowie walked through the house to the front door and paused in the open doorway to see how the porch was coming.

Ray saw him and stopped what he was doing. "Hey, Boss, did you get a delivery date on those two headers you ordered the other day?"

"Delivery is tomorrow before 10:00 a.m."

"Good. Once we get those in, we can open up the spaces even more."

"Will you be through with the porch by quitting time?" Bowie asked.

"Oh yeah…for sure, and then we can replace the posts first thing tomorrow."

"Good. I've got a couple more things to do, but I'll be back before quitting time to lock up. As always, call if you need me."

"Sure thing," Ray said. "You can come out this door. The floor joists are safe to walk on."

Bowie was off the porch in three steps and headed for his car. He needed to find a body shop and get an estimate on fixing his car, and then he was going to get a haircut.

After a discussion with the owner of the only body shop in town, Bowie would be delivering his car to the shop tomorrow afternoon and renting a loaner for the week.

Next stop, the Curl Up and Dye for a much needed haircut.

―᠁―

Ruby Butterman had just finished styling Rachel Goodhope's hair and was cleaning up around her chair when the front door chimed.

Vera and Vesta, the Conklin twins, were still working on clients, so Ruby set her broom aside and walked up front.

The man at the desk was a stranger, but she liked his smile.

"Welcome to the Curl Up and Dye. I'm Ruby," she said.

"Thanks," Bowie said. "I saw you take walk-ins, and as you can see, I'm way past needing a haircut. Does anyone have time to work me in?"

"Actually, I do," Ruby said. "I don't have another client for forty-five minutes. If you'll follow me, we'll get started."

Bowie liked her on sight, and when she led him to the shampoo station, he plopped down in the chair.

She draped a cape around his shoulders and fastened it at the neck.

"Is that too tight for you?" she asked.

"No, ma'am. It's fine."

"Okay, lean back, and you can put the footrest up if you want but I'm afraid it's going to be a little short for those long legs of yours."

"I'm good," Bowie said and leaned back.

"What's your name?" Ruby asked as she was adjusting the water temperature.

"Bowie James. Pearl James is my grandma. Ella is my aunt."

The chatter that had been going on between Vera and Vesta and their clients suddenly stopped. Every woman in the place turned to look. They'd all heard about the set-to between the Boone brothers and a man named Bowie James, but none of them knew who he was—until now.

It was his long muscled legs, wide shoulders, and flat belly they saw first, and then they saw him and for a few naughty moments let their imaginations run loose.

Vera glanced at her twin. "Ben Affleck," she whispered.

Vesta shook her head. "No, more like that actor who married that little Miley Cyrus girl."

Hope Talbot raised her hand like a little kid in school ready with the answer to the teacher's question.

"Liam Hemsworth!" she whispered.

They all nodded, caught the frown Ruby was giving them, and immediately returned to what they'd been doing.

Not only did Ruby know what was going on, but she secretly agreed with them. However, it wasn't proper to be ogling the customers, and she hoped the water rushing over Bowie's head had drowned out their nonsense.

As soon as she finished, she moved him to her workstation.

Now all four women were watching as Ruby combed out his hair, then ran her fingers through it a couple of times to get the feel of the texture and length.

Vera sighed, and Vesta rolled her eyes, picturing her fingers in that thick black hair.

"So, what are we doing here?" Ruby asked. "How do you usually wear it?"

"Not real short, but definitely not hanging down the back of my neck, either."

"What about the sides?" Ruby asked.

"Don't want to be tucking any hair behind my ears, and I don't want it falling in my eyes."

Ruby grinned. "How about I begin, and you call the shots as we go?"

"Yes, ma'am," Bowie said.

"Call me Ruby," she said. "Everybody does."

Bowie grinned at her, which turned up the volume on the heat the girls were generating.

"Lord love a duck," Vera muttered.

Vesta frowned. "Where on earth did you come up with that?"

"Oh, I heard it on a TV show."

As soon as they finished, they each got a bottle of pop from their mini-fridge and swiveled their chairs toward Ruby.

Front-row seats, with refreshments, for the ongoing show.

Ruby didn't hold back as she wielded her scissors, aiming first for the length and took a good portion of it off. The twins watched the black hair dropping onto the white tiled floor and took another swig of pop.

A couple of times Bowie stopped Ruby to discuss the process. Then she would resume the haircut, until she finally stopped and stepped back.

"So, what do you think?" she asked as she handed him a mirror and turned the chair so he could see it from all sides.

"Perfect," Bowie said.

Ruby smiled. She did enjoy pleasing her customers. "Sit tight just a couple of minutes while I use the clippers on the back of your neck, and we'll be through."

Bowie was happy with the end result as she finished, and when he caught the twins staring at him, he winked.

They blushed in unison.

Ruby removed the cape. "You're good to go. And just for the record, what you're doing for Miss Pearl and for Ella is wonderful. So many good people lost so much during that hurricane and then the flooding that came with it. It's going to take Blessings a long time to recover from that."

"It comes in handy that my company builds houses," Bowie said as he stood. "How much do I owe you?"

"Haircuts are twenty dollars," Ruby said.

He handed her thirty dollars. "Ruby, it was a pleasure to meet you." He turned to acknowledge his audience. "And you ladies as well."

"It was nice meeting you," they said, and then he was gone.

Vera leaned back in her chair, and when she did she burped.

"Oh good lord…excuse me. It's this pop. Thank goodness I did not do that while he was still here."

Vesta giggled.

Ruby was still smiling as she began to sweep up the hair she'd cut off.

A few minutes later, her next appointment arrived, and the day moved along at the Curl Up and Dye.

The day was moving along for Bowie as well. By the time he got back to the jobsite, the men were gathering up tools.

Samuel saw him get out of his car. "Hey, guys! The boss got a haircut."

Ray turned around and whistled. "You turned

yourself back into that pretty boy hiding behind all the hair and whiskers."

Bowie grinned. It was nothing he didn't expect. It's what they always did when he finally broke down and got it cut.

"I bet I know why. I bet that pretty girl who's staying with you is getting under your skin," Joe said.

Bowie ignored him. "The porch looks great. Anything happen I need to know about before I lock up for the night?"

"The plumber came by to get a look at what he'll be replacing, plus what he'll need to add. He wanted to make sure he had all of the supplies on hand to get the job finished in a timely fashion."

Bowie nodded. "Good. So, bright and early tomorrow, we're going be putting in headers as soon as they arrive, then taking down studs and reframing. You guys have a good evening. Get some rest. Both those headers are monsters. It will take all seven of us to get them in."

They loaded up and left, while Bowie took a walk across the new porch deck and into the house. He went through the rooms, making sure all the windows were down and locked and the back door was locked as well, then walked to the front door. He paused in the doorway, thinking he heard someone saying his name, but when he turned around there was no one there.

The evening sun coming through the west windows lit up the dust motes hanging in the air, turning them into glitter. The light pattern on the floor was disappearing with the setting sun.

He stood within the silence, thinking about the happy years he'd lived here, innocent of the tragedy that had brought him into this world. He was almost ten when his mother told him about what had happened to her, but that his arrival in her life had been what healed her and made her life whole. She'd given him all the confidence he needed to grow up without a father in his life, and Ella and his gran had reinforced the belief he had in himself.

He thought about the journal she'd left behind and the phrase *wish he hadn't been born*, and standing here, he suddenly got what she'd meant.

His birth had made him a target. And the attack that drove them away from Blessings had nearly killed him. That's what she meant. She'd loved him so much that she couldn't give him up, and then it had nearly gotten him killed.

"Sorry I doubted you, Mom. I miss you. Wish you were here."

Then he walked out, locked the door, and headed home. He was driving down Main Street when his phone suddenly signaled a text, and then a second, and then a third. He pulled over to the curb to read them and then burst out laughing.

> This is Gran. I sent this by myself.
> Mama nearly drove me to drink. Brag on the damn text when you see her.
> It's me saying Hello, and thank you. It's my first phone. I feel like a teenager but with no one to call, so you're it. Come home hungry.

He laughed. "I might have just created a three-headed monster." Then his belly growled. "And it appears I am coming home hungry. For you, Dark Eyes, I'll eat anything you cook."

He backed away from the curb and headed home.

———~~~———

Rowan was wearing the same old shorts and big T-shirt, standing barefoot at the stove, stirring gravy.

The oven timer went off.

"Ella, come check the roast. See if it's done, please."

Ella opened the oven door for a peek. "It looks done to me and smells wonderful. Where are those pot holders?"

"The little drawer to my right," Rowan said and stepped aside, still stirring as Ella got out the pork roast and set it on a wooden cutting board they were using as a hot pad to let the juices set before they cut it.

Pearl was watching the evening news in Bowie's recliner, with her feet up and a glass of sweet tea in her hand.

All three of them heard Bowie's car.

"He's home!" Pearl crowed. "I wonder if he got my text?"

Ella rolled her eyes. "Lord, I hope so."

Pearl sniffed. "Don't judge. I grew up when the phone was huge and hanging on a wall and you had to crank it to make it work, and everyone on the line had a different ring."

Rowan hid a grin. This afternoon had been an experience, all of them trying to figure out the new phones with Ella as their teacher. She was pretty sure they'd both tried Ella's patience to the limit.

And then the front door opened and Bowie came

inside, bringing a blast of hot air and immediately dwarfing the space with his larger-than-life persona.

The women were momentarily speechless. The haircut turned him into someone else—a cosmopolitan mover and shaker, not the builder of other people's mansions.

"Something smells good!" he said and smiled at Rowan.

"Pork roast. You have time to shower first," she said, and then added, "Nice haircut."

"It feels better," he said, then hugged Ella and gave his gran a kiss on the cheek. "You guys are great to come home to. I got all the texts. Way to go, girls! I won't be long," he said and headed for the shower.

Pearl was watching the evening news and weather, and turned up the volume as the weatherman came on.

"Look at that," she said. "We're going to get thunderstorms tonight. We don't really need the rain, but since when does the weather give us what we need on command?"

Rowan turned the fire off under the gravy, set it aside, and moved closer to the television. The weather map was a maze of different colors. Rain, strong winds, lots of lightning predicted with the storm, and possible flooding in low areas.

She shuddered. This would be the first really big thunderstorm since the hurricane and subsequent flood.

"Is the trailer park in a low area?" she asked.

"No more than any other part of town," Ella said, and then saw the fear in Rowan's eyes. "Honey, it will be okay. It's not a hurricane. They're not even predicting tornadoes or hail with this. I've lived here all my life, and the town never once flooded before Hurricane Fanny. We're safe."

Rowan nodded, then heard the water go off in the shower and knew Bowie would be out soon.

"I guess we'd better finish up supper," she said, and went back to the little kitchen island where she and Ella began assembling a tossed salad.

Bowie was out less than five minutes later. Pearl began filling him in on the approaching weather.

"There's a big thunderstorm coming. Is everything watertight?" she asked.

"The house is fine, Gran. The roof is solid. The old windows are still there, so nothing is open to the elements, and everything is locked up."

Pearl nodded, then held out her hand. "Help me up, honey. My lower back is giving me fits today."

Bowie frowned. "Is there anything you need? Do you have something to take that would alleviate the pain?"

"No, I'm out. Do you have anything? Just over-the-counter stuff?"

"Yes, ma'am, it's in the bedroom you've been sleeping in. I'll get the bottle for you, then you can keep it where you want."

Ella called out from the kitchen. "Supper's ready!"

"Be right there," Bowie said. "I'm getting Gran some pain meds."

Ella frowned. "Mama, you didn't tell me you were hurting today."

Pearl shrugged. "I hurt every day, Daughter. No need to complain about it."

Bowie came back with two kinds of pain pills. "I don't know which you'd prefer, but keep both of them handy for yourself."

Pearl shook out a couple from one of the bottles,

then carried them to the table. As soon as she sat down, Rowan appeared with a small glass of water.

"Thank you, darling," Pearl said, and downed the pain pills and handed the glass back to Rowan.

The comfort of being here was beyond explanation. Pearl had always imagined home as her sanctuary—until the flood. She still had dreams about the water coming into the house and the horror of knowing they couldn't stop it. They'd evacuated to one of the churches that was on higher ground, and even then her car had floated right out of the parking lot below it. After that had been the nursing home, which for her had always seemed like the last stop before heaven.

Life as she'd known it was over, and then Bowie came back all full of it, so strong and happy, and gave her reason to care about living again. And now, there was the simple act of seeing her daughter and grandson together—and knowing because she'd been born, so too had they. It was an affirmation of life coming full circle.

And there was Rowan. She already felt like the gift they'd been given. But if Rowan and Bowie did become the couple Pearl hoped they would be, Rowan was the final piece of the circle. The woman who would bear the next generation.

Chapter 12

THE FIRST ROLL OF DISTANT THUNDER SOUNDED IN THE middle of supper. They all heard it, and for a moment talk ceased. Then the conversation shifted to their house. Thanks to Bowie, it was safe now, and Bowie's motor home was so heavy that strong winds didn't faze it.

Rowan listened to them talk with her heart in her throat. The panic she was feeling was real, and she desperately needed to think about something else. She caught Bowie watching her, saw the look of concern in his eyes, and smiled, hoping to shift his focus.

"Remember there's leftover peach cobbler for dessert, which I reheated earlier to freshen the crust," she said.

The mention of food did what she wanted. Pearl began talking about Bowie getting into the desserts she used to bake, even before the meals were eaten.

Bowie rolled his eyes. "If I've heard this once, I've heard it a thousand times. Rowan...let me cut to the chase and save Gran the misery of telling it again. I ate the middles out of the pies and tunneled bites out of Gran's coconut cakes and covered up the crime by stuffing more coconut in the holes to hide the deed. But it only lasted until the cakes were cut, at which point the pile of coconut fell away, leaving a great big-ass hole at the bottom of at least two slices."

Rowan grinned.

"Oh, and don't forget the embarrassed look on Billie's face the day the preacher had dinner with us after church. Being the guest, he was served the first piece of dessert, and only by chance Mama cut right into the spot you'd tried to hide. When Billie saw it, we all knew you'd done it. She gave you such a look," Ella said.

Rowan laughed imagining the sight. "What were you thinking?"

"Thinking about that cake, I guess," he said.

She laughed, and for a few precious minutes, the panic was gone.

They finished the meal and were dishing up dessert when it thundered again, and much closer. Rowan took a deep breath and kept scooping cobbler into bowls.

Ella was adding the ice cream, and Bowie had gotten up from the table to take a call. He came back just as his bowl was set at his place.

"I already know how good this is," he said. "It's the perfect end to such a great meal."

Rowan took a quick bite of ice cream from the top, just as a bolt of lightning struck somewhere nearby.

"I used to think that sound was the sky breaking," she said, and scooped up a bite of cobbler, focusing on the taste of sugar and peaches.

"It does sound like something breaking!" Pearl said. "I swear, I learn something new every day."

"Yes, like that phone," Ella said.

Pearl frowned. "Don't remind me. I figured out texts and phone calls, but I still don't know where FaceTiming is on the thing, and I have to know how to do that to keep up with Bowie's travels."

"I'll help you, Gran. I can show you later, before you go to bed, and then we'll practice tomorrow when I'm at work by you FaceTiming me at your house. How's that?" Bowie said.

Pearl grinned. "Yes. That's good. I can do that."

They heard the rain beginning to fall as it peppered both the top of the motor home and the west windows.

"Well, it's finally here. Maybe it will have blown over by bedtime," Ella said.

"I hope so," Rowan added, and got up to refill their glasses of tea.

"No more for me," Pearl said. "I don't want to wet the bed."

Bowie laughed.

"Mama! For the love of God…really?" Ella muttered.

Rowan giggled as she moved on around the table.

"How about you, BowieMan?" she asked.

Bowie liked the nickname. "I'll take whatever you're handing out," he said, and laughed when her cheeks turned pink.

Ella frowned at him. "You're no better than Mama. You're both outrageous."

For the time being, the thunderstorm played second fiddle to the laughter, and that was all Rowan needed.

———∿∿∿———

Unfortunately, the storm had stalled out in the area. Bowie spent a little over an hour helping Pearl with the phone, and by the time everyone was in bed, thunder was still rumbling and lightning was popping and cracking. Everyone was asleep but Rowan, and when the night-lights flickered, her stomach knotted.

She knew Bowie was asleep from the way he was lying—flat on his back, with one arm flung over his head and the other on top of the covers over his chest.

She rolled over, trying to find a comfortable position, until exhaustion claimed her and she finally fell asleep.

The sound of the wind and thunder outside turned into the roar of floodwater in her dream, and the intermittent crack of lightning became the sounds of wood on the barn giving way to the water's force. When she rolled over onto her belly in her sleep, the sheet beneath her turned into the hay-strewn floor of the barn loft.

Rowan moaned. Daddy was gone. No one knew what had happened. No one would think to check on her. No one would ever know what had happened to them. The story of their life and death would be buried with them, and people would forget they had ever been born.

And into the dream she went.

The sun was gone, and with it went light. Rowan was belly down on the loft floor, afraid to move for fear she'd accidentally roll off into the rushing water below. She could feel the floor vibrating from the water moving through the structure.

Her fingers were cramping from hanging onto the hay door in the loft, but she was afraid to let go, for fear the barn would sway too far one way and dump her out into the roiling water of the black abyss below.

When something rammed against the outside of the barn with enough force that she heard wood breaking, she closed her eyes and began repeating the silent prayer she'd been saying for hours. Please God, please... Don't let me die.

Suddenly, she heard a flapping sound from some-where behind her, like the wings of a very large bird, then the stir of air above her. There was an earsplitting screech—the only warning she would get before some-thing slammed into the back of her head.

Pain followed shock as she began to scream, and then kept on screaming because the creature was caught in her hair.

There was terror in the screams that broke the silence in the room. Bowie knew it was Rowan before he even opened his eyes. He was at her side in seconds, scooping her up into his arms, covers and all, just as Ella came flying out of the bedroom.

Rowan knew she was moving, and even though she saw Bowie as she opened her eyes, she was still caught up in the dream and couldn't tell what was real and what was not.

"Is she okay? Was she dreaming again?" Ella asked.

"I think so," Bowie said. "Turn on the lights." He sat down on his bed with Rowan in his lap.

The tension in her muscles was intense. He could see her eyes moving from bed to chair to the walls, as if she was trying to find a familiar object on which to focus.

"Rowan, honey! You're safe! You're safe! Look at me!"

Light flooded the room. And in that instant, the barn was gone. Rowan looked down at the floor and saw only the dark hardwood, not the flood. She saw Bowie's face, felt the warmth of his bare chest and the fierce grip with which he was holding her. She put her hand on his chest.

"Is this real or am I still dreaming?"

"It's real. I'm real, and you're in my arms," he said.

"I'm going to make her some hot chocolate," Ella said.

Rowan saw Ella at the stove, then ran her hands up the back of her neck, searching for the small, healing scars, but when she looked at her hands there was no blood.

Bowie pulled her closer. "Talk to me, Rowan. What happened to you?"

"Water was in the house. Daddy sent me to the barn loft. I begged him to come with me, but he told me to run and he would be right behind me. He was too slow. By the time he came out, the water was deeper. He was halfway to the barn when it hit him chest high. He went under and didn't come up."

"Oh my God, I am so sorry," Bowie said, and held her even tighter.

But once she'd begun talking about it, she couldn't seem to stop. The horror of what she'd endured was finally coming out.

"I was flat on my stomach, holding onto the hay door, screaming for help. I cried for a long time, then the sun went down. It was so dark I couldn't see anything—not even stars—but I could hear the water moving down below. The loft floor was vibrating from the power of the flow." Then she looked up at Bowie. "I was just waiting for the barn to wash away, taking me with it."

Ella appeared over Bowie's shoulder, then offered the mug. Rowan took it, cradling the warm crockery within her hands as she took a small sip. The warmth and the sweetness slid down her throat and into her stomach, settling the panic.

"What happened to you there?" Bowie asked.

"I was too afraid to sleep and afraid to move away from the hay door in the dark, for fear I'd take a wrong step and fall out of it. So I didn't move. I lay there for hours, until sometime toward morning. I thought I heard something behind me, and then there was the sound of flapping wings and a brief rush of air above my head. Before I could react, there was a piercing screech, and then something hit me hard in the back of my head. The pain was sudden and intense. All I could tell was that it was a big bird of some kind, and its talons had become tangled up in my hair. I was screaming and hitting at it, trying to make it fly away, and then all of a sudden it was gone, and I'd lost my sense of direction."

"Bless your sweet heart," Ella said softly.

"What did you do?" Bowie asked.

"I felt what I assumed was blood running out of my hair and down my neck, so I knew the talons had cut my scalp. I dropped to my hands and knees and crawled until I felt a wall, then inched my way to the back of the loft and waited for daylight. When it came, I went back to the hay door. Our house was gone, and I was too numb to care."

"How long were you there?" Bowie asked.

"Until that evening. A neighbor came in his bass boat to check on us. He took me to his home. They'd suffered a lot of damage and were in the process of packing up to leave. I spent the night with them, and the next day, a sheriff's deputy came looking for me. They'd found Daddy's body. But Blessings was still flooded and without power, so they took the body to a neighboring town. I buried him in a cemetery among strangers."

"But if you were already out of the flood, how did you wind up back where you'd lived?" Ella asked.

"A car from the funeral home was taking me back to my neighbors but couldn't get up the hill because part of the road had collapsed while I was gone. So I got out and walked up. But the house was empty. Part of their roof had fallen in, and they were gone. I turned around and started walking to Blessings. It was closer, and the only place where I knew people. It was almost dark when the sheriff spotted me and took me to the nursing home, and you know the rest." She shuddered, then covered her face with her hands. "I can't find my way out of sad. I can't stop dreaming of what happened. I'm broken."

Bowie laid his cheek against the top of her head. "Honey, we're all broken. That's what life does to us. Time doesn't make anything better. It doesn't make the sad stuff go away. But we figure out how to live within the new person we've become, and that's where you are."

"I just want the nightmare to end," Rowan said.

"And it will," Bowie said.

Rowan took a few more sips of the hot chocolate, then leaned against Bowie's chest, and closed her eyes.

Ella rescued the mug and carried it back to the kitchen.

"Aunt Ella, do me a favor and turn out all the lights except the one over the dining table," Bowie asked.

Ella began flipping switches, then turned the chandelier over the table down to dim.

"I'm going back to bed," she said.

Bowie glanced down. Rowan was already asleep.

"I'm not putting her down again," he said.

Ella nodded, then slipped back into the bedroom and shut the door.

Bowie settled himself into a more comfortable

position and leaned against the headboard, listening to the thunderstorm still rumbling overhead.

Sometime around 3:00 a.m., he laid Rowan down, then stretched out beside her and covered them up. When he rolled over onto his side and pulled her close, she sighed.

Minutes later, he was asleep.

―――――⁓⁓⁓―――――

Rowan woke up just before daybreak and saw Bowie watching her sleep. She hadn't started the night in his bed.

"What happened?" she asked.

"The storm triggered you. You called it a nightmare, but it's more like PTSD."

"Oh no… Was it bad? Did I wake everyone up?"

He reached out and brushed a lock of hair away from her eyes and smiled.

"Pearl slept right through it."

Rowan threw back the covers and sat up.

"What's wrong?" Bowie asked.

"They're not going to want me living with them if I can't even sleep through the night without losing it."

"They managed to live with newborn me, and all the years of crying at night, and potty training, so I'm real sure a few nightmares aren't going to faze them."

She looked back at him, imagining him as a toddler being potty trained, and grinned.

"What?" he asked.

"Potty training," she said.

He chuckled. "Well, it's a fact of every adult's life, right?"

Before she could answer, his alarm went off. He silenced it.

"I need to shower and shave. Got a new hand coming this morning so I don't want to be late."

"Really? Who?" she asked.

"Junior Boone."

Her eyes widened in surprise. "The kid who keyed your car?"

"Yes. He showed up yesterday, wanting to work off some of the cost of fixing the car to lessen his debt. He seemed sincere and struck me as a decent enough kid. We'll see how it goes."

Bowie got up and was across the room in three strides, shutting the bathroom door behind him as he went.

Rowan watched, thinking he was as good-looking going as he was coming toward her, then got up and slipped into the girls' room and that bathroom to get dressed.

She came out minutes later and headed for the kitchen. She heard the shower go off and knew Bowie would be out soon. After starting a pot of coffee to brew, she got out two bowls and two spoons and then a box of cereal. She liked the look of their bowls side by side, and the nesting spoons added to the image of togetherness.

Then she sighed. He'd already indicated his intentions, but she needed to confess something before it went any further.

He came out, saw her waiting, and greeted her with a smile and a kiss.

"Good morning, lady."

"Good morning. Do you have time to eat?"

"With you? Always."

She got milk from the refrigerator and then sat down.

Bowie chose the chair across from her and poured his bowl full of cereal, then added milk.

Rowan did the same and waited a couple of minutes before she broached the subject.

"If we're going to be more than 'not family,' I have something to confess," Rowan said.

Bowie laid down his spoon, giving her his full attention. "Okay, but you need to know that I have no need to know anything about your past."

She sighed. "Just let me say this. I don't like surprises, so I don't want to spring this one on you, either."

"Duly noted," he said. "You have my full attention."

"I have never made love," she said.

He reached across the table, his hand extended palm up. When she laid her hand in his, he grasped it gently.

"If we're starting off on full honesty, then I need to confess something to you as well."

"I'm listening," she said.

He grinned. "With regards to lovemaking…I have. So if one of us knows what we're doing, the rest will all fall into place, don't you think?"

Rowan sighed. "I know it sounds ridiculous."

"Not at all. What you don't seem to realize is that from my perspective, the trust that takes for you to choose me is a gift. And in return, I can promise you won't be sorry. Okay?"

"Okay," she said.

"Feel better now?" he asked.

She nodded.

"So finish your cereal, and don't worry about details."

She scooped up another spoonful of cereal. A few

minutes later, Bowie carried his bowl to the sink, kissed the back of her neck, then whispered in her ear. "You are an entrancing little witch, and I adore you. Have a good day."

She blushed. "You, too, Bowie."

He pretended surprise. "Are you saying I am also an entrancing little witch?"

She laughed. "No, but you are a sexy hunk, which is exactly what you were fishing for. So go to work before you get me in trouble, and be careful."

"Always," he said, and was out the door.

As was their routine, she stood in the doorway, waiting for him to look back. When he did, she waved.

Bowie grinned and then instead of waving blew her a kiss.

She was smiling as she stepped back and locked the door. As she did, she heard the girls stirring and went to the kitchen to make some oatmeal with raisins for Pearl and Ella.

―――

Junior Boone was in the kitchen making a sandwich and chips to take with him to work. It was the first day since he keyed Bowie's car that he felt good about himself. As soon as he finished making his lunch, he sacked it up and set it beside his cap and gloves, and poured himself a bowl of cereal, added milk but stopped before it began to float, and sat down to eat.

He was almost finished when his mother entered the kitchen. She wasn't in her robe and nightgown as usual. She was dressed and carrying her purse and keys.

"Morning, Mom. Where are you going?" he asked.

"I'm taking you to work," she said.

"Oh, you don't have to. I can walk."

"It's all the way on the other side of town. I won't embarrass you. I'll drop you off at the corner. You can walk the rest of the way, okay?"

He was pleased she understood his need to be doing this without the aid of anyone else. He'd caused the problem. He wanted to be the one to fix it.

"Okay, and thanks for understanding," he said.

Tiny shrugged. "I miss a lot of signals, but not when it comes to you."

Junior carried his bowl to the sink, rinsed it out, then left it there. He put on his cap, grabbed the work gloves and his lunch, and followed his mom to the car. Minutes later, they were on their way across town.

Bowie was still reeling from what Rowan had told him. At the same time, when he considered the depths to which her father had gone to keep her cloistered, he shouldn't have been surprised. But the heads-up had not only given him something to think about, but also made him wonder where the hell they could go and ever be alone.

The drive through town was interrupted when he stopped to pick up yet another twenty-four-count pack of bottled water and ice it down before continuing on to the house.

He was surprised to drive up and see Junior Boone already there sitting on the porch. That was a good sign of the kid's intent.

He waved as he got out and then carried the ice chest full of bottled water back to the shade tree.

"Morning," Bowie said.

Junior nodded. "Morning, Boss. Is there a good place to set my lunch?"

"You brought your lunch?" Bowie said.

"Yes, sir. Made it this morning before breakfast. There's nothing in it that heat will spoil. I just need to keep it out of the way."

"Bring it on in the house with you for now, but when Ray and Joe Tuttle get here with the tool trailer, you can set it in there on any of the shelves. And tomorrow… don't worry about lunch. I give the men an hour off to go eat, and because this trip is for my gran, I'm paying their way. You'll be included. Okay?"

"Okay, and thanks," Junior said. He was surprised and proud that Bowie was calling him one of the guys.

"Come on in, and we'll walk the house to look for any roof leaks," Bowie said, and in they went, with Bowie pointing out what the rooms were and where the layout was changing. By the time they had gone all the way through the house and unlocked the back door, Bowie was pleased they hadn't found even one leak.

"There's the port-a-potty. Keep it clean."

"Yeah, nobody messes up Mama's bathroom, either," Junior said.

Bowie grinned. "Women are fussy about that, aren't they?"

By the time the rest of the crew arrived, Junior Boone had an official man crush. And when Bowie introduced him to the crew and then called him his cousin, it sealed the deal.

They began the day by verifying that the headers were on the way, and then began preparing the openings, using temporary braces when necessary to make sure the roof would be secure while the transfers were being made.

Bowie kept Junior occupied running back and forth to the tool trailer and helping carry lumber in and trash out to the roll-off. It was nearly full, so Bowie was back on the phone ordering a pickup on the one they had so the company could bring the replacement.

Junior loved football and had easily learned the plays. It came naturally to him. The way he looked at it, this was a similar setup. There was safety protocol, paying attention to what he was told, and quickly asking if he didn't immediately understand. And it was all about the team. There wasn't any room for outstanding players... just the team.

Chapter 13

THE HEADERS ARRIVED ON SCHEDULE, AND AFTER HELPING carry them inside, Junior stood out of the way and watched, intrigued by the placement of each one and how it was going to be put in such a position as to bear the weight of the roof. With the drywall removed from the ceilings, he could see all the way up past the rafters to the roof. It was like looking at the skeleton of a home. Then they removed the temporary braces, revealing the space they would use to create an open-concept living area. Junior Boone was hooked on the engineering aspects of being a builder.

It was nearing noon when Bowie called a halt.

"I'm taking my car to the body shop and picking up a rental. Then I'll swing by and check on the girls before I come back. Ray, you've got this until I return. Next thing we start on is framing up the new layout and getting everything ready for the plumber. Junior, I know you brought your lunch today, but why don't you go eat with the rest of the crew instead. Ray has a credit card to cover it. No money required. Okay?"

"Yeah, come with us, kid," Presley said. "I'm going through the menu at Granny's, trying something new every day, and so far it's all thumbs-up for me."

Junior was still stinging from the weight of Bowie's words, knowing he was the reason the boss even needed a body shop, but being included with the rest of the crew was as good as making the football team.

"Yeah, sure," Junior said. "And thanks."

"No problem. I'll see you all later. You know the drill."

Joe Tuttle grinned. "Yes, we'll call if we need you."

Bowie just shook his head and headed for the car, but the sound of their laughter made him smile.

———∿∿∿———

Bowie arrived at Newton's Body Shop just before noon, got his insurance info out of the glove box, and took the car key off the fob and gave it to Douglas Newton.

"We should have this ready by the end of the week," Douglas said. "And the car rental is next door in the same office as the insurance agency."

"Thanks again," Bowie said. "I sent photos to my insurance agent, and he's already okayed the work order. You have his number."

"Yes, sir," Doug said. "We've got it covered."

They shook hands, and then Bowie went into the insurance agency next door. He presented his driver's license and his proof of insurance, and fifteen minutes later drove out of the back parking lot in a tan 2017 Chevrolet Equinox.

He had his cell phone on speaker when he called Ella. She answered on the second ring, which told him she probably had her phone near to hand.

"Hey, Aunt Ella, is everything going okay?"

"Yes, we're fine. Just getting ready to figure out something for dinner. Want to come eat with us?"

"If you haven't started anything, how about I bring some food to you?"

"Oh yes! That's a great idea."

"What sounds good to you?" he asked.

"Just a minute and I'll ask."

He heard bits and pieces of the conversation and then Ella was back on the phone.

"We can't agree, so you surprise us."

"What if I bring something you don't want?" he asked.

"Oh, we'll like it. Today, you're the chef."

"You asked for it," he said, and headed for the old Broyles Dairy Freeze. He'd seen it on the way home the other day and was surprised it was still in business.

It was a true moment of déjà vu when he pulled up, noticed a drive-through had been added to the side, then backed up and drove up to the window.

A middle-aged woman with rainbow hair and one skull earring in her right ear came to the window.

"What'll it be?" she asked.

"Do you still make chili dogs like you did back in the day?"

She grinned. "We sure do."

"Awesome. I need six chili dogs and four orders of fries."

She rang it up and then pointed to a small parking spot just to the right of the drive-through.

"If you'll park over there, someone will bring it to you."

Bowie pulled up and parked, and then began checking out the car's controls. Within a few minutes, his order was delivered. He drove out of the parking lot and headed home with dinner on the seat beside him.

Rowan had already set the table and was putting ice in their drinking glasses when he drove up.

"He's here!" she yelled, and Ella got up from the sofa to open the door.

Bowie was looking forward to one more meal with his girls. He'd taken a few pictures of the open space and couldn't wait to show them, so he picked up the sack and got out.

Yancy Scott, the big redhead, was on a riding lawn mower, mowing grass. It appeared he was mowing all of the yards in the trailer park because more than a dozen yards had already been done. His little girl was riding her bike up and down the road close by him.

Ella opened the door. Bowie came inside with his hands full.

"Oh my word! Do I smell chili?" Pearl asked.

"Chili dogs from Broyles Dairy Freeze," Bowie said. "Remember when Mama always treated us to chili dogs on half-price Thursday?"

"Oh, that's right!" Ella said. "You brought a little bit of Billie home with you today. That's wonderful!"

Bowie put the sack down on the table and let the girls fix all the plates. He turned around to go wash up, and as he walked past Rowan he leaned down and stole a kiss.

She grinned.

He winked.

And the girls never saw a thing.

⁕

Bowie got back to the jobsite ahead of the crew. He noticed the old roll-off was gone and a new empty one was in place, so he went in the back door to look around. They already had the studs up for the new bath and walk-in closet and had a doorway framed up for the door leading into the master bedroom. He walked the house, checking the layout and the old plumbing that was being replaced, then moved on into the kitchen, making sure all of the utility hookups were going into the right places for the new appliances.

During the past twenty years, he'd worked on more homes than he could count, but none was more important to him than this one. For a time, three generations of James men and their women had lived in this house. It felt good to be fixing it rather than tearing it down.

When he heard vehicles pulling up, he knew the crew was back. He moved to a window to look out and smiled. Junior Boone was right in the middle of them like he belonged there. Confirmation for Bowie that he'd make the right call.

The crew was still out in the yard when a truck from the lumberyard pulled up. Bowie walked out onto the porch and then jumped off the side and jogged to the truck as the driver got out.

"Delivery for the James location," the driver said. "Who's Bowie James?"

"That's me," Bowie said, and together they verified the delivery order and then unloaded the forklift and began offloading the stacks of subfloor and lumber, cartridges for nail guns, and everything else on the list.

As soon as something was off the truck, the crew carried it inside.

"Now we can begin putting this place back together," Bowie said.

Cora Boone had cleaned every surface of the house and hauled out years of needless accumulation. Part of it had gone into the garbage and the rest was donated.

The fact that she had the only keys to the house now made her feel safe. Even when she was gone running errands, she had no fear of coming back to find Judson waiting inside.

It felt strange to be holding such fear of him when she'd slept in the bed beside him for almost fifty years and birthed him all the sons that he'd wanted. She'd seen the hard side of him plenty of times, but she'd been completely unaware of the cruelty that coexisted with it.

She was putting a skillet of cornbread in the oven to bake when someone knocked at her back door. She turned around and saw Nellie through the window in the door.

Nellie knocked again, then called out, "I just want to tell you goodbye."

Cora went to the door, hesitated, then turned the lock and opened it. There was a locked storm door between them and it was going to stay that way.

"What do you want?" Cora asked.

Nellie had tears in her eyes. "I'm leaving for Kentucky. I'm going home, but I couldn't leave without telling you how much I love you, Cora. You were like a mother to me, and I need you to know that I knew nothing about any of this and I am as horrified by what I've learned as you seem to be."

Sorrow welled, but Cora wouldn't give way.

"Is Mel going with you?" she asked.

"No, ma'am. He wasn't invited. I won't see you

again, but I'll never forget you," Nellie said, and then turned and ran.

Cora watched her get into a car with someone she didn't recognize, but as they drove away she saw a Kentucky license plate on the car. Looked like Nellie's family had come to her rescue.

Cora sighed, then relocked the door and set the time for the cornbread to come out of the oven.

She had beans reheating on the stove and a pitcher of sweet tea in the fridge. There was nothing left to do but wait for the timer to go off, so she picked up the newspaper, turned it to the crossword puzzle, and sat down at the kitchen table to work it, then had to quit because of the tears blurring her vision.

Jud Boone had just signed a one-year lease on a furnished one-bedroom apartment in the old part of Savannah. It wasn't fancy, but it felt comfortable enough. The utilities were already on and it was a simple matter to get them switched into his name tomorrow. He was back at the motel packing up his belongings. When he finished, he paid up as he checked out, then stopped by a supermarket to buy a few groceries to tide him over until he could make a more thorough list. He had never shopped for groceries in Blessings and considered that woman's work. But he was about to get a dose of what being without a woman was like.

He'd called Emmitt and Mel to give them his new address, but neither of them had returned his calls. It made him wonder what was happening. The lack of contact with them was unusual. His sons had always answered his calls or returned them promptly. He didn't realize his absence in their lives was also going to mean a loss of control.

He stopped at a red light, glancing around as he waited for it to change. This was the first time in his life that he was living in a place where everyone he saw was a stranger. The light turned green and he proceeded through the intersection, then missed his turn. When he tried to circle back, there was no "going around the block" in his area. The city was old, and many of the streets were one-way. Back in Blessings, he could go around a block and come back out on the street he'd turned on, but not so here. It didn't take long for him to figure out he was lost.

He knew there was a GPS app on his phone, but he'd never had occasion to use it in Blessings. And being lost in Savannah was no time to try to learn how to use it. Finally, he stopped and asked for directions. Getting from the supermarket to his apartment should have taken fifteen minutes but had turned into an hour.

By the time he got home and carried his purchases up to the second floor, he was in something of a snit. And when he went to put up the groceries, he had to throw out the gallon of Rocky Road ice cream that had melted.

He was hot and frustrated and mad that this was happening. Today, he wasn't sure who made him madder, the bastard who didn't belong, or Cora for kicking him out.

The longer he thought about Cora, the angrier Jud became. He shouldn't have given up so easily. He should have dragged his things back in the house and shown her who was boss. By the time he went to bed that night, he'd added her to his mental hit list.

—⁓—

Pearl was taking a mid-afternoon nap and Ella was watching TV when Rowan announced she was going for a walk. Ella shooed her away with a smile, and out the door Rowan went.

It felt good to be out, even though last night's rain and today's blistering sun had the humidity set on sauna.

She'd put her hair up in a ponytail and was in the old shorts and oversize green T-shirt when she left the house. She was thankful for the tennis shoes, but wishing she had a cap as she gazed at the surrounding area, wondering where to start. It didn't take long for her to see the sidewalk behind where Bowie had parked his motor home, and since it was lined with trees, that would make the walk more pleasant.

She took off with a purposeful stride that set her ponytail to swinging, and with her long legs she could cover quite a distance in a short time.

As she walked past trailer after trailer, she could hear a baby crying in one trailer and a couple yelling at each other in the next. There was a little girl playing dolls beneath a tree. Rowan smiled as she passed, listening to the little girl's one-sided conversation, most of which consisted of punishment for her dolls for being naughty. When she stopped to retie a shoelace that had come loose, Rowan thought she heard running water. When she straightened up, she looked down into the woods and guessed there was a drop-off. She walked a short distance through the trees to look and saw a creek below. The current in the water was moving at a fast clip, which she attributed to the big rain they'd just had.

A little squirrel scolded her from a nearby tree, and when she looked up to see if it was visible, she was momentarily blinded by sunlight coming through the leafy branches. She gave up on the squirrel and walked back to the sidewalk.

As she continued on the path, passing trailer after trailer, she thought living in a trailer park was a bit like living in an apartment building—always hearing the neighbors on either side, as well as the ones above and the ones below.

Living that way seemed stifling to Rowan. She'd always known quiet, the privacy of rural living, and lots of land on which to roam. She thought of the farm, and the land that was now hers, and wondered what to do with it. There was no way she could ever afford to rebuild, and she didn't know how to go about pricing it and putting it up for sale. The only building standing was that barn, and even though it had been her refuge when she needed one, she never wanted to set foot in it again.

She noticed the sidewalk was taking a turn to the left, and as she kept moving forward, she came upon a small parklike patch of trees and grass. There were a couple of picnic tables and one large charcoal grill made of red bricks, as well as a rather dilapidated swing set. But there were fresh kid tracks all around the swings, so she knew it was still in use.

The sidewalk continued past the minipark and behind the trailers on the opposite side. It was more of the same from the people inside them. The sidewalk ended behind

Frank and Jewel Crockett's fifth wheel, and when she started across the driveway to get back to Bowie's home, Frank and Jewel were sitting beneath their awning. They saw her and waved her over.

"Hi, honey!" Jewel said. "You're Rowan, right?"

"Yes, ma'am. I went for a walk around the trailer park, but it's getting too hot to stay out much longer."

"Yes, it's hot, but as long as we're in the shade we don't mind it so much," Jewel said.

"Miss Rowan, would you care for a cold drink?" Frank lifted the lid on their little ice chest. "There are cold root beers and cold water."

Rowan smiled. "I'd take a water. I should have thought to take a bottle of water with me when I set out. I will next time."

Frank pulled a bottle out of the ice chest, opened the seal for her, and then handed it over.

"It even feels good to hold," Rowan said, and then removed the lid and took a big drink. "Oh, that's wonderful! Thank you so much," she said.

"Anytime," Jewel said.

Rowan glanced across the drive. "I'd better be getting back before Ella thinks I got lost. Thank you again for the drink."

She jogged across the driveway and then hurried inside. The shock of cool air was welcome, and she dropped down onto the sofa with her bottle of water.

Ella was in the kitchen getting herself a drink. "Is it very hot out?" she asked.

"Yes, ma'am! That rain made the humidity even worse. The couple across the driveway just gave me a bottle of water. Next time, I'll have the good sense to take one with me," Rowan said, and proceeded to drink until the water was gone.

"You also forgot your phone," Ella said. "And I know this because I heard it ringing. You might want to check your messages."

"Oh my gosh! I never even thought of it," Rowan said. "I never had one at home."

She went to the dining table and picked it up. It took her a bit to figure out where to look for saved messages, and then she sat down to listen.

"Miss Harper, this is Freddy Morse, your neighbor. My sincerest condolences on the loss of your father, and I hope you are well. I've had quite a time getting in touch with you. I saw what happened to your property and was wondering if you intend to build back or if you intend to put the place up for sale. If you do, I would be interested in knowing what you want for it because I might be able to buy it. As you know, my property adjoins yours, and I didn't want to miss a chance to add some land to mine. Let me know your decision when you can."

Rowan disconnected, then laid the phone aside and went to the sofa where Ella was sitting.

"Everything okay?" Ella asked.

"Yes. It was a neighbor wanting to know if I was going to rebuild the house or sell the property. He's interested if I put it up for sale."

"What are you going to do about it?" Ella asked.

"I can't rebuild, and I don't know that I would want to if I could. I'll sell, but I don't know what land is worth around here, or who to ask."

"You can talk to a real estate agent. They'd be the best ones to give you advice. There's a real estate business here in town. You can call them, now that you have a phone."

Rowan nodded. "Maybe tomorrow. I can't think about it now."

Ella hugged her. "You're having a hard time, aren't you?"

Rowan shrugged. "I didn't think I was, but the nightmares are proof that I am."

"It will get better," Ella said. "Mama and I had a lot of trouble facing Billie's passing and then losing track of Bowie for a time."

"How did you get over it?" Rowan asked.

"Oh, you never really get over it. But after a period of time, we saw we were concentrating more on her death than all the time we had her. So, we made her part of the family again. There were pictures of her all over the house, and sometimes we'd watch her favorite TV shows and do 'remember when' moments together. And we still celebrate her birthday."

"Those are wonderful ways to commemorate her life," Rowan said.

Ella nodded. "Whatever works, you know? Mama and I have been putting off reclaiming parts of our lives since the flood. We have money in the bank to buy a car and haven't done it. And we had homeowners insurance, but the flood insurance was too high, so we didn't have that. So there we sat in that nursing home, reeling from the shock of all that happened, and with nowhere to go and without the money to fix the house."

Rowan leaned her head on Ella's shoulder. "Thank you for giving me a place to live. I fully intend to go to work and pay you monthly rent."

Ella just smiled. "You can work all you want, but we'll not take a penny of your money. We aren't renting you a room, we're sharing our home." And then she chuckled. "And look what you got in the bargain! Bowie James."

Rowan blushed. "We'll see how it goes. He may decide I'm too much trouble to bother with."

"That'll be the day," Ella said. "You just keep an open heart and do what it tells you to do."

"Yes, ma'am," Rowan said, and then glanced at the clock. "I guess I need to be thinking about supper. I got those pork chops out of the freezer this morning and they've been thawing in the refrigerator. Should I fry them, or does he like them made another way?"

"This is the South. You can never go wrong if it's fried."

Rowan laughed. "True. Okay then, I need to check the pantry and see what else there is to go with them."

"Let me know if you need help later."

"I will," Rowan said, and as she got up, she shoved the idea of a farm sale to the back of her mind.

Bowie had been watching Junior off and on all day, taking note of how readily he took to whatever task he was given and how thorough he was in following through. He hadn't been afraid to ask for help if he was uncertain.

It was almost time for the workday to end. The men were packing up tools, and they'd sent Junior to lock the back door and close and lock all the windows.

Bowie watched, and when the kid got up to the front

of the house to close the last of the windows, Bowie walked up beside him and gave him a quick pat on the back.

"You did a good job today, Junior."

Junior smiled. "Thanks, Boss!"

"Hey, you earned the compliment. If anyone is picking you up, you might let them know it's about that time, or I can drop you off on my way home. It's up to you."

"Oh…I was gonna walk home, Boss."

"Want a ride?"

Junior nodded. "Yeah, sure."

"Good. Grab that lunch you didn't get to eat, and make sure you take everything you brought back home for the night."

"Yes, sir," he said, and finished locking the last of the windows. Then he went to get his lunch, his gloves, and his baseball cap, but when he turned around and saw Bowie was on the phone, he went out onto the porch to give his boss privacy.

The crew was driving away when Bowie locked the front door, and Junior was waiting for him on the top step.

"Okay, we're off," Bowie said.

Junior followed him to the rental car, got in, and buckled up, trying to be cool about the fact that he was riding with his cousin, while trying not to panic that the man his daddy viewed as the enemy was taking him home.

"I don't know where you live," Bowie said.

"Turn right just past the bank. I'll direct you from there."

Bowie nodded, and a few minutes later, he braked in front of the house Junior pointed out.

"Have a good evening," Bowie said.

Junior nodded. "See you in the morning," he said, and took off running up the driveway to the house.

Bowie drove away before anyone knew he'd been there and headed for home, thinking about Rowan. There was something about sleeping in the same bed with a woman that shifted just being acquaintances to more than good friends.

Chapter 14

As Bowie took the turn into the trailer park, he was struck by how anxious he was to get home. After spending so many years alone, this unexpected turn in his life had given him a glimpse into what family life and having someone like Rowan in his life could be like. He'd never felt like this about a woman before. Despite the fact that he was a grown-ass man of thirty-five, he felt like a lovestruck teen.

He parked, got out, and was halfway up the steps when Rowan opened the door to surprise him. Only she was the one who got the surprise.

Delighted by her sudden appearance, the first thing he did was cup the back of her head and kiss her. It was a surprise attack with unmistakable intensity.

"You're the best reason I've ever had to come home to," he said, then slid an arm across her shoulder as he entered.

Pearl was sitting at the dining room table, and Ella was at the stove.

"How are my girls?" Bowie asked, taking note of how fast Rowan went to help Ella.

"We're good. How are things going at the house?" Pearl asked.

"Really good, Gran. We got the headers in, so now the walls are all gone from the front door through the kitchen, and through the dining and living area."

Pearl was beaming. "I absolutely can't wait to see all that," she said.

"The crew got your master bath and walk-in closet framed up today, too, as well as opening up a door from your bedroom into the bathroom en suite," he added.

"Your day was far busier than ours. We're going to be spoiled by the time we move back in. We haven't had to do anything but cook a few meals and enjoy the luxuries of your home," Ella said. "Mama took a nap this afternoon, and I watched some of my shows. The only industrious one was Rowan, who got a little cabin fever and took a walk around the trailer park."

"You did? So, how was it?" Bowie asked.

"It was great and didn't take any effort to walk," Rowan said. "It felt good to be outside. Did you guys know there's a creek just behind this side of the trailer park? It's just a few yards into the woods. And there's also a tiny playground at the back of it. It has two picnic tables, a grill, and a swing set. I think there are quite a few kids who live here, too. I see one little redhead riding her bike a lot, and I hear others playing."

Bowie shook his head. "I haven't gone any farther here than where I parked. Was it hot?"

"Not too bad," Rowan said. "The sidewalk is shaded almost all the way around, so I didn't really feel the heat."

"If you're going to clean up before supper, get at it," Ella said. "It's almost ready."

Bowie laughed. "Yes, ma'am. Give me about ten minutes, and I'll be back."

He pulled his work shirt over his head as he headed for the shower. Rowan looked away, for fear the girls would see the shameless lust she was feeling for that man, and went to help Ella.

A few minutes later, they were seated and talking as they ate.

"So how did your new hired hand do today?" Rowan asked.

"He did good. Really good," Bowie said.

Pearl looked surprised. "You hired a new hand? Someone local?"

Bowie nodded. "The kid who keyed my car."

Ella gasped. "You hired a Boone?"

"I hired a kid who wanted to work off what he owed me," Bowie said. "He didn't know anything about me except that I broke his daddy's nose. We talked. He had no idea of the history between our families. The kid has a sense of honor or he wouldn't have faced me and asked if he could work off part of his debt. Without me going into all the ugly details, he gets the drift."

Pearl nodded. "Then you made the right call...for both of you."

Bowie paused. "One other thing. I dropped the charges against him. No one else knows this except Chief Pittman, so keep it within the family for now. My insurance will pay for the repairs, except the deductible, and Junior is working that off."

Ella smiled. "You are a good man, Bowie."

He shrugged. "I didn't do it to be magnanimous. I did it because of who his parents are. The Boone family has a tendency to raise their young with extreme prejudice. This boy is not what I expected. He didn't blame anyone but himself, is upset about what's happening within his family, and wants to do the right thing. I think he deserves a break."

"What is happening to his family?" Rowan asked.

"According to Junior, Cora kicked Judson out of the house and filed for divorce. His aunt Nellie, who's married to Melvin Boone, is leaving Mel and going back to Kentucky. And Junior's parents, Emmitt and Tiny, are at odds with each other, too."

"You're not serious?" Pearl said.

"Yes, ma'am. It appears the men in Cora's life, including Randall, all lied to her. They knew what Randall did to Mama. And they knew I was his. What shamed Cora most, from what she said to me, was they knew I was blood kin and denied me. They knew I was her grandson and lied to her."

Pearl was silent for a few moments, and then she sighed.

"I'm glad to know this. Cora and I were friends before we were married."

Rowan frowned. "And getting married made you enemies?"

Pearl nodded. "Because the men we married already hated each other. It was so ridiculous, but neither of us could fight a blood feud, and that's how the separation began."

"I understand being angry at someone," Rowan said. "But I don't understand not getting over it."

"That's good to know for the times in the future when I totally tick you off," Bowie said, and then grinned at the look on her face.

"You are impossible, aren't you, Bowie James?"

"Not impossible, by any means. But there's probably still some assembly required."

She fired right back at him. "Then somebody pass a screwdriver, please. I can't be hanging around with someone who has a screw loose."

He laughed.

"I do believe you've met your match," Pearl said.

"Lucky me," Bowie said.

Rowan didn't respond, but she was thinking it. *Oh no, Bowie James. Lucky me. Lucky, lucky me.*

Supper at Emmitt and Tiny's house was quiet. They both kept waiting for Junior to talk about work, but he hadn't said a word. Tiny noticed he'd brought back the lunch he'd taken with him, but he hadn't mentioned anything about that, either. So as his mother, she decided she had the right to question him.

"You haven't said a word about your day," Tiny said. "How did it go?"

Junior looked straight at his daddy. "Are you gonna lose it if I talk about him?"

Emmitt flushed. "No. Say what you want."

"I liked the work. All the guys on his crew were really nice to me, and so was the boss."

"He told you to call him Boss?" Tiny asked.

"No. He said I could call him Bowie or Boss, which is what his crew calls him. I chose to call him Boss because he is one."

Tiny shrugged. "Oh. Well, I just didn't want him to be ordering you around and lording it over you."

Junior frowned. "Mama. All bosses order their employees around. And I don't even know what 'lording it over me' means. Please pass the chicken."

He took another piece of fried chicken from the platter and took a big bite.

Tiny watched him licking his fingers and frowned. "Use your napkin, please, and what kind of work did you do?"

Junior wiped his hands and his mouth, then laid down his fork. "If I get all this said, then can I finish supper? I was starving, and the chicken is good."

Tiny didn't like the question, so she ignored it.

"Why were you so hungry? Didn't he even let you eat the lunch you took?"

Junior rolled his eyes. "You guys are just looking for something to disapprove of, and I already told you he was nice. He sent me to eat with the rest of the guys, and he paid for everything. We went to Granny's. I had a burger and fries and a piece of chocolate pie. As for the work, I did a lot of lifting and carrying because the lumberyard delivered some supplies and me and the guys carried them into the house. I watched them hang two big headers. I did whatever they asked, and being a builder is something special, Mama. They fix people's homes, or they build new ones. Homes aren't just pretty to look at. They furnish shelter and safety for people, and I might want to do that someday when I grow up."

Emmitt was in a state of shock. He knew why Bowie had come back, but he didn't know that was what he did for a living.

"So, how many men work for him?" he asked.

"I'm not sure, but I know it's a lot. The guys said they're only one crew, and that he has about twenty more, working on different projects at the same time."

"Twenty more men?" Emmitt asked.

"No, twenty more crews. There are six men with him here, but there are lots more in each of the other crews."

Tiny was thinking of the money, and the greedy side of her kicked in before she thought.

"If you get in good with him, you could have access to a rich lifestyle someday."

Junior blinked, then looked at her as if he was seeing her as someone other than his mother. And he didn't much like what he saw. His words were measured, but the tone in his voice was about one shade short of angry.

"Right now, Mama, I'm trying to work off a debt I owe him for messing up his car. So you and Daddy need to get on the same page here. Are you still hating him because he's the bastard son Uncle Randall didn't want…or has he become more appealing because of the money you think he has?"

Tiny gasped. "Emmitt Lee, you do not talk to me like that!"

Junior pushed his plate away and stood up. "Well, I know I'm not discussing him with either of you again, and I'm not hungry anymore. Excuse me."

Tiny was pissed. Now that she couldn't fuss with her son anymore, she turned on her husband. "Well, you just sat there like a bump on a log and didn't say a word to him about how rude he was to me!"

Emmitt shrugged. "You're the one who wanted to talk about it, and now you messed up his supper. Just because you didn't like the answers doesn't mean what he said was wrong. And I still don't want to talk about him, so this discussion is over."

Tiny started yelling, and Emmitt started yelling back. Junior sat on the side of his bed, wondering which parent he'd wind up with when they divorced. From the sounds of the fighting, it wouldn't be long in coming.

He was still in shock about a whole other side to his family that he'd never known about and was struggling not to be ashamed of the lot of them.

He was tired, and sad, and a little sick to his stomach. He kicked off his shoes, stripped down to his undershorts, and turned back the covers. He'd showered when he first got home and wanted nothing more to do with his parents tonight. So he set his alarm for work and crawled into bed and closed his eyes.

Judson was drinking a beer and watching television in his underwear, something he'd never done at home. Cora was all about propriety and wouldn't have put up with that.

He'd spent all day waiting for his sons to return his calls, but it had never happened. He couldn't stand not knowing what was going on, but it was beginning to appear that if he wanted answers he was going to have to get them for himself, and tomorrow was as good a time as any. He just had to figure out how to go about it, because he didn't intend to advertise his presence to anyone. He was going to show up unannounced and find out what the hell was going on that they didn't want him to know.

Mel was alone, and he was drunk. Nellie was gone, and he never got to say goodbye. He was trying to envision the rest of his life alone, but nothing had occurred to him yet that would be considered positive.

Nellie had left a note—of sorts. Not really a note, just a tying-up-loose-ends kind of thing. Basically, all it said was "These are yours," and left her debit card from their bank, her keys to the house and car, her cell phone that was under his phone plan, her wedding ring, and her checkbook to the bank account on the table.

She hadn't taken one damn thing from this house but her clothes and makeup. Her car was still in the driveway. He had no idea how she got out of town, but she took nothing with her of their lives together. Every connection they had was left behind.

Mel tried to pour himself another shot of whiskey but the bottle was empty, so he set it back on the table, kicked back in the recliner, and meant to turn on the TV. But somewhere between pressing the Power button and cognizance, he passed out.

———

Cora was picking up a few things from the Piggly Wiggly before it closed for the day, and as she was going down the baking aisle, Mavis West, the secretary at Blessings Elementary, was coming from the other direction. She and Mavis sat side by side every Sunday in Sunday School class. Cora was expecting a smile. Instead, she got a frown and a rude interrogation.

"Well, hello, Cora. Didn't expect to see you out and about," Mavis said.

Cora frowned. "Why in the world not?"

"I would have thought, after what I heard about you and Judson, that you wouldn't be showing your face in town."

Cora's eyes narrowed angrily. "Exactly what did you hear that led you to believe such a preposterous thing?"

Mavis's face turned red, and her voice rose just the tiniest bit.

"I heard you kicked him out of the house for a little fuss down at Granny's. Granted it wasn't Judson's best day, but hardly worth breaking up a fifty-year marriage."

Cora was stunned. "This is what's going around Blessings?"

Mavis nodded.

"And you believed it? Not that it was any of your business to begin with…but that just tells me you weren't the friend I thought you were."

Mavis glared. "So you're not denying it?"

Cora lifted her chin in defiance. "How long have you lived in Blessings?"

"Nearly eighteen years," Mavis said.

"Then, as Judson used to say, you don't know hell from high water. There's been an ongoing feud between those families that goes back three generations. And what Jud did at Granny's was part of that. The man he assaulted—the one he threatened to kill—is his oldest grandson, who he has rejected since the day he was born. So you take your hateful self on down the road and don't talk to me again unless it's to apologize," Cora said, then moved past Mavis with her head held high.

Two hours later, Cora was still angry, and after cleaning up the kitchen from her supper, she went out onto the back porch to watch the sun go down.

She'd been thinking back over her life all afternoon and had come to the conclusion that it could have been worse, and it could have been better. There was a huge hole in her heart where her family had been, but the family she thought she had was only in her mind's eye.

So she grieved for the loss of her innocence, and for their culpability in such brutal crimes, and wondered if she'd ever be happy again.

Tears fell freely as the setting sun turned the sky a brilliant wash of pinks and orange.

"I see it, Lord. I know you're trying to cheer me up, but it's going to take more than one sunset to right the wrongs."

Cora sat until light began fading to dark, and when the first stars came out, she went back inside. Had she seen the shadow she cast as she entered the kitchen, she wouldn't have recognized herself.

The stoop to her shoulders and the dragging steps she was taking didn't fit the woman she'd been. Jud wasn't the only person suffering through a divorce. Just because she'd been the one to file didn't mean it didn't hurt.

Bowie came out of the bathroom, thinking Rowan would already be asleep, but she was sitting up in bed with her legs crossed, staring off into space.

"Hey. Is everything all right?" he asked.

Rowan had been so lost in thought she hadn't heard him come out. "Oh, yes, I was just thinking. I got a call today from one of our neighbors asking to let him know if I was going to sell my property."

Bowie sat down on the side of her bed and slipped his fingers between hers.

"Are you conflicted about it? Were you thinking about keeping it?"

"I actually hadn't thought about it at all, other than I never wanted to set foot on it again," she said.

Bowie was startled by the vehemence in her voice. "Because of what happened during the flood?"

"I guess," she said, and looked away again.

He stayed with her in her quiet space, fully understanding where she was coming from but so sorry that it had happened.

Finally, she looked up at him again. "I guess if I'm going to sell it, then I need to see what's left. The real estate agent will want to know."

"Whoever you use, they'll take their own pictures for advertising it, but I'll take you. All you have to do is say the word."

She took a deep breath, as if she was about to jump in deep water, and nodded. "Yes, I need to go. Who knows? Maybe it will settle some of the horror that's locked in my mind. Maybe seeing it again will help."

Bowie lifted her hand to his lips and brushed a kiss across her knuckles. "Good for you."

"You pick a day when you feel comfortable enough to leave the jobsite. It won't matter to me. You do need to know it's about ten miles from Blessings," she said.

"I'll see how tomorrow begins, and if it looks like I can get away for a couple of hours, I'll call. It'll give you time to get dressed."

"Thank you, Bowie."

"You're welcome," he said, and then leaned forward and kissed her—gently at first, then longer, more intensely, until Rowan moaned.

At that point, Bowie stopped. They couldn't take this any farther, and he didn't want to tease.

"Believe me, stopping is the last thing on my mind,

but here we are, with the best chaperones ever behind that door."

"I know. I guess I don't have a stop button where you're concerned."

"You weren't on that trip alone," Bowie said. "Do you feel like you can sleep now? If not, feel free to watch television. I can sleep through anything."

"No, I'm ready to sleep, and I'm sure you are, too. I kept everyone up last night."

"You don't really expect me to complain about holding you in my arms all night. Or waking up beside you this morning, do you?" he asked.

She smiled shyly. "I guess I didn't think about it like that."

"Well, I thought about it enough for both of us," Bowie said. "Sleep well, sweetheart."

Rowan pulled back the covers and then slipped between them and stretched out. She was reaching down to pull up the covers when Bowie did it for her, then kissed her forehead as he tucked her in.

Rowan sighed as she closed her eyes. "I haven't been tucked into bed since my mother died."

Bowie stopped. "I thought you said you were ten when she passed."

"Yes…ten," she murmured.

"Your dad didn't ever—"

"Never… 'Be a big girl. Big girls don't cry.'"

Bowie stood over her for a moment, waiting, watching for her to pull the covers up under her chin. And she did. Her breathing was changing. He knew she was already drifting off to sleep, but the farther away she went, the tighter the hold.

The more he learned about her father, the less he liked him. Still bothered by what she'd revealed, Bowie went to get a drink, then settled for a beer instead. He popped the top, then turned out the lights, letting the dark settle around him as he took the first sip.

He could hear the soft sounds of her breathing and ached for the lonely child and then the isolated woman she'd been. She didn't know it yet, but that hurricane didn't destroy her life. It had released her. Bowie knew his life hadn't been easy, but he'd known his enemies' faces. She'd never recognized the deceit or the covert aspects behind her own father's smile.

He sighed, wondering what the odds were of two broken people having a successful relationship, but he didn't really care. Bowie wasn't a betting man, but for him, Rowan Harper was the dark horse who'd come out of nowhere. He was about to lay every card he had on the table for her. If he'd learned one thing in the past twenty years, it was never pass up a sure thing.

He finally finished his beer, trashed the bottle, set the alarm on his phone, and crawled into bed. Sleep came easy. He dreamed of the house he was renovating as if it were a person, seeing the old woman she'd been, and then him giving her a key that began turning back the clock of her life to new again, but in a different way.

He woke up when the alarm went off and silenced it quickly, then sat up on the side of the bed and began thinking about the day. He looked across the room at Rowan, wishing he could crawl in bed with her and love her awake, then headed for the bathroom to dress.

When he came out, coffee was made and she was sitting at the dining table holding a steaming mug cupped between her hands. The curtains were pulled back to let in the sunshine, and she was sitting motionless—again staring off into space.

He crossed the distance between them, laid a hand on the back of her head, and leaned down for a quick morning kiss.

"Good morning, sunshine."

She smiled. "It is a good morning, isn't it?"

"Yes, ma'am. I'm going to make a peanut butter and jelly sandwich. Want one?"

"I can do it for you," she said and started to get up, but he stopped her.

"I'm cooking this morning. Just sit tight. It won't take but a couple of minutes, okay?"

"Light on the peanut butter, heavy on the jelly, please."

He gave her a thumbs-up, then moved to the counter. He banged a door, rattled dishes, and opened and closed the refrigerator twice for one jar of jelly, but the sandwiches were finally made.

He put Rowan's sandwich down in front of her. One side had peanut butter, the other piece of bread had the jelly. And he'd left them open for her to put together.

She grinned when she saw what he'd done. He'd drawn a big heart in the jelly, and put *Bowie + Rowan* in the peanut butter. When she put them together, the heart would be complete.

"I love it," she said.

"Thanks. I was always really good in art."

She laughed as he sat down beside her and took his first bite. But once again, she was staring out the window. He stopped and tracked her line of vision.

"What do you see out there?"

"Oh, nothing…everything. The world and all of its possibilities, I guess."

"Am I included in your possibilities?" he asked.

"Yes."

"How do my chances look?" he asked.

She laughed. "You just carved our initials in a heart in my PB&J sandwich, so I would never have taken you as the indecisive type."

"Not indecisive at all, but a hurtin', lovestruck sap would pretty much cover it."

"Just my type, so I'd say your chances look good, real good."

He leaned over and whispered in her ear, "Thank you, baby. I promise you won't be sorry. Oh…and don't forget we're going to your farm today, okay?"

"I'm not likely to forget. The knot in my stomach is a great reminder."

"I'm sorry this is hard for you. All you have to do is say the word and we'll leave whenever you say. Oh… and make a new grocery list. I'm sure there are things that need replacing."

"It is what it is," Rowan said. "I'll make the list and check with the girls to see if they need anything in particular. I'll be ready whenever you call."

He nodded.

They finished their sandwiches, and Bowie checked to make sure he had his phone and car keys, then shut off the security alarm at the front door.

"Do I get a goodbye kiss?" he asked.

Rowan threw her arms around his neck, centered her lips on his mouth, and kissed him senseless. When she heard him groan, she stopped.

"Will that work?" she asked.

Bowie slid an arm around her waist to pull her close. "It'll hold me, but I want one more for the road."

And this time, she was the one whose head was spinning when he left. She stood in the doorway, waiting for him to look back. When he did, she waved.

He just pointed at her and grinned.

Chapter 15

AFTER LAST NIGHT'S DEBACLE, JUNIOR GOT UP EARLY, quietly made himself some breakfast, then left the house while his parents were still asleep, giving himself plenty of time to walk to work. He had no desire to be alone with either parent right now. All he wanted was to do the right thing and get to know his cousin better.

He thought about telling Grandma Boone what he was doing, then let it go. It would be worse to be refused entrance to her house than to let her think he was a hoodlum, the name she'd called him when he and Grandpa were both in jail.

He got to the jobsite a little before eight, but this morning, Bowie was already there. Junior jumped up on the porch and went inside, seeing Bowie near the back of the house where they would be adding new plumbing for the master bath.

"Morning, Boss."

Bowie turned around, then smiled. "Morning yourself. Are you ready for today?"

"I'm ready for whatever you need me to do," Junior said.

"We're going to have plumbers here during the morning hours. I'm hoping they don't run into issues, but with old plumbing, there's never any way to tell until they start pulling out what's there. Watch where you step back here today. We're all going to be walking on the two-by-fours below the subfloor until the plumbers are finished."

Junior eyed the open spaces with the missing sub-flooring and looked at how far down it was to dirt. Far enough he knew he did not want to slip and drop. He'd be riding a two-by-four if that happened, and in a world of hurt.

Bowie glanced out the door. "The crew is arriving. You'll be answering to Ray for part of the day. I have to run an errand for a friend."

"Okay with me, Boss."

Bowie pointed. "There's the plumber. Come on. We may need to help him carry supplies inside," and out the door they went.

⁓

Junior wasn't the only Boone who was up early. It was a little past eight when Jud turned off the street and up into Mel's driveway. Both cars were under the carport. Exactly what he was looking for. They were both still there, and now so was he.

He combed his hair away from his face with both hands, then swaggered up onto the porch like he owned it. As he was heading toward the front door, Jud noticed the shades were already up, and a light was on in the living room. He peered through the glass and was surprised to see Mel asleep in his recliner. He saw an empty whiskey bottle beside the chair and frowned. This didn't look good.

He knocked loudly, then checked to see if Mel was up. It didn't appear that he'd even heard the sound. Jud knocked again, then made a fist and pounded on the door, and this time got results. He heard the sound of the recliner as Mel put it in an upright position and then heard him stumbling toward the door.

Success.

Mel woke with a start and was up and moving toward the door before it occurred to him to look and see who was out there first. When he opened the door and saw his daddy, he sighed. Hopefully, he was here with money... or a suggestion of where to get some, Mel thought as he unlocked the storm door.

Jud yanked it open and strode inside as if nothing had ever happened. He picked up the whiskey bottle and then turned around and waited for Mel to explain. But Mel didn't have anything positive to say, so he said nothing at all.

"What's going on?" Jud asked. "Did you and Nellie get into a fight? Is that why you're sleeping in the recliner?"

"There's nobody here but me, so I sleep where I want." Mel took the empty whiskey bottle out of Jud's hand and walked into the kitchen.

Surprised by Mel's answer, Jud followed, watching as Mel put the empty bottle in a wastebasket they used for recycling.

"So where's Nellie?"

It was the combination of a throbbing hangover and the fact that Jud had left them all without a word that gave Mel the nerve to challenge him.

"Why do you care? For all you knew, we could all be gone," he muttered, and began making a pot of coffee.

Jud frowned. "Look, I'm here now, so what the hell's going on?"

"Uh…let's see… Where do I begin?" Mel said. "I guess I'll start with me. Nellie left me. She went back home to her people in Kentucky, and I was not invited to go with her."

Jud's surprise was evident. "You mean, as in just a visit, or what?"

"She's divorcing me! Just like Mama dumped you. And for the same damn reason. I'd leave, too, but I not only can't afford to move but will also be evicted when my landlord realizes I can't pay the rent I owe. So unless you came to tell me you're putting my monthly salary in the bank, we're done here."

Jud shrugged. "I'd tell you to come live with me, but I just signed a lease on a one-bedroom apartment."

"How convenient," Mel said.

Jud didn't like where this was going and changed the subject. "What's going on with Emmitt and Tiny? Has Junior been sentenced yet?"

"You want information about them, then go knock on their door."

Jud didn't know how to take this. His boys had never been defiant or questioned his authority. He didn't know who to be mad at, but he was well aware that none of it would have happened if he'd left Bowie James the hell alone.

"I'm not cutting my boys off," Jud said. "Your money will be in your account like always."

Mel just looked at him.

Jud was put so off-balance by this behavior that he didn't know what to do. "I guess I'd better be going," he said.

"You can see yourself to the door," Mel said and turned back to the coffee maker.

Jud stood for a moment, staring at the stiff, unyielding set of his youngest son's back, and then left.

Mel locked the door after he heard Jud backing out of the drive. He thought about texting Emmitt to let him know their daddy was in town, and then changed his mind and took a shower instead.

———∞∞———

Emmitt got up with heartburn and wandered through the house to the kitchen to take something for it. Then he noticed a dirty bowl and glass in the sink. Junior was already gone.

He stood there a minute, thinking of the growing gap between him and his only son, when he caught sight of a car pulling up into the drive.

Holy hell. It's Daddy!

Moments later, the doorbell rang.

Emmitt hurried to answer, hoping the sound didn't wake Tiny. She was already angry with him and he didn't want a repeat of the fit she'd had last night.

He opened the door, trying to gauge his father's mood.

Jud eyed Emmitt's pajama bottoms, his bare beer belly, and bare feet.

"Did I get you out of bed?"

"No. I was in the kitchen. What do you want?"

Jud glared. "This is the second time I've been asked that this morning."

"So you've already seen Mel. Was he sober?"

"Hungover," Jud muttered. "Where's Tiny? Did she leave Blessings like Nellie did?"

"I should be so lucky," Emmitt mumbled. "She's still sleeping, or she was."

"Oh. Well, the reason I'm here is to check on

everybody. Where's Junior? He hasn't already had his sentencing, has he?"

"We haven't been notified of a court date yet," Emmitt said.

"Go get him out of bed. I want to talk to him."

"Too late," Emmitt said. "He's already at work."

"What? Why did he go to work all of a sudden?"

"To help work off the debt he owes Bowie James— and we had nothing to do with it, so calm that rage. Your face is red as a beet. He did it because he thought you and Mama's divorce, and Nellie leaving Mel, and the fights me and Tiny have been having are all because of what he did. He now knows enough of the back story to be disgusted with all of us."

Jud's rage faded and was replaced with regret. He loved his grandson—at least the younger one—and was sorry this had all come out.

"Well, you can tell him he doesn't have to work. I'll pay off the debt for him and—"

"And then what? Turn him into Mel and me? We don't have enough job skills between us to get hired as dishwashers at Granny's. You aren't paying anybody off. Junior is proud of what he's doing. I don't want him growing up dependent on you, too."

Jud's heart was beginning to pound. He knew his blood pressure was rising. He could feel his face getting red all over again.

"I told Mel, and I'm reassuring you as well. Your monthly salary will be in your bank account as always. Nothing about that is changing."

Emmitt had never felt like more of a loser. "And what do I have to do to earn it?"

"Nothing now."

"Be warned. I'm never doing your dirty work again," Emmitt said.

Jud frowned. "Why are you both suddenly mad at me? You never once questioned or hesitated at anything I told you to do."

"I'm mad at myself," Emmitt said. "And just so you know, don't show your face anywhere in town without being prepared for the hard stares and cold shoulders. They've seen Bowie, too. They know what we did, know we all lied. If I could, me and Tiny would already be gone, but we can't because we're awaiting Junior's court date. So if you don't have anything else to talk about, then you better get while the gettin's good. Tiny is almost as mad at you as she is at me. And whatever you do, stay away from Junior. He's doing just fine without you."

Jud didn't have to be told twice. He was out of the house and in the car within seconds. He had a healthy respect for Tiny. She was hell on wheels when she got mad. He backed up and sped away, leaving rubber on the street behind him, and without hesitation drove straight home to have it out with Cora. He had no intention of knocking and was going to let himself in even if he had to break another safety chain to do it.

He was struck by new anger as their home came into view. She had no right to do what she did, and he'd been too lenient with her, but no more.

He parked in the driveway and stormed toward the front door with his key in hand, then shoved it in the lock, but it wouldn't go in. He frowned and turned it the other way, thinking he must have had it upside down, but it still didn't work.

"Sonofabitch. She changed the locks," he muttered and began banging on the front door, shouting. "Cora! Let me in now or I'll kick it in."

Cora was in the kitchen making her breakfast when she heard the shouting. Her heart sank. She knew Judson well enough not to be surprised by this. She had feared this might happen once he got over the shock of what she'd done. It appeared the bully in him was back.

She turned off the fire under her scrambled eggs just as he began to pound and kick on the door. In a panic now, and fearing for her physical safety, she grabbed her phone and dialed 911.

"911. What is your emergency?" Avery asked.

The moment she heard the familiar voice, she started crying. "Avery, this is Cora Boone. Judson is on my porch, beating on the door and yelling at me, threatening to kick it in if I don't let him in. Hurry! I'm afraid if he gets in, he will hurt me!"

"Stay on the phone with me, Cora. I'm going to dispatch this call out right now."

Cora heard the call going out and hoped they'd get there before Jud did his worst.

"Okay, they're on their way. Is he still there?" Avery asked.

Cora moaned. "Yes, please hurry!"

"Are you all right?" Avery asked.

"I am for now," she said.

"Don't hang up, whatever you do. I need to know if he does kick his way in."

"Yes, okay," Cora said.

Jud had already lost his cool and was unaware that neighbors on both sides of the house were now out on their porches.

"Jud! Leave her alone!" one of them shouted.

Jud turned on him. "Mind your own damned business," he shrieked and began hammering the door again, cursing and raging, promising all the ugly things he was going to do if she didn't obey.

All of a sudden, he began hearing sirens. *Dammit! She called the cops.* Jud jumped off the porch, ran back to his car, and sped out of the neighborhood.

Cora heard him leaving and rushed to the door in time to see the car take a quick right toward the school and disappear.

Her heart was racing and she felt like she was going to be sick. She was reaching for something to hold onto when the world began to spin, and then everything went black.

The next-door neighbor was still on his porch when he saw Cora look out, but she was only there a few seconds before she suddenly dropped. He knew by the way she went down that she was unconscious. He went down his front steps and was racing across his yard when the police arrived.

Chief Pittman saw the neighbor running and pointing, and then saw Cora was down. He got out on the run, calling dispatch to send an ambulance.

"Did you see what happened?" the chief asked as the neighbor ran up the steps behind him.

"I heard Jud carrying on and came outside. I yelled at him to leave her alone, and he pretty much told me to mind my own business. I guess Jud heard your sirens because he left in a rush. Then I saw Cora come to the door, probably to make sure he was gone. That's when I saw her drop."

"Did he touch her in any way?" Pittman asked as he felt for a pulse.

"No, sir. Just yelling and kicking on the door."

She was still breathing, which was a relief, but when the chief checked her pulse, it seemed irregular. Even if they found Jud Boone, unless Cora wanted to press charges for harassment they didn't have much of anything to arrest him for except disturbing the peace again. Family squabbles were the worst, and the chief needed to talk to Cora.

"Would you mind going into Cora's kitchen and bringing me a cold, wet cloth?" the chief asked.

The neighbor scooted past where Cora was lying, then raced toward the kitchen. He was back moments later with a dish towel that he'd gotten wet then wrung out.

Deputy Ralph pulled up on the scene as the chief carefully wiped down Cora's face and neck, then folded up the cloth and laid it across her forehead.

"What do you need me to do, Chief?"

"Make a quick patrol through town, and if you see Judson Boone anywhere, pick him up for questioning. I don't know the make and model of his car. You'll have to check the DMV."

"I know it," the neighbor said. "He drives a 2012 black Chevrolet Impala." And then he went home, as Ralph took off in a rush.

To Lon's relief, Cora began waking up.

"Lie still, Miss Cora," he said.

Cora recognized the chief, then felt something cold and wet on her head and reached up to feel it.

"It's just a wet cloth," Lon said, still worried. Her eyes were red and tear-filled, and she was far too pale for his liking. "What happened to you?" he asked.

"I just got dizzy. I think because I was so scared. I don't need an ambulance. I'll just sit here a bit and rest. I'll be all right," she said.

"No, ma'am. I can't do that. I need to make sure you're okay before I leave. The EMTs will check you out."

She didn't argue.

Lon kept watching her closely, and the moment he heard the ambulance coming, he began breathing a little easier.

"Is that them?" Cora asked.

Lon frowned. Her voice was weak and shaky.

"Yes, ma'am, that's them."

"Tell them if my heart stops, I refuse CPR."

Lon was stunned. "Cora! You don't want to think like that! What about your family? Your grandson! He got a job with Bowie so he could help work off some of the debt he owes, and he did it all on his own."

Cora was still for a moment. "He did? And Bowie hired him?"

"Yes, ma'am. And just between you and me, because nobody else knows this yet, Bowie already dropped all the charges against him. He just wants Junior to get to finish what he set out to do."

"He did all that? After what happened to him?" Cora asked.

Lon nodded. "But you can't tell. I already broke my word to Bowie by telling you, but you need something positive to get you through all this. And…I think the ambulance is just pulling up. You're gonna be fine. Just have a little faith."

Moments later, the EMTs came up on the run and began checking Cora's vitals. A few minutes later, when they told her they needed to transport her to the ER, she didn't argue.

Inside the house, the chief picked up Cora's phone from where she'd dropped it, scrolled through her contact list until he found Emmitt's name, and called him.

―――

Emmitt was in the shower when his phone began to ring. Tiny rolled over in bed to see who was calling, and when she saw it was the Blessings PD, she answered.

"Hello?"

"Tiny, this is Chief Pittman. Is Emmitt there?"

"Yes, Chief, but he's in the shower. What's wrong?"

"We're transporting Cora to the ER. I need you to let Emmitt know."

"Oh my God! What happened?" Tiny cried.

"Judson happened. I haven't been able to interview her since my arrival, but when she called 911, she said he was pounding on the door and threatening to kick it in. He was gone by the time we arrived, and she appeared to have passed out on the threshold. I think it scared her pretty badly. I'll leave it up to you to notify the rest of the family," he said.

"Yes, yes, oh my God, thank you for calling," Tiny said, and then jumped out of bed and ran into the bathroom, shouting. "Emmitt! Get out of the shower. Chief Pittman just called. They just took your mama to the ER!"

Emmitt gasped, in a panic as he quickly shut off the water, grabbed a towel, and began to dry off.

"What happened?" he asked.

"Your daddy happened! He scared her so bad trying to get in the house that they had to take her to the hospital. I don't know what all is wrong."

"Oh, for the love of God," Emmitt muttered. "I'll call Mel. Mama may not want us there, but we're gonna be there just the same."

Mel drove to the ER in the clothes he'd slept in. He needed a shave, and his head was pounding from the hangover, but all he could think about was his mama. She might hate him, but he still loved her and was gutted that this had happened.

He pulled up and parked just as Emmitt and Tiny parked a few spaces down. Emmitt saw him and waited for him to catch up so they could go in together.

Jud was furious as he drove the alleys and back roads around Blessings. His head was pounding from the blood rush. His sons had turned against him. His wife had betrayed him, and all because that damn bastard came back to Blessings.

He kept ranting as he drove. "It's Bowie James's fault. I told him if he ever came back, I would kill him. My mistake was sending Mel and Emmitt to scare him away."

When he got to a dead-end street, Jud stopped and reached beneath the seat, then pulled out his handgun.

He sat long enough to make sure it was loaded, then laid it in the seat beside him and turned around. Bowie James had put an end to Jud's world, so Jud was going to return the favor. And since Bowie was supposed to be renovating Pearl's house, he guessed that was where he would find him.

Jud's pulse was racing as he headed for the other side of town. He'd lost all sense of rational behavior, unconcerned with doing this in broad daylight and most likely in front of witnesses. But if he was going to spend the rest of his life alone, he'd gladly spend it in prison just to know he had fired the last shot in the feud.

He began to slow down as he came up on the street. There were vehicles parked on both sides of the street, a big roll-off dumpster in the yard, and a van from Ken's Electric parked beside it in the driveway. Jud had all the cover he needed and then some, so he slowed down even more, rolling past the house in near silence.

It appeared they were hanging new windows by the front door because there was a huge opening where a window had yet to be hung, and he could easily see men walking back and forth inside. He kept looking and waiting for sight of Bowie, and then it happened.

Bowie walked right into frame where the window would be and appeared to be looking at something on the wall above the opening. Then Jud saw him pointing up and heard him call out to someone behind him.

Jud reached for the handgun and then rolled down his window and took aim. Just as he was pulling the trigger, another man walked in between Bowie and the window. Jud watched him turn around and look up at where Bowie was pointing.

It was then he saw his grandson's face.

"*No!*" he screamed, and got out of the car and started running toward the house, as if he could stop what was already happening.

Chapter 16

BOWIE HEARD WHAT SOUNDED LIKE A LOUD POP ONLY A fraction of a second before Junior fell back against him. Still unaware the boy had been shot, Bowie grabbed him to keep him from falling and as he did, saw Jud Boone running toward the house with a gun in his hand and a look of horror on his face.

Then Bowie looked down and saw blood all over his hands, and that Junior was unconscious.

"Ray! Call the police and 911. The kid's been shot."

Men came running as Bowie laid Junior down.

"Put pressure on that entrance wound!" Bowie ordered, and bolted toward the door.

He arrived the same moment Jud crossed the threshold.

"I didn't mean to—" Jud said, and then the gun went flying and his jaw cracked from the impact of Bowie's fist.

Jud hit the floor like a felled ox.

Bowie rolled him over on his belly and yanked his arms behind his back.

"Someone bring me something to tie him up with!"

Presley and Joe came running. One held Jud's hands while the other one tied them up.

Bowie ran back to Junior, yanking off his T-shirt as he went, and dropped down on his knees. All of a sudden he was eighteen again and back in the kitchen, kneeling in his mother's blood. He was a breath away from a panic attack when Samuel, who was putting pressure on Junior's wound, went into panic mode first.

"I can't stop it, Bowie. He's gonna bleed out in front of us!"

Bowie shifted into trauma mode without thought. "Let me," he said as he shoved the wadded-up T-shirt against the wound and began applying all the pressure he dared.

The shriek of sirens was once again ripping through Blessings, and Deputy Ralph, who was on patrol, was the first cop on the scene. When he saw the car he'd been looking for, parked and still running with the door open in front of the address of the second 911 call, he quickly radioed in.

"This is Deputy Ralph. Advise the chief, man in question is on scene of current call." And then he got out and ran inside.

When he saw Jud Boone on the floor, bloody and unconscious, with hands and feet tied up like a hog going to butcher, then saw Junior Boone unconscious and lying in a pool of blood, he radioed for a second ambulance, then bagged and tagged the gun.

Emmitt and Tiny were standing by Cora's bed in the ER when Mel walked in. Cora's eyes were closed, and Mel immediately feared the worst.

"Is it bad? Did she have a heart attack?" he asked.

Cora opened her eyes. "I'm not dead or dying."

"Oh, thank God," Mel said, and went to her side and patted her shoulder. "I'm sorry this happened, Mama. I never thought Daddy would treat us all so bad."

Emmitt nodded. "I know! Right?"

Tiny sniffed. "He was always rough around the edges, but not cruel," she added.

Cora slapped the bed with the flat of her hand. "Oh, please! Just stop talking. The three of you seem to have conveniently forgotten the cruelty a teenage Bowie James received from this family. It wasn't just Judson who was mean to him. You all were. And you proved the mean streak ran deep and true when you tried the same old maneuvers on a full-grown man. I don't know why you assumed it would be comforting and reassuring to me to see your faces again, but you were mistaken."

"But Mama—"

It was as far as Mel got before all hell seemed to break loose out in the hall. They heard approaching sirens, then someone shouting orders as a woman called out, "They're here."

The open door in Cora's room left them free to observe all that passed by in the hall beyond. Within moments, a flurry of EMTs and nurses ran past, holding onto both sides of a gurney as they raced to save the patient on it.

"Oh my!" Tiny muttered, and then moments later, a second gurney followed, with more medical personnel accompanying that patient as well.

Just when they thought it was over, Bowie James strode past, minus a shirt and covered in blood, with Chief Pittman and a couple of deputies beside him.

Tiny got up from her chair and ran to the door to

look out. "Something must have happened at the job-site!" she said.

"But why the cops?" Mel asked. "And what the hell happened to the James dude? He was covered in blood."

Suddenly, Chief Pittman was in the doorway. The news he had to deliver might throw Cora back into another episode, and he had to be careful of how he said it as he entered the room.

"Cora, how are you doing?" he asked.

"I feel okay now, but they haven't come back with any test results."

He reached in his pocket. "I brought your phone and house keys and locked the house."

"Thank you," she said as he handed them to her.

"You're welcome," he said, then braced himself to deliver the news. "I have something to tell all of you that's going to be hard to hear. Are you up to this, Miss Cora?"

"Yes. What's wrong?"

"There's no easy way to say this. Judson went to Pearl James's house with the intention to shoot Bowie James and shot Junior instead."

Tiny screamed and fell into Emmitt's arms.

But it was Mel who asked the question they were all thinking.

"Is Junior alive?"

The chief nodded. "For now."

"What happened to Daddy?" Mel asked.

"Bowie disarmed him as he was running inside the house and knocked him out."

Emmitt reached toward his nose, feeling the brace and remembering the power of the blow that had broken it as the chief kept talking.

"And you have Mr. James to thank for the fact that Junior is still breathing," he added.

"Can we see Junior? I need to see my boy," Tiny begged.

"I don't know, but you might if we get there before he's taken to surgery. Come with me and we'll see."

Emmitt and Tiny followed the chief out of the room, holding on to each other for support, leaving Mel and Cora alone.

"Aren't you going to go check on your father?" Cora asked.

"No, ma'am. Will you let me stay with you?"

Cora was in shock and sick to her stomach. Her voice was shaking and she couldn't stop the tears.

"I don't want to talk," she said. "Go talk to your father. Ask him if he's happy now. Ask him if all the grief you've all caused was worth it."

Mel pulled a couple of tissues from a box on the counter and handed them to her.

"Look, Mama. I'm not asking you for forgiveness, and I understand how you must feel about us. But what you haven't taken into consideration is that we all still love you."

Cora heard the little boy he'd been in his voice and knew in that moment that even though she'd been unaware of their deceit, she had also ignored a lot of Judson's negativity in an effort just to get along. Acknowledging that, she could no longer claim total innocence. She wiped her eyes and pointed at an empty chair.

"Sit if you want."

"Thank you," Mel said.

Bowie was still in Junior's room and wasn't leaving until they either took him to surgery or family showed up. He wanted to be shocked or at least surprised this had happened, but he wasn't. He was just sorry the kid had been an unwitting victim of Jud's mania.

Two doctors and a roomful of nurses were trying to stabilize Junior enough to get him to surgery when Chief Pittman came back with Junior's parents.

Bowie could tell by the expressions on their faces that they were in shock, and when they weren't looking, he tried to slip out.

But Tiny Boone saw him and called out.

"Bowie James. How can we ever thank you?"

Bowie was having a hard time staying civil. He didn't want their thanks or anything to do with them.

"By leaving me and mine alone, that's how. Oh…and just so you know, I dropped the charges against Junior the day he came and asked me for a job. He has more strength of character than all of you put together, and I hope to God he survives this. I would hate to think the sole purpose of his life on this earth was to die for the karma you've all been collecting."

Then he walked out.

He had to pass Jud's exam room to get out of the ER and as he did, heard him wailing and moaning, claiming shooting his grandson was an accident and that he'd been aiming at Bowie James.

Bowie just kept walking. The man was certifiable. He'd just confessed to the attempted murder of one grandson in an effort to explain why he'd shot the other one.

He stopped in the public bathroom in the ER, grabbed a handful of paper towels, turned on the water at the sink, and began washing off the blood. He'd have to go home shirtless, and there was blood all over his jeans, but at least he no longer looked like a victim.

He drove straight back to the jobsite to check on the men, noticed they'd installed the window that was to go in the opening and were silently cleaning up the blood on the old hardwood floors. But when they saw him, they all began talking at once. He held up his hand for quiet.

"The kid's still alive. His grandfather confessed to the police that he was trying to kill me when he accidentally shot his grandson, so I'm betting he won't see another free day in Georgia until he dies. We're all safe here to finish the job. The rest of the family is in shock. I see the electrician and his crew are gone. Are they finished, or did this scare them off?"

"They ran out of something, but Ken said more was due today on the UPS truck, so they'll have everything to finish up tomorrow," Ray said.

"Good enough," Bowie said. "Let's call this a day. Rest up, get some good food in you, and we'll start again tomorrow."

They were all rattled by what they'd seen and glad to put some distance between them and the scene of the crime. As soon as they had their tools gathered up, they were gone.

Bowie walked back through the house, making sure windows were down and locked and that the back door was locked as well. Then he headed toward the front door, ready to put this behind him. He paused in front of the new window and looked up again. The little bird that had been sitting on the rafters was gone. Hopefully, it flew out the opening when all hell broke loose.

He locked the front door and then got in the car to go home. There was no need calling Rowan ahead of time to be ready because he was going to have to shower and change.

———

Ella had just taken a load of towels out of the dryer and was sitting on the side of the bed to fold them.

Pearl was in the recliner watching television, and Rowan was dressed and quietly waiting for Bowie's call. Part of her was dreading the trip because she knew going home would be hard. But being with Bowie made it better.

It would be the first time the two of them would be alone, which was ironic considering their brief history. She'd slept beside him in a bed, and Bowie kept teasing her about their future even though they'd never been on a date. This might not be a traditional relationship, but she would be the first one to admit there was something special between them.

Then she heard a car pull up outside. He'd said he would call. Maybe it wasn't him. She was waiting for a knock when she heard a key in the lock, and then he was already inside.

They all turned to look, and then reacted.

"What happened to your shirt?" Ella asked.

Rowan stood up. "Is that blood on your jeans?"

Bowie started to explain, and then stopped. If he started talking, he might lose it. He'd kept his cool through everything that had happened, but the simple act of coming home to people he knew and trusted had brought him to his safe place to fall.

He held up one finger, indicating he needed a moment, and got a cold bottle of Coke from the refrigerator and took a big drink, then set it down as he turned to face them.

"Judson came to the house this morning with the intention of killing me and accidentally shot Junior instead."

Pearl gasped.

Ella whispered a prayer.

But it was Rowan who heard the raw emotion in his voice. Without care for the audience, she went straight to him and hugged him.

"I'm so sorry," she said.

Bowie was shaking as she wrapped her arms around him. He pulled her close, holding on to the anchor she'd given him.

"Is he alive?" Pearl asked.

Bowie nodded. "He was when I left the hospital."

Rowan looked up at him, remembering the blue T-shirt he'd worn to work, and suddenly knew why it was gone.

"You used your shirt to stanch the flow of blood, didn't you?"

Bowie nodded, trying not to think of how pale Junior's face became the longer it flowed—the coppery scent, the warm gush of lifeblood on his skin, like the way he found his mother. Only she was already gone.

Pearl saw the tears in his eyes, and all of a sudden she was thrust back twenty years to the sound of Bowie's voice on the phone. "Mama killed herself." It was only later that she learned Billie had slit her wrists and bled out all over the kitchen floor.

Pearl came out of her chair and went to him, hugging both of them. "I needed to do this twenty years ago, but you were too far away. I love you, Grandson, more than you will ever know."

"I'm so sorry, Bowie," Ella said, and latched on from the other side.

Bowie held on to them all, taking comfort from their presence and from the love flowing from them to him. When he heard a knock at the door, he flinched.

"Are you expecting anyone?" Pearl asked.

"No, ma'am," he said, but then he opened the door, and Chief Pittman was on his doorstep with a box in his hands.

"I'm sorry to bother you, Bowie. But when my wife, Mercy, heard about what happened, she called and asked me to deliver this to you and your girls. And I'm to tell you that something sweet cures a whole lot of what ails you, so enjoy."

He handed Bowie the box, and then he was gone.

Bowie carried it to the dining table and opened it.

Pearl clapped her hands. "Oh, my goodness! One of Mercy Pittman's famous pies, and it's pecan pie, at that! What a sweet lady."

"Yes, ma'am," Bowie said. "But I need to clean up, so if you all will excuse me for a bit, you have my permission to ruin your lunch and eat dessert first."

"It's not close to lunchtime," Ella said. "We'll just call this a midmorning snack." She turned around to get a knife to cut it as Bowie headed for the bathroom.

But Rowan was behind him, and the soft touch of her hand on his back stopped him.

"We don't have to go back to the farm today," she said.

"Honey, you have no idea how much I need to do that," he said. "But thank you for being so thoughtful."

"I can't bear seeing you hurt," she whispered.

"That works both ways," he said. "Give me a few minutes, and then we'll be on our way."

"It won't mess up your workday too much?"

"I shut it down for the day. We were all a little too wired for our own good."

He went into his bedroom for clean clothes and then took them with him into the bathroom he and Rowan were sharing. A few moments later, he tossed the bloody jeans out the door.

Rowan saw him toss them out and put them in the washer, turned it to cold water only, added detergent, and started it up. It wouldn't wash away the memory, but at least he wouldn't have to look at blood on his clothes again. Then she washed up at the kitchen sink before sitting down with the girls.

"Want a piece of pie?" Ella asked.

Rowan shook her head. "Not now. I'll wait for Bowie. And can I ask you something?"

"Absolutely," Ella said, and laid down her fork.

"How did Billie die? I mean, I know she committed suicide, but how?"

Ella sighed. "She slit her wrists. Bowie found her on the kitchen floor in a pool of blood."

Rowan's eyes filled with tears as she nodded. "Thank you. That explains what I felt when I hugged him. I knew something about today had triggered an old memory for him. I just needed to know so I wouldn't unintentionally say something that would make him feel worse."

Pearl reached across the table and clasped Rowan's hand. "You are a gift to all of us, child. Thank you for being a part of our lives."

But Bowie wasn't going to be able to shower off what had happened. He managed to hold it together until he stepped beneath the scalding spray and felt himself coming undone. He reached out on instinct until he felt the tile on the shower walls and then flattened his hands against the cool, slick surface to keep from falling.

Maybe it was feeling safe within such a small enclosure that was part of how he healed himself of panic attacks, or maybe it was because the water on his face would hide his tears, but within seconds he was crying.

Today was the culmination of everything he'd feared about coming back, and worse. He didn't understand hate like that family held for him, but he was sick of it being the guiding factor in his life. All he'd ever wanted was to be accepted for who he was, not the bastard child who'd been born of rape, which was the tag he'd been branded with at birth.

He cried until there were no more tears left. Unaware of how long he'd been in there, he reached for the soap and a washcloth and began scrubbing every inch of his body. In his mind he was telling himself it was to wash away Junior's blood, but in his heart it was an unconscious effort to wash away the shame of being born. By the time he came out, he was clean and dressed, with his game face back in place, ready to face the rest of the day.

"Did you leave me a piece of that pie?" he asked as he moved to the table.

"That and more," Ella said. "Rowan made you two some sandwiches to take with you."

"A picnic, and with the perfect partner," he said, and winked at her, knowing she'd blush, and she did. "I have an old blanket I'll throw in the car. I have a cooler in the car that's already iced down with bottles of water."

Rowan saw the boy behind the man and knew he was struggling. "But we have to eat dessert first," she said. "Today has started off wrong in spite of trying to do the right things, so we're going to break rules for the rest of the day."

Pearl grinned. "I never heard that excuse for a picnic before."

"Oh...it's not an excuse," Rowan said. "It's a fact of the universe. When there's too much negativity, we have to break the cycle, and break rules like no dessert until after you eat, which is a terrible rule anyway. Sometimes you just need that sweet to reset your day."

"Like eating a piece of chocolate when I'm frustrated!" Ella said.

"You eat chocolate regardless of frustrations," Pearl muttered.

Ella started to fire back and then sighed. "I hate to admit it, but Mama's right."

"Mama's always right," Pearl said.

Ella rolled her eyes.

Rowan giggled and cut and plated two pieces of Mercy Pittman's famous Southern pecan pie.

"You two fight it out. Bowie and I are eating pie," she said.

Bowie laughed, and as he sat down at the table with them and took the first bite, hurt settled and horror faded.

These were his people.

They were the ones who mattered.

Then the pie was gone, and Bowie was standing at the door with the old blanket on one arm and Rowan on the other.

"Gran, Aunt Ella…are you two going to be okay while we're gone?"

"Of course we're going to be okay. We're not helpless," Pearl said, and in the same breath issued a request for assistance. "Ella, would you please put some more ice in my glass? My sweet tea is getting warm."

"No, we're not helpless until we want to be," Ella said, taking her mother's glass to the refrigerator.

Pearl snorted.

Ella ignored her. "You two be careful, and we'll see you later."

Bowie started to leave, and then remembered. "Oh… Gran, since you mentioned you and Cora Boone used to be friends, you might like to know they transported her to the emergency room this morning, too. I heard this while I was in the ER."

"Oh no! What happened?" Pearl asked.

"All I know is when Jud came back into Blessings this morning, he tried to get into the house. I guess Cora had locked him out. Anyway, they said he was beating on the door and shouting at her. She got scared and called the cops. He heard the sirens and took off, but it scared her enough that she suffered some kind of episode and passed out."

Pearl frowned. "Poor Cora. I'll keep her in my prayers."

"See you later," Rowan said, waving as she and Bowie started to the door.

"Oh, hey…Rowan, did you get the grocery list?" Pearl asked.

"Yes, ma'am," Rowan said, patting her hip pocket.

"Is there anything on there that you need before we get back?" Bowie asked.

They shook their heads.

"Then we'll shop later," Bowie said.

They drove out of Blessings, and even though Rowan dreaded the trip home, she was happy to be with Bowie. She was quietly admiring his profile when he caught her and winked.

"Sorry for staring, but all of this still feels like a dream," she said.

"All of what, honey?" Bowie asked.

"You. Me."

"Ahh, that. Well, if it will make you feel any better, you are the first woman who's ever made me feel like this. I keep thinking about what a short time we've known each other, but I feel like you've always been in my life."

Rowan sighed. "As isolated as my life has been, I should be afraid to even look you in the eye, and yet I don't want to look away." She blushed ever so slightly. "And it's probably shameless of me to admit that, but no guile comes along with inexperience."

"On the contrary, Rowan. True honesty is rare, just like you. Don't ever change," he said and reached for her hand.

When his fingers curled around her hand, she shivered, thinking about the hold he already had on her heart.

They rode in comfortable silence for a few miles, but when Rowan suddenly turned loose of his hand and leaned forward, Bowie frowned.

"What is it?" he asked.

"This property belongs to a neighbor. I'm just look-ing at what the flood did. All his fences are gone, and he had a large herd of sheep."

"That's a tough loss," Bowie said.

Rowan nodded, but her heart was beginning to pound. All this had done was resurrect the dread she'd had of going home.

"You'll have to tell me when to turn," Bowie reminded her.

"It's not far now," she said. "Oh…I didn't think. I hope that washed-out road has been repaired."

"We'll find out soon enough," Bowie said.

A few minutes later, Rowan pointed to a bank of rural mailboxes at the side of the road.

"If the road has been fixed, we turn on the far side of those mailboxes. If you'll stop for a moment, I'll check our mailbox. It's the last one on the end."

Bowie nodded and began to slow down just a bit, in case he needed to make a sudden stop. But when they got there, it was obvious recent roadwork had been done.

"Ah, it's been repaired," Rowan said, and then got out and ran to the box. The only thing in it was an elec-tric bill… for a house that was no longer there. She took it with her and got back into the car. "Turn right and follow the road. Our farm begins at the end of it."

Bowie glanced at her as he turned. She was pale and tight-lipped. He'd seen that look on her face before. Her memories couldn't be good.

Rowan's hands were clasped tightly in her lap as she leaned forward, anticipating each house, each mailbox, counting them down to home as she'd done so many times before.

And then, as they came around a curve, Rowan moaned. Silt and flood debris were all over everything. It was worse than she'd imagined, yet in the midst of the chaos, the old barn where she'd sought refuge was still standing. She finally leaned back, letting the emotions of what she was feeling wash over her.

Bowie stopped and parked. "Let's walk from here, okay? I don't want to ruin a tire on something that might be buried under the silt."

Rowan unbuckled her seat belt and got out, then walked to the front of the car where Bowie joined her. The sun was hot on her face, but there was a faint breeze. The landscape was familiar and yet somewhat deformed. Nearly every memory she had in her life had been linked to this place, and now the landmarks that had defined it were missing.

When Bowie slid an arm across her shoulders, she leaned against him and pointed.

"You see the chimney. That's where the house stood. And just to the west, a hog pen, a chicken house, and Daddy's old tool shed. We weren't feeding out a hog at the time, but we had about twenty laying hens." Her chin quivered. "My poor little hens. I couldn't see all of this from the loft, and I was so shaken and weak when I was rescued that all I cared about was the bottle of water I was given to drink."

Bowie pulled her close. "I saw something similar to this about ten years ago when we were on a build site in Oklahoma. A tornado came through the area. The debris looked something like this. I'm so sorry, baby. I'm so sorry," he said, and kissed the top of her head.

Rowan was crying and didn't know it. "That's the barn I was in."

"Do you want to go see it?" he asked.

"I think I have to, or I'll be afraid of these emotions for the rest of my life."

Then he brushed a kiss across her lips. "You lead the way, and at your pace."

About halfway there, Rowan paused.

"This is about where Daddy went under. The last thing I heard him say was 'I'm sorry.'" Then she suddenly gasped. "Oh my God... It just dawned on me. I thought he was saying that because I would be left all alone, but what if he was talking about how he had manipulated my life?"

"How would that make you feel, if that's why he said it?" Bowie asked.

"I wouldn't feel quite as betrayed, I think."

"Then why don't you accept that as your truth? It does no good to resent someone for past behavior. I'm living proof of that," Bowie said.

"I know you're right. I'm still going to have to come to terms with it, though. When I think back through all the years, and how he abused my trust in such a selfish way..." Her voice trailed off as she looked back at the barn and the hay door above the breezeway. "That's the loft I was in."

"Show me," Bowie said, and she did.

Chapter 17

THERE WERE WASHED-OUT POCKETS OF EARTH INSIDE THE barn and what looked like ruts in the breezeway, formed as the force of the water rushed through it.

Rowan stopped, looking around to see if the structure was still sound.

"Do you think the flood weakened the barn much? I ask because I'll need to tell the real estate agent the condition."

"I'll check," Bowie said, and started walking the interior, going in and out of stalls, checking the flooring in the granaries and the inner and outer walls themselves.

He found a couple of places where soil had washed away from some of the interior poles, then noticed they'd been seated in concrete.

"This is why your barn didn't wash away. The breezeway kept the water's force from pushing against much of the structure itself, and the poles were set in concrete."

Rowan looked up into the rafters, checking to see if any birds were roosting above them, but they were empty. The barn used to smell like sweet feed and hay, but no more.

"I played in here all of my life. I never dreamed it would be the shelter that saved me," she said.

"I don't want to stir up any more bad memories, but I need to climb up in the loft and see what the rest of it looks like. I know the water didn't get up that high, but when the hurricane hit, it could have damaged the roof or walls," Bowie said.

"I'll go with you," Rowan said.

"Honey, are you sure you want to do that? It's not necessary, if you don't."

She looked at the stairs built onto the outer side of a granary wall, then reached for the first handhold to pull herself up and took a deep breath.

"The last time I stood here, there was water above my knees. A woman faces her fears," she said, then took the first step and went up, with Bowie only a couple of steps behind her, testing his weight on each step as he went. They felt solid and sound to him, and in a few more steps, they were in the loft.

He immediately began walking around the perimeter, looking up through the rafters to the roof above, checking to see if he could see sunlight coming in through any holes or loose shingles.

Rowan was focused on what Bowie was doing when she thought she heard a dog bark. Without thinking, she turned around to look out and felt the floor tilt beneath her feet. She cried out, thinking she was going to fall.

Within seconds, Bowie was behind her, his arms around her, holding her close.

"Rowan, are you okay? What happened?"

"I think I turned too fast and lost my equilibrium. It felt like the floor was tilting and I was falling out of the loft."

"Come sit over here against the wall while I finish up, okay?"

"Yes, I'm sorry."

He frowned. "You don't apologize for reliving a valid fear."

She let him lead her away from the hay door. She sat, and as soon as she felt the wall at her back, she drew her knees up against her chest and closed her eyes—the same way she'd waited out the night when she was here before. But that was then, waiting for rescue. Today was for saying goodbye.

It was almost noon by the time the barn inspection was over. Rowan was second-guessing her decision to picnic, because there wasn't a single place on the farm that wasn't an ugly reminder of what had happened.

Bowie had already picked up on what a bad vibe the whole area had for her, and as they started back to the car, he reached for her hand. "I've been thinking about Grey Goose Lake for our picnic. Are you up for that?"

Rowan breathed a quick sigh of relief. "That sounds like a wonderful plan! I can't remember the last time I was there."

"It's been a long time for me as well. I'm sure it's changed some, but we can always find a good place in the shade."

Now that he'd removed the dread, Rowan was suddenly hungry again. "What a good idea! I'm excited."

Bowie laughed. "You have a kick-ass smile, Dark Eyes. You should get excited more often."

"I'll try to remember that," she said.

He got a couple of bottles of water from the cooler when they got back to the car.

"Thank you," she said, and took a big drink before she buckled up, while Bowie downed a good half of the bottle in one big drink, then rubbed the cold bottle against his forehead before getting in the car. But instead of starting the engine right away, he leaned over the console, and without a word she leaned toward him and met him halfway.

Their lips were cold and wet, but the heat between them was still there. Rowan felt weightless, like she was floating, and the only thing keeping her earthbound was him.

Bowie finally let go, then watched her eyelids fluttering open and saw everything in the depths that he'd hoped for. They hadn't said the word *love*, but it was there between them.

"Are you ready?" he asked.

Rowan had to pull herself back to realize he was talking about leaving the farm.

"Yes," she said, and then leaned back as he turned around and drove away. But the next time he asked, she would say yes to anything he asked. She was ready for him and so much more.

There was a breeze coming off the water as Bowie pulled up into a parking area at Gray Goose Lake. There wasn't another car in sight, and the dark shade from the trees surrounding the lake was a respite from the heat of the sunlit sky.

"I'll carry the food," Rowan said.

"And I'll follow the woman with the food," he said, and got out to open the rear door.

Rowan picked up the food, and he took the blanket and the small ice chest. He locked the doors, pocketed the keys, and then followed her into the woods.

"This place is beautiful," Rowan said. The path was narrow, so she walked a few steps ahead.

"I have the best view," he said, and waited for that to sink in. When it did, she paused and pivoted.

"Are you referring to my backside?"

"Lady! I am most certainly not…gonna lie. Yes. Yes, I am referring to the nice fit of those jeans."

Rowan was suddenly struggling with whether she could laugh or should blush.

"Just for that, you are now the leader of this pack."

"I was always the leader. I was just staying behind to protect your back," he said as he moved past her and struck out on the path.

Now Rowan had the best view.

"I have never seen such a fine specimen," she said.

Bowie burst into laughter and kept walking.

"Surely you didn't think I was talking about you?" Rowan said. "I was referring to that little hawk perched up on that tall pine."

"Oh, sure you were," he said and grinned, but he felt lighter than air—like he was ten feet tall. He'd known women, but he'd never had one touch his well-guarded heart before.

It wasn't lost on him that he would never have known her if the hurricane hadn't gone through Blessings, and if his gran's house had not been ruined, and if he'd let his dread of coming back again keep him away. The bottom line was that Rowan was worth it.

A few minutes later, he came upon a small clearing within the woods. There was one large, spreading oak tree out in the grass, with a generous amount of shade.

"What about here?" Bowie asked.

Rowan paused and then moved up beside him and whispered, "It looks like a place for faeries."

Bowie thought she was teasing until he saw the look of wonder in her eyes and accepted that there must still be things unseen on this earth that he had yet to meet.

"Do you think they would mind if we borrowed their tree?"

"Not at all. Faeries love all things happy and joyful. A picnic is all of those things."

"Then to the tree we go," he said.

When they stopped beneath the shade and spread the blanket, Rowan felt the magic. *Good things happen here*, she thought, then sat down cross-legged and began pulling out sandwiches and potato chips, while Bowie opened the cooler.

"Water or Coke?" he asked.

"Um, Coke, please. The sandwiches are peppered ham and Swiss cheese."

A slight breeze stirred the air around them, rustling the leaves above to the point they almost sounded like applause.

Rowan smiled, but Bowie was sorting out a sandwich and chips and didn't see her.

The morning had been stressful for both of them in different ways, and the relief of this quiet beauty, and the food, and their picnic partners made this moment feel perfect.

"Mmmm, this is good," Bowie said, and then picked up a small chip and offered it to her.

Rowan opened her mouth like a little bird, and he popped it in. As she ate, she kept looking up into the vast arbor of limbs and leaves above them as if waiting for a sign. Then she closed her eyes and breathed a prayer of thanks into the air.

For this day. For this man.

And when she was through, she opened her eyes and finished her food. Just as she was reaching for a drink, a tiny acorn dropped down into her lap, then rolled under her legs.

She smiled, unscrewed the lid, and took a drink.

"What was that?" Bowie asked.

"I thanked the faeries for allowing us their space, and that was our welcome."

Bowie stopped eating. "You're serious, aren't you?"

She nodded. "All Irish believe in faeries. My name is Rowan, after all. My mother was Irish, and she gave me the knowing the day I was born. It is the one precious thing I still hold of her that is mine alone. The one thing Daddy could never share, and the one thing he could never control."

Bowie was so touched he could hardly speak. Sitting here with her, beneath this tree, in the bright light of a beautiful day, he could almost forget there was evil in the world. He had to tell her now—when he could feel the magic—what was in his heart.

"You with the black hair and dark eyes...and that perfect curve to your cheek...are so very beautiful. But the beauty of your face will never match the beauty of your soul. I look at you and see light, Rowan Harper. I look at you and see my own salvation. If you ever want my heart, it is yours."

Rowan froze. The words came from love, but whether he'd meant them that way or not, they were poetry to her soul. Her hands were shaking as she began putting food back in the bag and screwing the lid back on her drink, as if she was packing up to leave.

Bowie panicked. "What are you doing? Did I say something wrong?"

Rowan looked up at him and knew her whole life had been preparing her for this moment and this man.

"You did nothing wrong and everything right. Yes, I want your heart, and I am clearing away a place to make love, so that you may have mine."

Something broke free in Bowie's chest as he reached for her and pulled her to him. In one smooth motion, she was beneath him, and when she wrapped her arms around his neck, he was lost.

One minute rolled into another, and another, as their kisses became urgent, and the touching and stroking was no longer enough.

Boots came off, then jeans, then they were bare and entwined in a tangle of arms and legs, and still Bowie didn't lay claim.

Rowan was trembling from the want of him, needing to give of herself, to be the woman she was meant to be.

"No more waiting, Bowie James," she whispered. "Do it now."

"Ah God, woman, I want you. But I can't bear to hurt you," he said.

"But, Bowie, it is the way of a woman. She suffers pain, but only for a moment when she is first taken, so that she may have a life of pleasure until she takes her last breath. The ecstasy of love is her gift, to make up for the pain of giving birth."

"Then God give me strength to make your pleasure ever more perfect than the pain," he whispered. He moved between her legs, then ever so slowly eased his way in.

In the moment of their joining, Rowan inhaled sharply, but he kept easing his way, giving her body time to adjust. The feeling of being whole in this way was an aphrodisiac she had not expected. She wanted more, but she didn't know what more felt like. All she knew was that every sad, lonely space within her was opening up to all the secrets of being a woman…and then he stopped.

"Forgive me, love. This is going to hurt," Bowie said, and with one hard, quick thrust, he took what she'd given him with all the love in his heart.

Rowan cried out as he tore through, but the pain was brief, and then it faded. The next time he moved, it was a whole new sensation, and in the most tender of ways, they made love. Her joy came in knowing the pleasure she was giving him, and when the climax was upon him, she gave herself up to his release.

Bowie was spent but still coming down when he pulled away from her.

Thinking it was done, Rowan lay in quiet satisfaction and closed her eyes, a little sore, but knowing that, too, would pass.

Then she felt Bowie's hand upon her thigh and then coaxing a little space between her legs. Her eyes flew open, and he was on his side, touching her.

"Surely, you did not think that's all there is?" he whispered.

Rowan couldn't move, couldn't breathe.

"Close your eyes, love, and let go. Your body knows what to do, even if you don't."

So she did, shocked by the pleasure she was feeling, having never known this existed within her being, and it grew, and it grew into a tight, painful coil of mindless need.

She was not prepared for the climax that slammed into her in a rippling wave of heat. She cried out as it went to the top of her head, and when it rolled back into her belly to detonate. It was a feeling unlike anything she'd ever known, and she cried from a pleasure so intense that she thought she'd died.

Then she felt Bowie's mouth on her lips, kissing the breath from her body, and then he leaned down and whispered in her ear.

"Thank you for your heart. I will love you forever."

———

Rowan slept all the way back to Blessings with her head on Bowie's leg, curled up on her side, occupying as little space as possible.

Bowie drove with one hand on the wheel and the other on her shoulder. He'd lost all sense of time and place. He had no idea what day it was and wasn't even sure about the month. There was only him, and there was Rowan, and it was the day he'd fallen the rest of the way in love.

He had just passed the City Limit sign and was coming into Blessings when he patted Rowan's shoulder to wake her. "Hey, baby, we're home."

Rowan sat up and began combing her fingers through her hair, then turned and looked at Bowie. "I didn't just dream this, did I?"

He shook his head.

"Thanks be to Jesus," she muttered.

He grinned.

Rowan blushed a little. "Well, it was the most beautiful day of my life, and I didn't want it to be just my imagination."

"We may have to live on that memory for a while. We share a home with the chaperones, remember?"

"Yes, but the memory was magic, and magic never dies," she said.

Bowie shook his head. "Beyond the fact that I'm out-of-my-mind in love with you, you're going to be so good for me."

Rowan's dark eyes were sparkling. "So, I'm going to be medicine now, am I? Then you should know that the direction for dosage is take me once at bedtime, and never on an empty stomach."

Bowie burst out laughing.

Rowan grinned and then began putting her tennis shoes back on and fumbling through her pockets for the grocery list.

He pulled into the parking lot, found a space near the door, and parked. It was almost two o'clock. Then he paused, his hand on the door handle.

"Will you be happy living like I live…on the move… in a home on wheels?"

Rowan sighed. The boy loved, but he still did not trust the girl.

"It's not about where you live, Bowie. It's who you're living with that makes it home."

Bowie felt her truth all the way to his bones. "I guess that might be the most perfect thing I've ever heard anyone say to me."

The energy between them was palpable.

She was caught in his gaze and couldn't look away. Then someone drove past in a pickup truck with a muffler dragging. The noise was enough to break the moment.

They gathered themselves enough to get out, and by the time they got into the store, their focus had returned to the task at hand.

~~~

Junior Boone survived the surgery and was in the intensive care unit in a medically induced coma, hooked up to so many machines that for the moment the only thing he was doing on his own was breathing.

Emmitt and Tiny were holding hands, sitting side by side in the waiting room down the hall from the ICU. They weren't talking, just watching the clock, waiting for the hour to roll around so when the next visiting time came they'd get to spend ten minutes at their son's bedside, just for the gift of knowing he still lived.

~~~

Cora's tests were inconclusive, so they had her admitted to the hospital for observation. While she had not suffered a heart attack, her doctor knew something was wrong and had ordered more testing for tomorrow. She didn't argue. She had nowhere else to be.

Once Mel knew his mama was holding her own, he went home.

He didn't know how their relationship was going to pan out, but he wasn't ready to give up hope that she would one day forgive him. His biggest issue, however, was finding a way to forgive himself.

Judson Boone was in jail.

He had a couple of stitches in the top of his nose and a jaw too sore to open. There was no mistaking where he was going, and he wasn't going to fight it.

The two people he'd loved most in this world were both in the hospital because of what he'd done, and Bowie James was still walking.

"I get it, Lord. I damn sure get it. Vengeance is Yours, not mine. Just please don't let them die."

He was sick at heart, and sick to his stomach from the pain. But pain pills weren't plentiful in jail, and he was left to cope with it on his own.

He tried to sleep, but the pain in his face never abated, and the simple act of walking exacerbated his throbbing headache. After four hours of sheer torture, he was sitting on his cot, his head down, crying like a baby and wishing God would strike him dead where he sat, when Chief Lon Pittman came into the jail, escorting his visitor.

"Jud, you're going to be arraigned at ten tomorrow morning. Mel, you have ten minutes with your father," Lon said, "and I'll be standing right up there beside the door."

Melvin Boone nodded. "Yes, sir, thank you," he said, and then walked up to the cell where his father was sitting.

Jud swiped at the tears on his face but didn't get up.

"I didn't expect to see you here," he said.

Mel shrugged. "Yeah, I'm having myself a magnanimous day."

"I don't know what that means, but I'm glad to see you," Jud said. "Can you tell me how Junior is doing?"

"He's alive, and so is Mama, no thanks to you."

To Mel's dismay, Jud covered his face and started crying again.

"Physical pain is the shits, isn't it, Daddy?" Mel asked.

Jud nodded. "And I deserve every bit of it."

Mel frowned. "Yes, you do. We all deserve what's happening. The only one who's truly innocent is Junior."

Jud dropped his head again. "I wish I was dead," he said, and cried a little harder.

Mel leaned one shoulder against the bars, staring at his daddy as if he'd never really seen him before, and he absolutely knew Jud Boone was lying when he said that.

"Well, Randall took himself out. I guess if you want it bad enough, you'll find a way."

Jud choked on a sob and stood up, looking at Mel in disbelief. "What the hell are you saying? Randall did not kill himself. It was just those drugs he was on."

"And Randall didn't get on those drugs until after you sent him after Billie James. You broke what was left of him when you made us beat the hell out of his own son."

Jud's face turned a deep, angry red. "Shut up."

"Yep, that's a fact you can't ignore. And one week to the day after Billie James's suicide, he was gone. Damn shame," Mel said.

"You just shut the hell up!" Jud said.

Mel shrugged. "Oh, I'm sorry. I thought since you were washing your conscience clean by admitting the guilt of putting Junior and Mama in the hospital that you would want to clear the rest of it, too."

"What about you?" Jud said. "You were a part of it all."

"I know, Daddy. My wife left me because of it, even though it happened before we each got married. When she found out, she looked at me like I was some monster and walked out and never looked back. So you know what I did? I looked at myself in the mirror, saw the same monster she saw, and I've been trying to drown it every night since in a bottle of booze. It'll happen. I'm just not sure when."

"Go home," Jud said. "And don't come back."

"I don't have a home anymore," Mel said. "But I'm going to hell. Want me to save you a seat?"

"Get out!" Jud screamed, then grabbed his jaw and dropped to his knees.

Mel stared. "Don't worry. I'm leaving, but since you're in the right position, while you're down there this would be a good time to pray," he said, and walked away.

Jud got up, went back to his cot to lie down, then turned his face to the wall.

Chapter 18

WORD WAS SPREADING ALL OVER BLESSINGS ABOUT WHAT had happened. They were talking about everything from Cora Boone being taken to the hospital to Judson Boone's failed attempt at murder.

And as was always the case when something untoward happened in Blessings, it was all the gossip at the Curl Up and Dye.

Ruby, loving soul that she was, had tried changing the subject multiple times with each client that came and went, but nobody was buying it today. She was numb from the arguments that popped up between clients because of it, and had given Vera and Vesta hard looks for encouraging it. But a part of her also understood. The revelation of the underbelly of the Boone family's world was both shocking and horrifying, and knowing that the only innocent Boone in the family was near death because of it was tragic.

Everyone had an opinion, and the conversation was verging on turning into another argument when Ruby called it all to a halt.

"Ladies! I don't know how much blame there is to assess to any of them, and it's not our business to figure that out anyway. But saying Cora Boone's decision to divorce her husband and kick him out of the house is the reason this all came to pass is just plain ignorant of all of you."

The gasps and then the sudden silence were telling.

Ruby never got mad, and she was still talking so they guessed it might be time to start listening.

"There is one basic fact that none of you have seen fit to mention, and that is Cora Boone's husband was admittedly being an abusive monster and neighbors witnessed it, which leads me to believe there was plenty that went on there behind closed doors as well. He was on her porch, beating on the door and threatening to kick it in, and it scared her so bad that she nearly had a heart attack. I can attest to what it's like to be married to an abusive man. He scared me every day we were together, and no matter how long someone has been married, it will never make that okay. So unless you've walked in Cora Boone's shoes and lived her life, you have no right to pass judgment on her."

Every woman there was remembering when Ruby was kidnapped out of her own home here in Blessings by her ex-husband, and how everyone in town had feared she might be dead. It was that fact alone that ended the fussing in the Curl Up and Dye.

"So, while all of you are certainly free to have your own thoughts and opinions on the subject, you won't be free to share them here, okay?"

They all nodded.

"And Cora Boone is one of my clients, so I will be going to visit her after work today, just like I would visit you should you find yourself in the hospital one day. I don't judge. I just love," Ruby said, and then glanced at herself in the mirror to make sure her blond hair was still in place and walked back up front. "Who's next?" she asked.

"That would be me," Melissa Dean said and stood up.

Ruby smiled. "Then let's get started. You said you wanted a trim before your style today, right?"

Melissa nodded. "Yes, please. I'm hosting a special dinner for all of the employees at my dry cleaners tonight at Granny's. She's even opening up that little banquet room she saves back for the group meetings."

"What fun!" Ruby said. "What's the occasion?"

"Just an appreciation dinner for how they've all helped me transition to owner."

"Ah. So let's make you all pretty then," Ruby said.

The gossip session was over at the Curl Up and Dye, but the clients' chatter about their own families was not.

———∿∿∿———

Making love was hungry business. Bowie and Rowan came home with everything on the list, plus two full sacks of impulse purchases.

Rowan felt like the world could take one look at the two of them and know they'd made love. She wasn't ashamed, but it was theirs to know, not something to share. However, when they came in the door carrying all the grocery sacks, plus a blanket that needed to be washed, there was so much going on trying to find places to store all the extra food that the girls never noticed anything different about either of them.

That gave Rowan time to put on her game face, and Bowie gave her the perfect opportunity to shower while the rest of them were putting up groceries.

He winked at her, then offered up the ruse.

"Rowan...honey...why don't you go ahead and shower off while we're doing this. That trip out to your farm was a dirty one."

"Yes, maybe it will wash away some of the bad memories as well," she said, and picked up some clean clothes on the way.

As soon as she was in the bathroom, both women began to grill Bowie.

"Is she okay? Was it hard for her to go back? We worried. We didn't want her to be sad," they said.

"She can't help but be sad, Gran. It looks like a war zone, and there's silt and flood debris lying around everywhere. The only things on that whole place that are still standing are a rock fireplace and the barn."

"Oh, my lord," Ella said, and shook her head. "Bless her heart."

"Rowan wanted me to inspect the barn so she could give the realtor as fair a description of its condition as possible, but it was hard for her to be in there, I could tell. And when I went up in the loft to check the roof for hurricane damage, she insisted on going up because she *was* afraid. She's a pretty awesome woman for wanting to conquer her fears and not give in to them."

"Then where on earth did you have the picnic, if the place was so awful?" Pearl asked. "I'm the one who suggested a picnic, and now I feel bad."

"No, don't feel bad, Gran. I could tell that was not a good place and suggested stopping by the lake on our way home. I could see how relieved she was at the suggestion, and we found a pretty place. By the time we were through eating, her whole attitude had changed. And she fell asleep on the way home, so she's had a big day."

Pearl clapped her hands. "Did you have a good time, too?" she asked.

"Are you asking me if I'm smitten yet?" he said.

Pearl shrugged. "Maybe."

He grinned. "Well, I won't keep either of you in suspense. I'm officially smitten."

He left them putting up groceries and went to put the blanket in the wash before either of them spotted the bloodstain. He dumped it in, adding detergent, and set it to wash in cold water so the stain wouldn't set in the fabric, but he didn't start it up until Rowan got a chance to put her clothes in with it, too.

Just as he sat down to take off his work boots, his phone signaled a text from Chief Pittman.

> Junior Boone survived the surgery. Condition guarded. In ICU. You saved his life. Judson Boone in lockup, facing attempted murder and more. Here's to happy hammering on Miss Pearl's house.

"Everything all right?" Pearl asked after he laid the phone aside.

"It was Chief Pittman letting me know the kid survived his surgery but is not out of the woods. He's in the ICU. Judson is in jail. Attempted murder charges being filed, plus more."

"You gave the boy a chance, Bowie. It's in God's hands now."

Bowie nodded. "I know." Then he heard the water go off in the bathroom. "Sounds like Rowan's out of the shower. I'm going in after she gets out, then we can have an early supper. I might even be tempted to play cards with you all later, if you aren't playing strip poker."

They both giggled, and then they sat down at the dining table to plan what they were going to cook for the evening meal, while Bowie finally got the boots off then got a beer from the fridge and sat down in his recliner with his laptop.

He began going through messages from some of the foremen on other jobsites, and after answering questions and problem solving through the lot, he logged out just as the bathroom door opened. Rowan came out carrying her clothes.

He pointed at the washer.

"It's ready to start. I waited so you could put your clothes in with the blanket. It's old and long past fading, so it won't hurt anything."

His thoughtfulness struck her. "Thank you, Bowie."

"You're welcome. I'm going in next, and since I'm off for the rest of the day, we're going to have an early supper."

"And he's going to play cards with us!" Pearl said.

"Oh, really?" Rowan said. "What are we playing?"

"Anything but strip poker," Bowie said, and then headed for the bathroom, while the sound of her laughter wiped Jud Boone and his madness slick out of his head.

It was just after 7:00 p.m. when Ruby locked the front door of the Curl Up and Dye. She went toward the back, turning off lights as she went, then took off her smock and hung it on a hook in the break room. She was still thinking about Cora Boone when she sat down to call Peanut. Being able to call him *husband* was still a rush she did not take for granted, and she smiled when she heard his deep, sexy voice.

"Hello, beautiful. Are you on your way home?" he asked.

"I'm locking up now, but I want to run by the hospital and check up on Cora Boone. She's probably a little short on family and visitors. I won't be there long, but I don't want her to think the world forgot about her in the middle of all this mess."

"You are a good woman, Ruby, and I am seriously proud you're mine. Unless you want to come home to eat, why don't we just meet up at Granny's around seven thirty?"

"Oh, sweetheart! What a wonderful suggestion. Yes, I'd love to. We've been swamped today, and I want nothing more than to get off my feet and enjoy someone else's cooking tonight."

"Then I'll see you soon," he said. "Love you. Drive safe."

"Love you, too," Ruby said, and then shivered as she disconnected. He so hung the stars in her sky.

She went out the back door to her car, then drove straight to the hospital and parked.

The sun was below the treetops, and shadows were long as she crossed the parking lot to the entrance. It was well-lit and far from empty, but after being kidnapped right out of her own home months earlier, she had lost her sense of safety. She was close to running by the time she reached the building, and then breathed a quiet sigh of relief once she was inside. She stopped in at the gift shop, picked out a small vase of flowers, and then remembered Cora often brought a *People* magazine to read when she got her hair done, so she picked up the latest copy and went to pay.

After inquiring as to the floor and room number, Ruby headed for the elevator, rode it to the second floor, and began looking for Room 214. The door was closed when she found it, so she knocked, then heard Cora call out, "Come in."

"I hope I didn't wake you," Ruby said. "I just got off work."

"No, I wasn't asleep. It's so kind of you to come."

"Of course I'd come. I'm so sorry this happened, and I understand how frightening it is to be threatened by someone you're supposed to be able to trust and love."

Cora was trying to control her emotions, but the kindness was both unexpected and touching.

Ruby handed her the flowers. "I picked out pink roses, for the rosy pink that's always in your cheeks, and a *People* magazine I hope you haven't read."

"The roses are beautiful. Thank you, and no, I haven't read this one yet. It will really help pass the time."

"I can't stay long, but I want to know how you're feeling, and if they've determined anything."

"Oh, I feel all right, and no, there's nothing specific yet, but they will run a few more tests tomorrow," Cora said. "Mostly, I just feel stupid, and guilty—and a whole host of other emotions I can't rightly name—for what amounts in my mind to harboring the devil." Then she started to cry.

"I'm sorry, sweetie," Ruby said.

Cora reached for a tissue to wipe her eyes. "Nothing for you to be sorry for. I still haven't figured out if I was just naive about what was happening under my nose all those years or just too big a coward to admit my fears and call Jud and the boys on them."

Ruby patted her arm. "We can't change the past. But we can always change what's happening now. We're not locked into stupid by default."

Cora sighed. "I know, but the hard part is if I have the guts to still live here with everyone knowing how and why my family just imploded. And we don't even know if Junior is going to survive. He's the only true innocent of all of us."

"I'll keep the both of you in my prayers," Ruby said. "And just for the record, I was ashamed to show my face in Blessings after I was kidnapped. I'd never talked about my past here, and then all of a sudden it was in everyone's face in all its ugly glory. And look at me now. As long as we draw breath, we have the option to change what we don't like."

Cora clasped Ruby's hand and gave it a squeeze. "You don't know how much this has meant to me. Thank you for taking the time out of your busy day to visit, and thank you for the gifts. I will think of you every time I look at those roses."

Ruby smiled. "I'll keep tabs on you, and I'll keep you in my prayers. Have a good rest tonight and I'll see you soon, okay?"

"Yes, okay," Cora said, and waved as Ruby went out the door, then turned on the light above her bed and reached for her glasses. *People* magazine beckoned.

Ruby rode down alone in the elevator and left the lobby alone. The parking lot lights were ablaze, and there were fewer cars than when she'd come in. She was telling herself all the way out the door not to panic, when she saw a very tall, very familiar figure walking toward her. The relief that went through her was huge.

She went to meet him and then walked into his open arms, hugging him ever so tight.

"It's things like this that make you absolutely irresistible. How do you always know?" she asked.

"You've seen my scars and I've seen yours. That's how the best love works, and you're my best love," Peanut said. "I'll follow you to Granny's."

Ruby looked up at him there, so tall and so beloved. "You might as well. You've already followed me to hell and back. Granny's isn't all that far."

Peanut held out his hand, and she took it. They walked hand in hand between the vehicles until she was in her car and it was running, and then he loped a few cars down to where he had parked and followed her out of the parking lot.

By the time they got to Granny's, the knot in Ruby's stomach was gone. She and Peanut walked in together, chattering like nothing had happened.

The next couple of days leveled out into a regular routine. Cora was sent home from the hospital with a prescription for high blood pressure, and the renovation on Pearl's house was getting ready for painting and cabinets.

She'd chosen white cabinets with burnished copper hardware and white quartz countertops with a faint gold thread running through, like what was in Bowie's kitchen. Pearl also opted for wide-plank, dark hardwood flooring throughout the house. Even though Bowie cautioned her that it would show every bit of dust and footprints on it, Pearl stayed firm. It reminded her of what the floors had looked like at her home when she was growing up, and she wanted that little love connection from her past.

———

The only members of the Boone family left in Blessings who weren't in the hospital or in jail were Mel, Emmitt, and Tiny.

Mel never went back to the hospital after one more visit to his mother.

After the first day and night at the hospital, Emmitt and Tiny began taking turns staying near Junior. Tiny stayed at the hospital during the day, and Emmitt stayed there at night. Tiny had set up their own little nest in the ICU waiting area, and despite all the other people who came and went, she'd laid claim to the three-cushion sofa. She had pulled it into the farthest corner of the room where she could nap during the day and Emmitt could sleep at night. And she kept a tote bag stocked with fruit and snacks, a little cooler of bottled water, and a blanket and a pillow.

They were helpless to do anything for their son, but they wouldn't leave him. What they had yet to find out was that Junior was showing signs of regaining consciousness.

———

Junior was only vaguely aware of existing. From time to time he would almost surface from the darkness into which he'd fallen, but either pain or drugs would send him toppling back down. And then things started to change. Junior was beginning to drift in and out of consciousness. The times he was waking, he felt bound to the bed, and then when the pain became intolerable, shadow people sent him back.

The first cognizant thought he had was *What's making that noise?* followed by *Why do I hurt?* But the only thing he remembered was his name.

Hope Talbot, Mercy Pittman's sister, was working the day shift in the ICU when Junior began showing signs of awakening. She checked a few readouts, then patted his arm and said his name.

When she saw his eyelids flicker and then his right hand moving, trying to flex, she immediately reported it.

A short while later, Dr. Hastings, who was Junior's attending physician, came down to assess the readouts as well as any physical responses he could get.

Junior had no idea of where he was or that the doctor had given orders thirty-six hours earlier to begin weaning him off of the drugs that kept him out. But as Junior was beginning to show signs of regaining consciousness, Dr. Hastings went to notify his parents.

It was almost noon on the third day since the shooting, and Emmitt had come up to have lunch with Tiny. He'd arrived with burgers and fries from Broyles Dairy Freeze and was dipping one of his french fries into the little pool of ketchup on Tiny's paper plate when Dr. Hastings walked in.

The food was immediately set aside.

"Don't let me interrupt your meal," he said. "I just came to give you an update. Your son is beginning to regain consciousness. Right now, it's just eye movement and some hand and finger movement. He has not responded to anyone verbally, but it appears he does react to footsteps and voices."

Tiny started to cry. "Oh, this is such good news."

Hastings nodded. "Yes. His blood pressure is still a bit high, but I attribute that to pain. I imagine when he begins waking up, the pain medication is going to be something we'll have to adjust. He had so many internal injuries that a lot of repairs were made during surgery."

Emmitt was sitting quietly. There were questions he wanted to ask, but he didn't want to trigger Tiny into one of her spells, so he started out cautiously.

"Will he heal back to the way he was?"

Hastings smiled. "Well, that's our intent. As he progresses, we'll begin removing tubes and monitoring kidney output and see how it goes. That's all I can tell you right now."

"Okay," Emmitt said. "It was something I've been thinking about, and I was hoping he wasn't going to be saddled with long-term health issues."

"Understood," Hastings said. "So, that's the update, and it's a positive one. I'll let you get back to your lunch, and you'll have the usual visiting time to talk to him. Just don't expect conversations. Right now, we just want him to wake up and tell us his name."

Tiny's eyes widened. She stared at Emmitt in horror as Hastings left.

"What did he mean by all that? Remember his name and all?"

"I don't know, Tiny. Junior nearly bled to death, remember? So I don't know what a lack of blood does to a body, but we'll just hope for the best and pray for a full recovery."

Tiny pushed her food aside. "When Junior is well, we can leave Blessings anytime we want."

Emmitt nodded. He was still trying to come to terms with Bowie James dropping the charges against Junior. And he'd done it before Junior was shot.

I told Junior we'd pay for everything and that he didn't need to work. I wonder if Bowie would have dropped the charges then? Was it really Junior's intent to take care of his own troubles that made the difference?

Emmitt remembered all too well how Junior didn't want anyone buying him out of trouble and had made it clear he didn't want a life like Emmitt and Mel had lived. So what had Junior said when he went to ask Bowie for a job? Whatever it was, it must have made an impact. Very few people would hire someone who'd already vandalized their property.

He got James's reasoning for not telling Junior the charges were dropped. In a way, he was still honoring his son's desire to pay off his own debt.

It didn't sit right with Emmitt that Bowie understood Junior's motives better than he did. It was a sobering thought. He didn't want to be beholden to Bowie James, but it appeared they were.

He thought about updating Mel and called him, but his brother didn't answer, so Emmitt sent him a text and hoped Mel wasn't laid out drunk and passed out on the floor.

He wanted to call his mama, but she never answered, so he guessed if she wanted to know how Junior was doing she'd find out on her own. He put the phone back in his pocket and glanced at Tiny.

"Are you through with your food?" he asked.

She nodded. "It was good, and thank you for bringing

it to me, but talking about Junior and what a long way he still has to go to get better sort of stole my appetite."

"I understand," Emmitt said as he gathered up what was left and took it to the trash can. "I tried to call Mel, but he doesn't answer."

Tiny rolled her eyes. "Likely as not, he's drunk and passed out."

"Maybe," Emmitt said. "But I think I'll go by his house and check on him before I go home. I do need to get some rest. I'll be back up here around six."

"Okay," Tiny said. "See you later."

Emmitt drove straight to Mel's house, but the car was gone. He almost didn't stop but then noticed something odd. All of the windows were up. He wondered why Mel didn't have the air-conditioning on. It was sure hot enough.

Curious, he pulled up into the drive and got out. He was starting up the steps when Mel's landlord, Danner Amos, came around the corner of the house and waved him down.

Emmitt pointed at the windows. "What happened? Did Mel's air conditioner quit?"

Danner pulled a handkerchief from a back pocket and wiped the sweat off his face.

"No. He told me his power was shut off for nonpayment," he said.

"Oh no! I'll help him get it back on," Emmitt said. "Where did he go?"

"He didn't say. He just called to tell me what happened, and that he was leaving town."

Emmitt gasped. "You mean, as in move away?"

Danner nodded. "He owed me for a month's back

rent and asked if I would be willing to settle up with him if he left the furniture. I told him the furniture was worth more than the rent, so we settled on a price and I paid him the difference."

Emmitt was stunned.

"Uh, well, thanks for the info," Emmitt said.

"Sure thing," Danner said. "We're praying for your son. He's a friend of my boy, Charlie."

"Thank you," Emmitt said. "You can tell Charlie that the doctor told us today that Junior is showing signs of regaining consciousness."

"That is really good news," Danner said. "I will be sure to let him know."

Emmitt lifted a hand in goodbye, his thoughts in freefall as he drove away. As soon as he got home, he sent Mel another text.

> You left? For good? Without even saying goodbye? Melvin, don't do this. You're my best friend. Text me when you get where you're going. I need to know you're still in the world.

After that, Emmitt went into his bedroom, kicked off his shoes, and lay down to get some rest. He fell asleep dreaming Junior was well and they were fishing off a dock at Gray Goose Lake.

Unaware of what was happening with his family, Jud Boone had concerns of his own and had asked to speak to the chief.

When Avery told the chief, Lon set aside the file

he was working on and went back to see what Jud wanted.

Judson had the makings of a five-day beard. He had two black eyes, and the stitches on his nose were beginning to itch. It still hurt to talk, and chewing on anything other than soft food was too painful to bother. When he saw the chief, he stood up and walked to the cell door.

"Okay, I'm here. What do you need?"

"I want to have a will drawn up. Will you call Peanut Butterman for me and ask if he would come here to do that?"

Jud had already been arraigned, pled guilty, and was awaiting sentencing. Technically, Lon didn't have to comply with prisoners' requests, but he didn't have a problem with it.

"I'll ask and let you know what he says," Lon said.

Jud sat back down.

Lon returned about an hour later. Jud was still sitting on the edge of the cot, staring at the floor.

"Mr. Butterman will come by the jail around three today, or sooner if he's done in court," he said.

Jud nodded.

Lon frowned and then left the jail area and went back to work.

As a lawyer, Peanut Butterman believed every person deserved their day in court and had the right to representation regarding all legal matters. But responding respectfully to Judson Boone's request was taking all he had.

It wasn't far from his office to the police station, so

Peanut decided to walk. He was going to record their conversation so that Betty could prepare the documents properly and had everything he needed in his briefcase as he stepped outside the building.

The sun was shining but there was just enough breeze to take away the slap of heat to the face. Someone honked at him and waved as he started across the street. They were gone before he got a good look at who it was, but he waved anyway and kept going.

He was thinking about Cora, who had been in his office just a short while back, filing for divorce from the man. Now she was in the hospital because of him. The fallout from Jud Boone's existence on earth was nothing short of appalling. But the man wanted a will and Peanut was going to make it happen.

Less than ten minutes later, he was walking into the station, in a good place in his head, determined to stay professional.

"I'm here to see Judson Boone," he told Avery.

Avery nodded. "I'll let the chief know you're here," he said and buzzed Lon's office. Moments later, Lon came up to the lobby.

"Thank you for coming," he said, then pointed at Peanut's briefcase. "I don't suppose you have any weapons in there?"

Peanut immediately placed the briefcase on the counter and opened it.

"I'll be recording our conversation for Betty so she'll have all the details he wants in his will directly from him and not my notes."

Lon scanned the contents, then gave Peanut a thumbs-up. "Sorry, but I have to ask," he said. "Follow me."

Peanut had been in the police station many times on behalf of different clients, and Jud Boone was just another to add to his list, but he never liked going to the jail. It was old, and despite being clean, the very faint odor of vomit and urine was always present.

"I had Avery set up a little table and chair in the aisle between the cells so you'll have something to work from," Lon said, and then opened the door and led him inside.

Jud was lying on his cot when they came in, so he sat up, waiting for this to begin.

When they reached the cell, the chief gave Jud a look.

"I expect nothing but courtesy from you," he said.

Jud nodded. "Yes, of course, and thanks."

"Ring the buzzer by the door when you're ready to go out," Lon said.

Peanut nodded, then looked Jud straight in the eyes.

"Good afternoon, Mr. Boone. I understand you want to draw up a will?"

"Yes," Jud said.

Peanut sat down at the table, pulled up the chair, and opened his briefcase.

"I'm going to record our conversation so that my secretary will have all the details of what you want in your will." Then he got the recorder ready, hit Play, and they began.

After they had all the details out of the way, Jud didn't waste time.

"Before we get into what happens after I die, I have been giving my sons money each month from a trust I set up when I sold my business years back. Can you fix it so the same amounts are directly deposited into their accounts at the bank?"

"There will be papers for you to sign, but we'll get that set up."

"Thanks. I don't own much else but my car and a small portfolio of stocks and bonds. I want the balance of my account and the portfolio bequeathed to my grandson, Emmitt Lee Boone, Jr."

"I will need a list of the stocks and bonds and their present value."

"My broker is in Savannah. If I give you his name and number, he can furnish that for you."

"Perfect," Peanut said. "Anything else?"

Jud shook his head. "No."

"Okay, then," Peanut said. "I'll get my secretary working on the paperwork ASAP, and when it's all ready, I'll be back to get everything signed."

"Much appreciated," Jud said, then watched Peanut pack up. He pressed the buzzer, the door opened, and he was gone.

Jud gripped the bars with both hands as he looked at all the empty cells, unable to believe he was actually here. He'd lived his whole life in Blessings—under his own terms, rough though they may have been—and never once saw this as the end of his life.

No more Thanksgivings with family. No more Christmases watching Cora wrapping gifts and making candy. He would never lie down at night beside her again.

The tragedy of his life was that he didn't see the pattern that had led him to this place. He was still the hard, judgmental man who had set the wheels in motion years ago, and his only regret was shooting Junior when he was aiming for Bowie James.

Chapter 19

BOWIE'S CHEROKEE WAS FINALLY REPAIRED AND READY TO pick up. Pearl and Ella rode with him when he went to turn in his rental, and as soon as he turned it in, Ella rented it back. She and Pearl were driving to Savannah to look at replacing the car they lost in the flood. Bowie was torn about watching them drive away, but they'd been on their own for twenty years without him, and insinuating they couldn't handle it would have been an insult.

So he picked up his car and went back to the trailer to get Rowan. With everyone getting ready to leave at the same time, she'd taken the last turn at a shower.

She was in her underwear in Bowie's master bath, drying her hair, and didn't hear him come in, but he heard the hair dryer and knew where to find her. He just hadn't expected to find her in such a delightful condition.

"Hey, hey, sweetheart! Your outfit is a knockout, but I can't take you to work with me like that."

She was blushing a bit as she turned off the dryer and laid it down. "I didn't expect you back so soon."

He just shook his head and held out his hand.

She took it without hesitation.

"You are so beautiful," Bowie said.

"Are Pearl and Ella gone?"

"Yes. About fifteen minutes ago."

"Then this is an opportunity we should definitely

take," she said as she reached behind her back and unhooked her bra.

Bowie turned around and locked the door behind him, and then began taking off clothes.

Rowan dropped her panties where she stood and stretched out on the bed to watch, shivering with longing when he was finally naked.

"You have a beautiful body, Bowie James."

"The better to love you with," he said, and lay down beside her. "I've imagined this every night as I watched you sleeping. I love you, Rowan...so very much."

"I think I've been in love with you since the moment I saw you. You were the knight in shining armor that we all needed, and you have grown dearer to me by the day. Make love to me, Bowie. Teach me how to make love to you."

Without wasting a moment, he did just that, watching her every expression until he knew where to touch that made her lose her breath—learning how sensitive the rosy nipples were on her breasts, and watching for the moment when her eyes shut on a moan. That's when he knew that she was gone.

He took her to a climax once before he took her to him, and this time they fit in every possible way. Whatever joy he was giving her increased a hundredfold for him. No man had ever needed to be loved more. She was healing every broken piece of his heart.

Later, after getting dressed, Rowan took great care in smoothing out the sheets beneath the bedspread and then straightened the spread itself.

"Does it look okay?" she asked.

"It's fine," Bowie said.

"What's happening between us is still ours, and I'm not ready to share," she said.

When she finally stopped fussing with the bed, he gave a little tug to her ponytail and then brushed a kiss across her lips.

"It's too hot to wear the sweatpants, and I'm not wearing my new clothes to work in, so it's the old shorts and T-shirt for me. Is that okay?"

"It's fine, but we could always get more clothes."

"You've already given many things to me, not the least of which is food and shelter. I can wait."

He understood the need to be self-sufficient more than most.

"Okay, but you are going to marry me, right? I mean…I'll be giving you all kinds of things then."

Rowan's eyes widened and then suddenly filled with tears.

"Did you just propose?"

He grinned. "I guess I did. Is it too soon?"

"No, it's not too soon, and yes, I am going to marry you and follow you to the ends of the earth if that's where you take me."

Bowie scooped her off her feet, laughing.

She wrapped her arms around his neck and started peppering his face with kisses and tears. If his phone hadn't started ringing, they might have made another trip back to bed.

"It's them," he said, and answered quickly. "Hey, Aunt Ella. Are you already there?"

"Yes, and already cruising the car lots. It's been so long since Mama and I have been able to run around that we're having too much fun to make it back at noon."

"That's wonderful," Bowie said. "Don't worry about Rowan. I took her to work with me," he said, and winked at Rowan. He'd intentionally led Ella to believe they were already there, to keep Rowan's cover.

"Great. I didn't like to think about her there on her own."

"We're fine. Have fun. Text or call me when you two start for home."

"We will. Love you, honey."

"Love you, too," he said, then disconnected and put the phone back in his pocket. "Are you ready to go to work?" he asked.

"Yes."

"Then we're out of here," he said, and out the door they went.

Once he was outside, Bowie set the security alarm and headed for the Jeep.

Frank Crockett was washing his car as they got into the Cherokee and drove away, and Yancy Scott's little redheaded girl was riding her bike up and down the road between the trailers.

It was a little after nine by the time they arrived, and when the crew saw Rowan get out of the car in shorts and the Salvation Army T-shirt, work came to a halt.

They were standing inside the house with big grins on their faces when he and Rowan walked in. He already knew Rowan would be a distraction, and they already knew she existed because he'd talked about her. Now, they were going to meet her.

Bowie noticed Rowan's smile was a little shy, so he slid his hand across her back, wanting her to feel comfortable.

"Honey, these guys are my friends. Ray and Joe Tuttle are brothers. They're the ones with the silly grins on their faces. The one in the red shirt is Matt Roller, and next to him on his right is Presley Smith. You share a hairstyle with Samuel Hooper, and Walter Adams is the one with the beard. Guys, this is Rowan Harper. She's going to spend the day with us, so can the dirty jokes and try not to stare."

Rowan laughed. "It's nice to meet you guys."

"It's our pleasure," Ray said, and the rest of them nodded, suddenly at a loss for words.

"Okay, as you were," Bowie said, and they all went back to what they'd been doing. "I'll walk you through the place, just so you'll have an idea of the layout, before I grab a hammer."

As soon as she'd had the tour, she looked around at what was going on.

"Is there anything in here that I could help with in any way?" she asked.

"No, honey, not right now until we get the rest of this trim up."

"Then do you have some big garbage bags?"

Ray piped up before Bowie could answer. "Yes, ma'am. There are several boxes of them in the tool van. Just open up the back door and look on the shelf to your left."

"Thank you," Rowan said. She wiggled her fingers goodbye at Bowie and left him standing.

He didn't know what was up until he looked out a few minutes later and saw her picking up building trash from the front yard. Pleased by her take-charge attitude, he dug around until he found a pair of gloves that should fit her and took them outside.

"For you," he said, and tossed them off the porch.

"Thanks!" Rowan said as she put them on, then went back to work.

She liked being outside, and she liked being useful, so the time passed quickly. She had one trash bag full before she'd gone halfway around. She tied off the bag and threw it in their big dumpster, then got another bag and finished the other half of the yard.

Bowie was proud of her initiative and her willingness to get her hands dirty.

His crew was interested in the length of those long, tan legs and the way her eyes crinkled up at the corners when she laughed.

After catching them moving from window to window so they could watch what she was doing, Bowie frowned.

"Guys! What the hell? You act like you never saw a woman before. You haven't done a third of what needed to be done today and it's already nearly noon."

They turned to face him, wearing equally guilty looks but without bothering to hide their smiles.

"Well, don't get mad at us," Joe said. "You're the one who brought her to work, and we're not dead. She's pretty, Boss. She's real pretty."

"Yes, I'm aware of that. But give me a break. She's my girl, and you're expecting me to ignore all this blatant adoration?"

Samuel frowned. "What's 'blatant' mean?"

Ray laughed. "It means stop standing around staring at her."

"Oh! Right! Sorry, Boss," Samuel said, "but I'm done tiling the shower in the master bath, and I'm going to start on the bathroom in the hall after lunch."

Bowie shook his head and found something to hammer, while Rowan continued picking up trash, unaware of the commotion her presence had caused.

When they stopped for lunch, Bowie took Rowan with him to Broyles Dairy Freeze to pick up the order he'd called in.

"It sure feels good in here," she said. "This is like how it was at home. We'd be all hot and sweaty outside and then go in to eat. It was twice as hard to go back out to work once we were cool and our tummies were full."

"Is this too much for you, baby? I will happily take you back home if you want."

"No, I don't want to go back. I'm used to this. I want to stay with you. So I have the trash all picked up. What are you going to be doing this afternoon?"

"We'll probably start painting in the back of the house. The tape and bedding got dry on the new drywall. The new cabinets will be delivered day after tomorrow, and I want everything painted before we bring them in."

"This is so exciting for Pearl and Ella. They are going to be living in style."

"It's no more than they deserve," Bowie said, and then pulled into the drive-through, picked up the order, and headed back.

A good breeze had picked up, so they all ate out on the porch, laughing and talking, the men doing their best not to flirt with the boss's girl.

Rowan sat with her back against the wall, listening to the banter and watching how Bowie was with them—how he straddled the line between boss and friend with such ease.

She ate her burger, but not all the fries. "Hey, Bowie, do you want the rest of my fries?"

Before he could answer, Joe raised his hand. "I call dibs if the boss doesn't want them."

Bowie grinned. "Give them to Joe. He's always hungry."

Joe jumped up, took the little paper boat with the fries out of her hands, and grinned. "Thanks."

Rowan smiled. "You're most welcome."

———ᴧᴧᴧ———

Tiny was standing by Junior's bed, holding his hand and watching his face for even the tiniest hints of his awakening. Her thoughts kept going back to special moments when he was a baby—when he was learning to walk, and the time when he was three and put a whole roll of toilet paper in the toilet then tried to flush. Water flooded the bathroom, and when it did, he hid under the bed.

He'd been such a happy little guy. She couldn't believe where life had taken him. All she knew was that crying wouldn't help, but God might. According to their preacher, God cared for good and bad people alike, so she started to pray.

She was halfway through the Twenty-Third Psalm, her go-to prayer, when she thought she felt his finger twitch. She stopped right in the middle of "I will fear no evil," and looked down at his hand lying in hers.

"Junior? It's Mama. Can you hear me, sweetheart? This is me squeezing your hand. Do you feel it? Can you squeeze mine back?"

She felt another twitch, and then all his fingers

moved. It wasn't a squeeze, but it was an acknowledgment of the request.

"Oh, Junior! Oh, baby! You're waking up! Praise the Lord, praise the Lord!"

~~~

Melvin Boone was heading south, going as fast as the law would allow. He wanted to be as far away from his past as he could, where no one knew anything about him or his family.

Sitting at his mother's side in the ER and seeing true revulsion on her face had been his undoing. He'd gone home after they moved her into a room that day and thought about killing himself. The only thing that stopped him was knowing they'd bury him in Blessings. How could he get away from what he'd done if they put him six feet deep in Georgia soil?

It wasn't until they turned his power off that Mel made a move. Fate had decided for him. He hadn't expected to leave town with any money. But he also didn't want to skip out owing any, either. Being able to pay off his past-due rent by leaving all his furniture behind would get him out of debt, but the landlord took the furniture for past rent, then gave Mel the difference. Having money in his pocket had been a godsend. He had more than enough to get to Florida. He was damn good at cleaning fish. Maybe he could get a job on the docks. But whatever he did, he would do it on his own.

He'd been ignoring the calls from Emmitt, but when he read the text, Mel cried. No, he wasn't going to let anyone know where he was. How could he start over if he stayed connected to the past? This exodus from all he loved was his punishment. He knew it. He accepted it.

He stopped at the Georgia–Florida border to fuel up, picked up a snack and a cold drink to take with him, and then he was back on the road. When the highway took him on into Florida, his fingers tightened on the wheel. He was scared as hell, but there was no looking back.

It was midafternoon when Bowie got a text from Ella, telling him they were on their way home. He sent one back and went to find Rowan.

She was in Ella's room, running painter's tape around the windows to prepare the room for painting.

He walked up behind her and kissed the back of her neck.

"Good job, honey!"

"Thanks."

"Aunt Ella just called. They're on their way home, and they don't have a key to get in. It's less than two hours before quitting time. How about I take you home now so you can let them in? You can clean up before they get there, and I'll bring supper home with me from Granny's so no one has to cook."

"Okay. I've finished in here, anyway."

They walked back to where Ray was working. "Ray, I'm going to drop Rowan off at home, and then I'll be right back."

Ray gave him a thumbs-up, then pointed at Rowan. "You, pretty lady, are one hard worker, and it was a pleasure to meet you."

"Thanks. Tell the guys I said goodbye," she said, and

then they headed out to the car. "I hope I'm not too dirty to ride in this."

He laughed. "I ride home in this every night needing a bath and clean clothes."

She grinned. "Oh, right."

As they started home, she reached across the console and patted Bowie's leg.

"What's that for?" he asked.

"For… Because I love you."

The sudden lump in Bowie's throat caught him by surprise.

"And for that, I am truly grateful. I love you, too."

She nodded. "I know."

"Am I that transparent?" he asked.

"Oh, no, nothing like that. The faeries would never have let us under their tree if you hadn't been my true love."

"Really?" Bowie said, and then shook his head. "I think I keep saying that, don't I?"

"It's okay," Rowan said. "You had no way of knowing."

She was right, and he still didn't know what made her tick, but he also didn't give a damn. She was his and that was all that mattered.

The little redhead wasn't riding her bike anymore, but she and another girl appeared to be running races as Bowie drove into the park.

"I don't think that little girl runs out of energy," Rowan said. "She was on her bike when we left, and look at her now."

Bowie glanced up the road. "I remember being like that. I'd go out to play in the morning and only come back inside for meals or when it got dark."

"All of my friends were at school, so when we were out for the summer I was on my own for entertainment, only I never ran out of things to do," Rowan said. She hopped out of the car and yelled "Race you!" and headed for the steps.

He caught her before she got there, threw her over his shoulder, and left her hanging upside down as he unlocked the door.

Rowan was laughing so hard she could barely breathe when he dumped her onto the sofa and stole a kiss.

"You beat me!" she said.

Bowie grinned. "Come lock the door after me. The girls should be back within the next forty minutes or so, and I won't be far behind."

"See you soon," she said, then stood in the door, waited for him to wave, then watched him drive away. As soon as the door was locked, she danced herself across the floor, stripped off her clothes and tossed them in the washer, and headed for the shower to clean up.

Cora was pouring herself a glass of sweet tea when her phone signaled a text. When she saw Emmitt's name as the sender, she read it anyway, only because she was hoping it might be news about Junior.

> Mama, thought you would want to know that Junior is showing signs of regaining consciousness. He remains in guarded but stable condition. Mel is gone. He left town without intent of coming back. He does not return my calls or texts. My heart tells me we'll never see him again.

Cora put her phone back in her pocket and took her sweet tea to her recliner. She took a sip and then set it aside as she turned on the TV. She found the show she wanted to watch and turned up the volume.

She liked Ellen DeGeneres. Ellen made her laugh. But the longer she watched, the less Cora felt like laughing. In fact, laughing right now felt wrong. She changed the channel to a cooking show, then took another drink and put her feet up.

Before she knew it, she was crying again.

It was either cry, or die from the pain swelling up inside of her. She knew why Mel was gone, and that was going to be one more blot on her conscience to deal with. Today, life was just a little too hard. Maybe tomorrow would be better.

Rowan was squeaky clean and sitting with her feet up, enjoying the cool air, her Coke, and Bowie's book on constellations when she heard a car. She jumped up to see if it was Pearl and Ella, and it was.

"Need any help?" she asked as they began gathering up all kinds of shopping bags.

"We've got it," Ella said.

They came inside, grinning from ear to ear.

"What's the secret?" she asked.

"No secret. Come with us to the bedroom. We have something to show you."

"Okay."

They dumped all the bags onto the bed, and then pointed.

"Open them," Ella said.

"They're all for you," Pearl added.

Rowan's expression must have registered her shock, because the girls high-fived each other and grinned.

"Go on!" Pearl urged.

Rowan emptied the first bag onto the bed and squealed in pure delight. Then she did the same to the next, and to the next, until all seven bags were empty. By the time she spread the contents out all over the bed, she was crying.

"I can't believe you did this," she said, and hugged Pearl and then Ella. "They're beautiful, and all my size!"

"It's the most fun we've had in ages," Ella said. "Start trying them on. We want to see you model every one of them, while we go start supper."

"Oh! Bowie said he was bringing supper home."

Ella sighed. "I knew there was a reason why I love him so much. I am seriously too tired to cook. So, Mama and I will just go sit on the sofa and wait for the runway show to begin."

Rowan was beside herself. It was like Christmas, only better, and so she began.

By the time Bowie came home with their food, the show was over and she was wearing new shorts that fit and a pink cotton blouse that hung loosely around her waist.

"Look what they brought me from Savannah!" Rowan said. "This and so much more."

Bowie forgot what he'd been going to say and just stood there, watching the joy on her face and the pleased looks from his girls.

"You look way too cute to take back to work," he said as Ella took the food out of his hands.

Rowan laughed and did a little pirouette to give him the full effect.

Bowie gave Ella and Pearl two thumbs up. "You rock."

"It was our pleasure," Pearl said, then began looking through the food sacks. "What are we having?"

"Fried catfish dinner. I'm going to clean up real quick, but if you're too hungry to wait, dig in."

"I'll always wait for you," Rowan said.

Pearl and Ella glanced at each other and then grinned. They'd talked about Rowan and Bowie all day and the growing possibility that she was going to become a real part of the family. It was the best day they'd had since before Hurricane Fanny.

Chapter 20

THE FRIED CATFISH WAS A HIT. IT CAME WITH PINTO BEANS and coleslaw and hush puppies, and as they ate Pearl and Ella discussed the cars and the house.

"We found a car," Pearl said. "We're going back tomorrow and get it."

"What did you choose?" Bowie asked.

"Well, I told you we had the insurance money from the one we lost, so we just shopped for cars within that amount and found a 2014 Chevrolet Equinox with only 45,000 miles on it. The dealer said the lady who owned it had passed away and her niece inherited it and the rest of her property. The niece used it as a trade-in on a new car, so it's a one-owner. The dealer is holding it for us."

"How are the tires?"

"Nearly new," Ella said. "And it drives like a dream— quiet and a really smooth ride. It's kind of a champagne color, so it won't show dust easily, and Mama wants it, so there's that."

Pearl grinned, which made the rest of them laugh. "Pass the beans, please," she said.

Rowan passed the container and popped another hush puppy in her mouth.

"Anyway, that's our plan for tomorrow," Pearl said. "And we'll be gone pretty early in the morning."

"One of you has to drive the rental car back," Bowie said.

"We know," Pearl said. "I don't drive much anymore, but I still do okay. I'm sure we'll be fine."

"I'll go with you tomorrow!" Rowan said. "I can drive the rental back, then call Bowie to pick me up there and take me home."

Bowie looked relieved. "That's a great idea, honey."

Ella agreed. "It would really be appreciated! Thank you!"

"After all you've done for me, it's the least I can do," Rowan said. "It will feel good to get behind the wheel again."

"Then it's settled," Pearl said. "On the home front, how's the house going?"

"Ah…well, we began painting today and got the first coat on in all the rooms. Tomorrow, we'll apply a second coat and do the trim. Cabinets arrive the day after, so we'll be setting up the layout in the kitchen and the vanities in both bathrooms."

"I can't believe I am so excited about two bathrooms," Pearl said. "When I grew up, we had one and it was outside."

"I seem to remember a story about you and a raccoon in that outhouse," Bowie said.

"Oh, tell me," Rowan begged. "I'm the only one who doesn't know this."

Pearl rolled her eyes. "It's nothing to brag about, but here goes. I was twelve, and sitting there doing my business when I heard scratching at the door. I grabbed a page out of the old Sears catalog (that's what we used for toilet paper in those days) and then pulled up my drawers and got ready to run, then heard it again. I was scared to death. I didn't know what it was and kept

praying for it to go away, but it didn't. Then I saw one
black claw trying to dig underneath the door, and I guess
I lost my mind.

"I start screaming my head off, and Daddy comes
running with his hunting rifle. Opens the door, sees me
all upset, and asks me what's wrong. I told him there
was something scratching at the door and I was afraid it
was Old Nick, the devil that the preacher talked about in
church. Daddy laughed, told me there wasn't any devil
at the door but he did see a raccoon waddling off as he
was running to my aid."

Rowan laughed. "Bless your heart."

Pearl nodded. "I never did live that down."

"Don't feel bad. We women all have our breaking
points. I was a teenager and got trapped in the chicken
house once when a big snake dropped from the rafters.
It landed between me and the door, and Daddy told me
later that he thought I was being murdered. It was just
a black snake, likely wanting eggs, but it might as well
have been a dragon. I don't do snakes. Daddy had to
come rescue me as well."

"If you run into any more critters, I'll save you,"
Bowie said.

Rowan blushed a little, knowing the girls were
already reading between the lines of everything they
said to each other, but it didn't matter. They'd find out
soon enough.

"Well, I cooked," Bowie said. "So who's doing
dishes?"

Pearl threw what was left of her bread roll at him.

Ella wadded up her paper napkin and threw it at
his head.

And Rowan just sat and watched, thinking of all the years she and her daddy sat at table. Those were somber years, years of everything but foolishness and laughter.

She couldn't wait to belong—really belong—to these people.

―――∽∽∽―――

There were only two patients in the ICU now—Junior Boone and a cancer patient.

Emmitt hated to see the gray color to the old man's skin and his emaciated body. Of all the things Emmitt Boone feared in life, dying was the big one. But he had to pass the man to get to Junior, so he looked away and kept walking.

A nurse was at Junior's bed when Emmitt arrived. "Everything okay?" he asked.

She nodded. "Just checking his IV."

Emmitt waited until she was gone and then gently patted Junior's shoulder.

"Hey, son. I'm here. They told us you are waking up, so I'm hoping you hear me, wherever you are. Mama and I love you. We can't wait for you to come home."

He waited a few seconds, then took Junior by the hand. "I dreamed you and I went fishing out at Gray Goose Lake. In the dream, I caught the biggest fish, but you know that's never the case. You always beat me."

And so it went, talking without response until his time was up. Then he told Junior goodbye and that he would see him again soon, and left the room.

But Junior had heard his daddy's voice and was trying to figure out how to find him when the voice went silent. After that, it was too hard for Junior to focus, so he slid back into the dark.

He didn't rouse again until sometime toward morning.

The nurse on duty heard what sounded like a moan. She glanced at the readouts on the monitors and took off down the aisle of beds to check on Junior Boone.

She turned on the light over his bed and saw his eyelids fluttering and his fingers moving against the sheets, as if he was trying to grasp something.

"Junior, can you hear me?" she asked.

He moaned again.

"Can you open your eyes for me? Open your eyes. Follow the sound of my voice, and open your eyes," she said.

There was a hitch in his breath, and he muttered something unintelligible.

"That's good. That's the way. Open your eyes and tell me what's wrong."

His eyelashes fluttered like the wings on a resting butterfly, and then he uttered one single word.

"Hurt."

"You hurt. Okay. I can fix that," she said softly, and ran back to check his chart, then called Dr. Hastings at home.

He answered on the second ring. "Hello?"

"Dr. Hastings, this is Nina in the ICU. Junior Boone is on the verge of opening his eyes. He's been twitching and mumbling, and he just now said one word. 'Hurt.'" Then she reminded the doctor of the dosage Junior was getting through the IV and waited for instructions.

"Okay," Dr. Hastings said. "I don't want to dope him up so much that we keep putting him out, but at the same time, I certainly don't want to stress his body any more than it already is by waking up to pain. How long until the next pain meds are due?"

"Less than thirty minutes."

"Oh, then that's not a problem. Give the regular dosage to him now, and I'll be in shortly to check on him."

"Yes, Doctor, thank you."

Nina scrambled around to pull Junior's med dosage, then hurried back. He was still trying to pick something up off the bed, which meant he hadn't gone back to sleep. She injected the pain meds into the IV, then touched his arm.

"Junior, I just gave you something for the pain. You'll feel better soon."

His voice was barely above a whisper, but the message was the same. "Hurt."

"I know, honey. I know."

She stood by his bed until he quit digging on the sheet and watched the muscles in his body beginning to relax. Within minutes, she could tell that the meds had kicked in.

She checked his stats one last time, then stopped by her other patient before going back to her desk.

Dr. Hastings arrived an hour later and went straight to Junior's bed. He wanted to look at the dressings over the incision and then studied the readouts for the past twenty-four hours.

"I'm pleased with his progress," the doctor said. "Best-guess scenario, he'll be awake sometime today. Is his dad still here?"

"Yes, Doctor. In the waiting room."

"I'll talk to him on my way out, and I'm leaving orders to adjust Junior's meds."

Emmitt had been awake for almost an hour and was on his second cup of vending-machine coffee when the doctor walked into the waiting room.

He jumped to his feet in panic, knowing they must have called him in because Hastings did not make rounds this early.

"What happened? Is my son worse?"

"No, on the contrary. He is waking up. He spoke to the nurse, and he has been exhibiting more motor function."

"He spoke? What did he say?" Emmitt asked.

"He said 'hurt.' He's been given pain meds and will likely not wake up again for a couple of hours."

"That's wonderful news, Dr. Hastings. Thank you!"

"Of course. We'll talk again."

Emmitt was already on the phone to Tiny as Hastings walked out the door. As predicted, Junior did wake up that afternoon. He opened his eyes for a brief time, saw his parents, heard what they were saying, and fell back asleep.

Early the next morning, Bowie saw the girls off to Savannah to pick up Pearl's new car, then went back inside to finish getting ready for work. It was the first time he'd been alone since they'd come to stay with him, and the whole place felt empty. It had always been his place of refuge but nothing more. It had needed love to become a home.

He left early to eat breakfast at Granny's and was still early getting to the jobsite. Today was the last day of painting and he was anxious to get started.

As soon as Ray and the rest of the crew arrived with the equipment, they began at the back of the house again and painted their way forward, while Samuel and Walter followed behind them, doing touch-ups and painting the trim.

It was ten minutes after ten when Rowan called. She'd made it back to Blessings and needed a ride.

Bowie took off his paint mask, handed the spray rig over to Joe, and headed out the door. Rowan was standing at the curb in front of the building, and when she saw him coming, she waved.

As Bowie pulled up, she hopped off the curb, got in, and started talking.

"I didn't have any problems. I'm supposed to tell you that it'll be at least a couple of hours before all the paperwork is done and the car is serviced for them to drive. But I saw it, and it's really pretty. I think they did a good job."

"Good to know," Bowie said, and reached for her hand. "I want you to know that it is official. You are forever entrenched into my life. After all of you left this morning, my home felt empty. I can't imagine how I would be feeling, leaving Blessings without you when this is all over. So this is me thanking you for loving me."

"Oh, Bowie! That's so beautiful. You say the sweetest things to me, and you are very welcome. Believe me, the pleasure is all mine."

He winked and then backed away from the curb and drove to the trailer park.

He handed her the spare door key as he disarmed the alarm, then leaned over the console and kissed her.

"I'm not getting out, or we both know what will happen. We're halfway through the house with painting, so I need to get back. See you this evening. I love you, and take care."

"I love you more, and I will," Rowan said and got out.

Bowie watched until she was inside and then left.

––––

Peanut Butterman was back at the jail, this time accompanied by his secretary, Betty. He'd asked to be in the cell with his client, so Betty waited outside at the little table as Lon let Peanut in, then locked the door behind him. Peanut and Jud both sat on the cot while Peanut had him signing papers.

"This is paperwork from the bank, giving permission to withdraw this amount of money from your account each month and transfer it into both Emmitt and Melvin's personal checking accounts. Sign here, and then here. You can use the top of my briefcase for a table."

Jud signed all the copies and handed them to Peanut, who immediately handed them to Betty.

"Chief, are you signing as the witness?" she asked.

"I can. Show me where to sign."

Afterward, Betty notarized the documents and waited for the will.

"This is your last will and testament," Peanut said. "First read it over."

Jud nodded and read the pages carefully, making sure every one of his wishes had properly been included, then looked up.

"Where do I sign?"

Again, Jud showed him and then passed the will to Betty.

As soon as all the papers were signed, Peanut stood and shook Judson's hand.

"It's been a pleasure doing business with you," he said, and turned around to be let out of the cell.

When the door slammed shut behind them, Jud flinched. It was symbolic of his situation. The door to his freedom was not only shut but locked, and he was alone.

All signs of their presence had been removed, right down to the little table in the aisle. And tomorrow he would be back in court to be sentenced. He thought about a cold beer and his recliner, and Cora cooking something good in the kitchen for them to eat, and cried. If he knew how to make himself stop breathing, he would do it.

The moment Pearl and Ella got back to Blessings, they drove straight to their home to see the progress. When they pulled up at the far end of the driveway, they were speechless, but the more they saw, the more they wanted to see.

"Well, are we getting out or are we just gonna sit here?" Pearl asked.

Ella turned off the motor and got out, dropped the car keys in her pocket, and met Pearl at the front of the car.

"Should we let Bowie know we're here?" Ella asked.

"Why? It's my house," Pearl said and started walking.

Bowie just happened to glance out the front window, and when he saw them coming he grinned.

"Boys! Prepare yourselves. My girls are here," he

said, and went out to meet them. "Hi, Gran. Hi, Aunt Ella," he said, gave them each a hug and then looked down the drive. "Nice car. Did you come to take me for a ride?"

Pearl grinned. "You know why we're here. The last time I saw home, it was awful. I know you're not through, but I need a different picture in my mind."

"I'd love to show you," he said. "Both of you grab an elbow and I'll walk you in. There's so much building stuff lying around that I don't want you to fall."

They each grabbed an arm, and in the door they went—to find all six of the men waiting.

"Gran, this is my crew, and none of this would have been possible without them." He pointed them out, telling her their names, just like he'd done when he introduced them to Rowan. And then he introduced the women to the crew. "And these pretty ladies are my girls," he said. "This is my gran, Pearl James, and this is my aunt, Ella James, who is Pearl's daughter."

Pearl was almost in tears. "I'm proud to meet all of you," she said. "I can't believe what a transformation this has become. What a wonderful, wonderful thing you are doing for me, Bowie. Show us around."

"Glad to, but one warning. The paint isn't quite dry, so don't touch."

He began where they were standing and went all the way through the house, pointing out the details and modifications. But it was the master bedroom with the bath en suite and walk-in closet that got the biggest reaction from Pearl.

"Imagine, Ella! We won't have to share a bathroom again."

"I know," Ella said. "I don't know how you did it, Bowie, but my closet is twice the size it was."

"I said, 'Alakazam,' snapped my fingers, and there it was."

Ella laughed. "I'm not buying that story, but it all looks wonderful, and we have lingered long enough. We'll let you all get back to work."

He walked them back to their car. "Rowan is home, so she'll let you in, and I'll see everyone later."

He watched until they'd driven out of sight and then went back inside.

"Your gran and Aunt Ella are awesome," Samuel said. "I don't think we've ever done a house for anyone quite as appreciative as they are."

Bowie nodded. "This is going to be at a level of elegance they'd never imagined would be in their home, and they deserve it. So what's left to do this evening?"

"We're finishing up in the kitchen, and the living room/dining room is all that's left. After that, we'll clean up our stuff and be done."

"Then I'm going to be out here on the porch for a bit, following up on deliveries."

~~~

Bowie arrived home to find something of a celebration taking place. All three women were at the dining room table playing cards, and every time one of them won a hand, they toasted each other and then burst into laughter.

"What's going on?" he asked. "Gran, are you sitting on your underwear again?"

That set them off laughing again.

Finally, Rowan caught her breath enough to explain.

"I sold the farm. There was a bidding war, and I got ten thousand dollars over the asking price."

"Oh wow! Honey! That's awesome," he said, and pulled her up from the chair and danced her across the room and back, with her laughing all the way. "So, I get the toasting, but what's so funny about the sale?" he asked.

"On, there's nothing funny about the sale, and this isn't Coke in our glasses."

He blinked, then picked up Rowan's glass, smelled it, then took a sip and grinned.

"Y'all found the liquor cabinet, and if I'm not mistaken you're drinking Gentleman Jack, one of Jack Daniel's finer whiskeys."

The girls lifted their glasses. "He's right!" Ella said, and they took another sip.

Rowan giggled. "We're laughing 'cause we might be a bit tipsy."

"She's right!" Pearl said, and they lifted their glasses again and took another sip.

"Is there any left?" he asked.

"Oh my goodness, yes. It's right where we found it."

"Then I believe I might join you."

"Yay!" they all said, and had another tiny sip.

Bowie was trying not to laugh at them as he poured himself a shot, then came back to the table.

"To the three finest women I know," he said, and downed the shot neat.

"Oooh! Look what he did!" Rowan mumbled, eyeing the quarter inch of whiskey left in her glass. "What is it they say? Asses up?"

Pearl snorted. "No, girl. Lord, you can tell you're not a drinker. It's bottoms up."

"Oh. Anyway, in my mouth and all the way to my toes, that's as far as the whiskey can go!" Then she downed what was left in her glass, just like Bowie.

Not to be outdone, Pearl and Ella emptied their glasses, too, and then they all three laughed until they were gasping for breath.

Bowie kept grinning. They were a sorry lot as far as drinkers go. He shook his head and then leaned down in front of all of them and kissed Rowan soundly on the lips.

An immediate hush fell over the room.

Rowan gasped. "Did you just tell?"

"It appears I might have given them a big hint. I'm going to shower. Don't drink any more. I don't want to eat supper by myself." He started to the bathroom and then stopped. "I'm cooking tonight. There's not a one of you sober enough to be trusted with fire."

They looked at each other, then nodded at him in agreement. But he had no more than closed the bathroom door when he heard them burst into laughter again. It was all the warning he needed to hurry. They were too tipsy to remember what he said about fires.

Bowie was out of the shower in record time, then made bacon and tomato sandwiches for supper and a huge pot of coffee. They were all going to have hangovers, but he could at least get some food in their bellies and a little caffeine to boot.

As it turned out, the food should have been in their bellies before the drinking began, but it was too late now.

They spent the night either throwing up or meandering

through the room looking for something for a headache, and when Bowie left for work the next morning, they were all still in bed asleep.

He leaned down, planted a soft kiss on Rowan's forehead, and whispered "Love you" in her ear, then slipped out.

Chapter 21

TWO DAYS LATER, JUNIOR WAS NOT ONLY AWAKE BUT HAD been moved to his own room and was cognizant of the fact that he'd had some kind of stomach surgery. But every time he asked for details, the nurses gave him the runaround or his parents just kept saying he got hurt on the job.

But today, he wasn't buying that anymore. It was just before noon when they arrived. He waited as the greetings were made. Mama kissed him, and his dad patted him on the shoulder and grinned, and then he hit them with his complaint.

"We need to talk. Have a seat."

"What's wrong?" Tiny asked.

"You two have beat around the bush enough. I want the real truth about what happened to me."

Emmitt sighed and looked at Tiny, but she didn't hesitate.

"We weren't trying to keep it a secret, but we needed to make sure you were strong enough to hear it."

"My God, Mama. Hear what? What could possibly be that bad?"

"Your grandpa had another fight with your grandma, raising all kinds of a ruckus that scared her enough she called the police. He heard the sirens and drove away, but it upset her enough that she passed out. She was already in the ER when Jud went looking for Bowie

James. He drove to the house where you were all working, saw Bowie through a window, and pulled out his gun. He took aim, but just as he was pulling the trigger, you walked in front of Bowie and he shot you instead."

Junior gasped and laid his hands over his belly.

"Grandpa shot me?"

"Oh, he didn't mean to, and he freaked out when he saw what he'd done. He went running toward the house, still carrying his gun. Bowie knocked him out at the door, then took off his shirt and used it for a compress on your wound until the ambulance arrived. He saved your life. The EMTs said it. The doctor said it."

"Oh my God! Mama! Grandpa was really going to kill him?"

"He'd already be gone if you hadn't stopped the bullet," Tiny said.

Junior lay there, trying to collect his thoughts.

"And there's one other thing you need to know," Emmitt said. "Bowie James dropped all the charges against you the day he hired you. Chief Pittman told us. I don't know why Bowie didn't tell you, too. Then you wouldn't have had to work, and you wouldn't have been there when this happened."

Junior shook his head. "Dad. You're never going to understand people like him. He wouldn't have dropped the charges if I hadn't asked him for the job. You paying for everything still wouldn't have made him drop the charges against me. He was giving me a chance to do the right thing. And if I hadn't, he would be dead, and I don't know if I could have lived with myself, knowing I'd vandalized his car and then my grandpa killed him in cold blood."

"I get it, I guess," Emmitt said. "But you nearly died."

"I didn't because of him," Junior said. "And by the way, where's Grandpa? Jail, I hope."

"He's there," Tiny said. "But not for long. He's in court being sentenced as we speak."

Junior leaned back, suddenly exhausted. "Is Grandma okay?"

"She's out of the hospital. We don't know any more. She's not talking to us. But it is what it is. We can't wait for you to come home. The house feels empty without you in it."

"I'm tired, Mama. I think I need to rest a while," he said.

Emmitt and Tiny were instantly on their feet, hugging him goodbye and promising they'd be back later that evening to spend a little time with him before he went to sleep.

He waved but didn't comment. He didn't know what to say.

While Junior was trying to sleep off the horror of what he'd learned, Judson Boone was in court.

Since the State of Georgia did not have an attempted murder charge on the books, he was officially found guilty of aggravated assault and sentenced to twenty years, which was the maximum penalty allowed by law.

Chief Pittman was leading Jud out of the courtroom in handcuffs when Jud looked up and nearly stumbled.

Cora was sitting in the courtroom, just as she had the day he and Junior were first arrested. His heart sank. He couldn't look at her without shame for what he'd done to her, so he ducked his head and walked out of her sight.

Cora sat motionless for almost ten minutes after Jud

was gone, but she'd had to see this for herself. He was seventy-two years old. He wouldn't live twenty more years, not in prison. So that's where his life would end.

She got up and walked out of the courthouse and into the sunlight, pausing a moment to look around at the little town of Blessings, and then sighed.

"And this is where my life will end, right where I belong."

She lifted her chin, took the handicap ramp down from the steps, and went to her car.

Today was the first day of the rest of her life.

Less than a week later, and two days after Junior's sixteenth birthday, Emmitt and Tiny took him home. They talked all the way home about moving away now, and where they might go. But every time they asked Junior for input, he had nothing to say. Even as they were going into the house, they were still talking about leaving it.

"I'm gonna go lie down for a bit," Junior said, and Tiny went with him to his room and tucked him in for a rest.

"I'll bet it feels good to be home, doesn't it?"

He shrugged. "It can't be home if you and Daddy are already talking about leaving it."

Tiny frowned. "Well, you know why. People in Blessings don't want us here anymore, and I don't stay where I'm not wanted," she said. "Don't worry about grown-up things. That's for your daddy and me to decide."

Junior eased himself into a more comfortable

position and closed his eyes, but sleep didn't come. And the longer he stared at the ceiling, the more certain he became.

Supper that night was something of a celebration. Tiny made Junior's favorite spaghetti and meat sauce, and lemon pie for dessert, then couldn't stop touching him and talking, as if she sensed the growing distance between them.

Emmitt was quiet but he knew something was going on, and halfway through his piece of pie he laid down his fork and looked up.

"Junior, what's wrong?"

"I'm not going with you," he said.

Tiny's mouth opened, but nothing came out. She cast a frantic look at Emmitt as if to say, *Do something*.

"What are you talking about? You sure as hell are going with us."

"No, sir. I'm not. Blessings is my home. I belong here. I'm not guilty of anything, and I'm not running away from nothing."

"I have to find work, and no one in this town is going to hire me."

"Then go. Grandma is alone. I'm alone. Nobody is mad at us, and I'm going to live with her. I don't want her growing old alone."

Tiny started crying, but not her usual tirade. Just the quiet tears of a broken heart.

"Do you hate us, too?" Emmitt asked.

"I don't hate either of you," Junior said. "But I also don't know who either of you are. What I do know is you're not who I thought you were. It's like we're from two different planets, Daddy. I don't understand the way you think and speak, and you don't understand me or my language."

"That's bullshit! You'll go with us if I have to tie your ass down to do it!" Emmitt shouted.

Junior just sat there, watching his daddy's face turning red like it always did when orders weren't followed. And his mother was crying. Just like she always did to get her way.

"You can't make me, Daddy. Not anymore. I'm sixteen. I have the option of choosing where I want to live now, and I choose Grandma. She knows how to be quiet, and she knows how to love."

"She damn sure does not!" Emmitt shouted. "She quit on Daddy, and she quit on us."

Junior flinched as if he'd just been slapped.

"Your daddy shot me, put Grandma in the hospital, and you're still taking up for him? I don't speak that language, Daddy. I can't understand what you're saying anymore."

He pushed himself away from the table, put his hand against his belly, and walked out of the room.

Tiny looked at Emmitt in disbelief. "I can't believe you just said that."

Emmitt glared.

Tiny stared.

And Junior was in his room, texting Cora.

Cora had just finished her supper dishes and settled into her recliner when her phone signaled a text. She picked it up, then read it in shock. Then she read it again, and again, until everything she was reading made sense.

Mama and Daddy are moving away from
Blessings because they said they don't belong
here anymore. But I still belong here. You still
belong here. You're alone. I'm alone. I think
we need each other. Bowie showed me what
being a man of honor meant. I will be good for
the rest of my life. Could I please live with you?

Cora typed in one word, then hit Send.

Yes.

Two days later Emmitt dropped his son at his mother's doorstep, waited until she opened the door, and then
watched her wrap her arms around him. The door shut,
and just like that his son was out of their lives.

He drove home to get Tiny. They were packed and
ready to go. They left town pulling a small U-Haul trailer.

Tiny was sobbing, and Emmitt felt like it, but he just
kept driving north. He wanted to be somewhere without
hurricanes, somewhere that had snow.

He'd heard the other day that Jud had already been
transported to some prison where he would be for the
rest of his life. All the men in Emmitt's life were gone.
Tiny was all he had, which wasn't saying much. But she
was better than nothing, and that's how he rolled.

Pearl's house was nearing completion. Electricians and
plumbers had come back to finish up. All the light fix-
tures were in place, the quartz countertops had gone in
that morning, and the last bits of connecting plumbing to

appliances were finished. After that came flooring and then cleanup. The furniture they'd ordered would be here in two days, and after that was move-in day.

Rowan had come to work with Bowie that morning and was sweeping so they'd be ready for new flooring to go down.

She was working in the kitchen when she heard the first clap of thunder. Her heart started to pound, and she was trying not to panic when Bowie came running.

She dropped the broom and walked straight into his arms.

"It's just thunder. It's supposed to rain. Just some rain, honey. No big winds, no tornado warnings. Just some wind, rain, and noise."

"Okay," she said. "Just noise and rain."

"Yes. Do you want to go home? Before the rain starts?"

She couldn't look at him. She hated how this made her feel. But she couldn't control it.

"Yes."

"Hey, Ray!" Bowie shouted.

Ray came running. "Yeah, Boss. What's up?"

"I'm taking Rowan home before it starts to rain. I'll be right back."

"Okay," Ray said, and followed them out to make sure all the windows on the crew's vehicles were rolled up.

It thundered again just after they were inside the car, and Rowan jumped.

"I'm sorry."

"No apologies. You're allowed to feel how you feel."

The first drops were already falling when he pulled into the trailer park. He was walking her to the door when Pearl swung it inward. She saw the look on Rowan's face and took her by the hand.

"Honey, Ella is making hot chocolate and I'm baking cookies. You're going to be fine," she said.

Bowie was surprised by the preparations they'd already made.

"How did you know to do this?" he asked.

"We watched the weather report and hedged our bets," Ella said. "Even if the thunderstorm missed us, we still had cookies and hot chocolate, and that's always a good thing."

He hated to leave Rowan, but they were so close to being done at Pearl's house that he didn't want to overlook a thing.

"I'm just a phone call away if you need me," he said.

Rowan hugged him. "I'll be fine."

He frowned at the three of them. "This is not a good time for Gentleman Jack."

Rowan made a face. "I don't care if I never drink another drop of anything alcoholic as long as I live."

"Not even champagne on our wedding day?" Bowie said, and laughed when she shuddered.

Ella groaned. "I threw up more that night than I have in my whole life. Please don't mention whiskey again."

Pearl rolled her eyes. "Ella told me I talked about my wedding night with her daddy, so I have sworn off of liquor for the rest of my life."

Ella snickered.

"Hush it, Ella May," Pearl said.

Bowie left laughing.

It took the girls a minute for what he'd said to sink in, and then Ella squealed.

"Bowie asked you to marry him?"

"Yes," she said, then braced herself for the onslaught of hugs, kisses, and giggles, and so many questions for which she had no answers. "We haven't set a date. And we're going to be living in the motor home and traveling to his jobsites, just like he does right now. I don't need a house or a white picket fence or two cars in the garage and a set of china. All I want in this world is him, and he's already mine."

The first wave of rain that came through didn't amount to much. But another round came through after midnight, and that one lasted for at least an hour.

Rowan wound up in a blanket, asleep on the couch, and when Bowie woke up and saw her, he carried her to his bed, laid her down as she was, still wrapped up like a baby in swaddling blankets, and crawled back beneath his covers.

Daylight brought a clearing sky and sun peeking through the clouds.

"It's going to be nothing short of a sauna today," Bowie said as he and Rowan were eating breakfast together. "I'm grateful that we now have air conditioning and working plumbing."

"Does that mean the port-a-potty has to go?" she asked.

He nodded. "And probably none too soon for the neighbors. What are you going to do, honey?"

"I don't know. I didn't sleep much last night, so I might just take it easy for a while."

"Call me anytime you want to, and I'll stop by when we break at noon."

"I will."

"When this renovation is over, how about we take a little side trip to Savannah on our own and pick out rings?"

Rowan shivered from the joy of the turn her life had taken.

"Yes! Oh, Bowie! The proudest moment of my life will be becoming your wife."

He pulled her into his lap, waited for her arms to lock around his neck.

"Sealed with a kiss," he said softly and kissed her, then kissed her again because he could.

He left a few minutes later, and Rowan stretched out on the sofa and dozed off. She was dreaming about the flood again, and watching her daddy go under, when the sound of a car door slamming woke her up. It was already after nine and the girls weren't up, but they'd slept later than that before so she thought nothing of it.

The door was still shut to the bedroom, and she didn't want to make any noise. She was also sure she didn't want to go back to sleep and dream that again. Maybe all she needed was a little fresh air. That would wake her up.

She left the girls a note that she was going for a walk and not to lock her out if they left. Then she got a bottle of water, dropped her phone in the pocket of her shorts, and slipped out.

The morning was already warming up and the sky was clearing. Her thoughts were on that trip to Savannah to pick out rings as she stepped onto the sidewalk behind the motor home and started walking.

The first thing she noticed was the sound of rushing water coming from the creek. Likely runoff from last night's thunderstorm, and she was thinking about breaking into a little jog when her phone rang. She saw Bowie's name pop up and smiled.

"Hello, handsome. Miss me already?" she said.

Bowie's chuckle sent shivers all through her.

"Something like that," he said, and braked for a stop sign as he drove back home. "Did you happen to notice if I left a file folder on the table or the kitchen counter? It would have been a yellow one."

"Yes! I saw it on the counter earlier."

"Oh good. I was beginning to think I'd lost it. I need it, so I'll see you in a few."

"I'm out walking. I'll head back."

"You don't have to. Enjoy your walk because I can't stay anyway. I'll just talk to you now while you're walking, how's that?"

She smiled. "Good. Oh…you should hear the water down in the creek! I haven't gone to look, but it must be run-off from last night because it's making a rushing noise and it never does that."

"I think someone said this morning we got almost an inch. Are the girls up?"

"They weren't when I left. I left them a note. Oh…I see the little redhead on her bike already. Only she's riding on the sidewalk today, probably because the drive through the park is muddy. Oh, wait, Bowie, she just swerved and…oh my God! She just lost control. She's still on her bike, but it's rolling down that steep slope leading down to the creek. I need to—"

Bowie heard Rowan shouting, "Jump off your bike! Jump off!" and then he heard her running. All of a sudden Rowan was shouting in his ear. "She went into the creek! I can hear her screaming. Call 911. If she can't swim, she might drown."

Bowie didn't want to lose the connection to Rowan, so he put her on hold, made the 911 call, and then was connected to her again. All he could hear were bits and pieces of what was happening. Rowan must be at the creek now. He could hear her shouting to the little girl to hang on.

Then there was a moment of silence, and then he heard a big splash and knew without seeing it happen that Rowan had jumped into the water. He stomped the accelerator and started to pray.

———

Lorene couldn't believe she was in the water. One minute she'd been riding her bike like she always did, and then that snake had crawled across the sidewalk in front of her. All she remembered was swerving to keep from running over it, and then she was going downhill too fast. She heard someone screaming "jump off," but then she was in the trees and over the edge before she knew it was happening. She hit the water, went under, and then bobbed up a few feet from a branch and grabbed it as the water was carrying her past it. Surprised that she'd caught it, she began screaming for help, and she kept screaming until she looked up, saw a lady waving her arms, and pointing up the creek. When she momentarily disappeared, Lorene cried out.

"No, no! Don't leave me!"

Seconds later, she caught a flash of long legs and a red T-shirt, and then the woman was in the water.

Rowan couldn't believe the water was over her head,

but the moment her feet touched the creek bed, she pushed up and immediately surfaced. The little girl was only yards away, and Rowan began swimming with the current to get to her. Seconds later, she swam up behind the girl, grabbed onto another bush with one hand, and grabbed onto her with the other. The little girl was shaking so hard Rowan didn't know if it was from pain or fear.

"Are you okay?" Rowan asked.

"I think so. I'm scared. Are we gonna die?"

"No, ma'am, we are not," Rowan said. "What's your name, honey?"

"Lorene, but my mama calls me Reenie." Then she broke into sobs. "I want my mama."

"I know, Reenie. And she'll be here soon, I'm sure. But for now, you have me. My name is Rowan. Don't tell anyone, but I'm a princess, and I have a knight in shining armor who's coming to rescue us."

Before Reenie could respond, Rowan saw a small branch coming toward them and swung herself around so that it would hit her back instead of the little red-head's face.

The impact jarred both of them, and Reenie lost her grip. The only thing keeping her from going downstream was Rowan, and Reenie began screaming again.

"Put your arms around my neck!" Rowan shouted. "I won't let you go, I promise. Just hold onto me!"

Reenie wrapped her arms around Rowan's neck and her legs around her waist, and buried her face against her shoulder.

"I hear sirens!" Rowan shouted. "That means my brave knight has sent us a rescue! We're going to be fine, just fine. You just keep holding onto me," Rowan said, and then gasped. "Listen, Reenie! Do you hear the man shouting?"

Reenie nodded.

"That's my brave knight! I told you he would save us!"

———

Bowie took the turn sideways into the trailer park, drove up to his home, killed the engine, and got out running, leaving the door open and the keys in the ignition.

Pearl had seen him drive up and opened the door to greet him, but he ran past her shouting.

"Rowan's in the water. Rescue is on the way!" he said, and flew past the door and kept running.

"Oh lord, oh lord," Pearl cried, and then saw his car and ran out to get the key and shut the door.

Ella was right behind her. "What's happening, Mama?"

"Rowan's in trouble," Pearl said. They took off behind Bowie, moving as fast as they dared while listening to the fear in Bowie's voice as he began to shout. He knew something they didn't.

"Rowan! Rowan! Answer me! Where are you? Rowan!"

Then he heard her. "Here! We're down here!"

"I'm coming!" he said, and then saw a little bicycle in the trees about twenty yards farther. The first thing that went through his head was that the water would have already taken them downstream beyond the fall, and he leaped off the sidewalk and started running through the trees.

"We're here! We're here!" Rowan kept shouting, and then heard a voice above them. She saw Bowie standing in a ray of light coming through the trees and, for a heartbeat, thought it was an angel. Then she saw him kick off his boots and start sliding down the bank, then into the water.

His feet touched bottom, but the water was just below his armpits and rushing fast enough it was difficult to move against the flow. Moments later, he had them encircled within his arms, and the feel of her living, breathing body against him was the answer to his prayer.

"Sweet Jesus, Rowan. Are you two all right?"

The relief of him holding both of them was over-whelming. "We're okay. Sir Bowie, this is Lorene, but you may call her Reenie. She knows I'm a princess and that you are my brave knight in shining armor."

The pain in Bowie's heart was so suddenly sharp that he lost his breath. Rowan had no way of knowing how hard he'd tried to save his mother after he found her on the floor, and that he'd lived with that guilt for the last twenty years. But Fate had just given him a second chance to save a woman he loved, and this time he'd done it.

He could see that the fantasy she'd given the little girl had helped keep her calm and he wasn't about to screw up a good thing.

"It's always an honor to serve you, Princess Rowan, and your friend, Reenie, as well. Listen! Do you hear how loud the sirens are?"

Reenie nodded.

"They will help us get out," Bowie said.

Along with the sirens, Bowie began hearing a lot of voices and guessed a crowd was gathering above. Then he heard a scream and someone shouting the little girl's name.

"That's my mama."

"I told you she would come," Rowan said.

And then Bowie heard more voices, coming closer, and looked up just as Chief Pittman looked over the edge.

"They're here!" he shouted, then gave Bowie a thumbs-up.

It didn't take long for the firemen to get set up. When they sent the first rig down, Bowie fastened it around the little redhead and they hoisted her up. The moment she was safe up top, Rowan's legs went weak.

"Oh my God," she mumbled and fell against Bowie.

He couldn't talk. He just held her.

They lowered the rig again, and Bowie fastened it around Rowan. Kissed her once hard and fast, saw forever in her eyes, and then waved his hand and up the bank she went.

He waited, buffeted by the water, while his heartbeat finally settled into a normal rhythm. And when they sent the rig down one last time, he fastened himself into it and they pulled him up as well, until he was out onto solid ground.

"Are they both okay?" he asked.

"It appears so, but the little girl's parents took her to the ER to be checked out. Rowan's up top with Pearl and Ella."

He nodded, then looked around for his boots.

"Oh, Rowan saw them and took them up with her," Lon said.

Bowie looked up at the gathered crowd and then started making his way up the steep slope, just as it began to sprinkle.

Raining again? And the sun was shining.

The crowd had mostly dispersed by the time he got back on the sidewalk. All three of his girls met him with open arms and then surrounded him without words, hugging him, holding him tight.

"It's time to get you two warm and in dry clothes," Pearl said. "Ella and I will go ahead to get some coffee going. I have Rowan's phone. The chief found it. Where is yours?"

"Still in the car."

"Are you two okay?" Ella added.

"We will be," Rowan said, and slid her arm around Bowie's waist as they started walking back.

Bowie was holding onto Rowan as if she were about to blow away, and yet there was nothing but the sprinkles slowly turning into something of a drizzle. The farther they went, the tighter his hold became. Rowan felt the fear he'd had of losing her.

"I love you, Bowie James, and you can't lose me. I'm a princess, and they always live happily ever after, remember?"

He inhaled slowly. "How do you always know what to say?"

"I'm a little fae, remember, along with being a princess. What the faeries know, I know, and they always send signs. There will be one. Wait and see."

They'd walked all the way out from beneath the shaded sidewalk, making their way to the door, when Rowan gasped and then pointed.

"Look up, Bowie! See that?"

Bowie looked and then stopped. "A rainbow. I see a rainbow through the rain."

"Yes, yes! That's our sign from the faeries. For all the

rest of our lives, even when we can't see it there will be a rainbow above us."

He reached for her hand, and she gave it.

Epilogue

THE DAY OF THE BIG REVEAL WAS AT HAND. BOWIE'S CREW had gone home, ready to be with their families again. Before they left, everything of value Pearl had put in storage after the flood had been cleaned up and set in place about the house. Her grandmother's sideboard was in the dining room and somehow fit among the new furniture she and Bowie had picked out. Everything else in that house, except Pearl and Ella, was brand spanking new.

They'd moved in last night and kept walking through the house in all its glory, unable to grasp the fact that it was their home. And today, because Pearl wanted it so, they were having an open house for people to come see what Bowie had done for them.

Bowie and Rowan had spent their first night together without the chaperones. But with the engagement ring on her finger, and the man who'd put it there asleep in the bed beside her, she felt a quiet satisfaction that her world had stopped rocking and she was settled into place.

Pearl and Ella had given up on the idea of seeing them married in a church here in Blessings. They'd come to accept how deep the scars of life were on Bowie. He didn't have enough happy memories in this town to have it mark the beginning of his and Rowan's life together, and Rowan wanted nothing in life but to be with him.

"'Whither thou goest,'" she said the day he put the engagement ring on her finger, and as soon as the open house was underway, they would be going.

———∿∿———

Rowan and Bowie arrived in his red Cherokee and parked at the curb in front of the house so they could leave when they chose, then walked up the drive.

"It's beautiful, you know," Rowan said, eyeing the green roof and white siding and the welcoming porch with delicate spindles and matching porch posts of the same turn but bigger and stronger—the kind needed to hold up the porch roof for the next hundred years. The white wicker furniture with big, fluffy pillows invited you to sit a spell, and six baskets of dark-green ferns hung from the edges of the porch like oversize eyelashes the grand lady had chosen to wear for her unveiling.

Bowie walked up the steps with Rowan on his arm and then into the house he'd saved from dying. Subdued colors of off-white and pale-gray blended with a navy sofa and one bright armchair upholstered in a fabric of red and gold birds on a navy background.

Pearl met them at the door wearing a new pink dress, and the long braid of her hair wound on top of her head instead of at the back gave her the appearance of wearing a crown.

"You look beautiful, Gran," Bowie said and kissed her cheek, inhaling the scent of Estée Lauder powder that she'd always worn and a faint aroma of lilac.

Ella came running, kissed Rowan's cheek, and threw her arms around Bowie.

"We're still pinching ourselves that we live here,"

she said. "Thank you for responding to my SOS. This is vastly more help than I ever dreamed."

"You're my girls," Bowie said. "I love you both, and this is nothing more than you deserve."

"Here come the first of your guests," Rowan said, pointing to the trio coming up the walk.

"And there are more parking," Ella said as she looked out the big picture window. "Mama, have we set out all the goodies?"

Pearl nodded. "Just calm down. Everything is perfect. Bowie, you and Rowan will stay for just a bit, won't you? I want to make sure the people who come know it was you who did this."

"Oh! There comes the photographer from the newspaper," Ella said. "Good. We'll get the picture taken before you two leave. And just so you know, we'll be expecting all kinds of postcards and pictures. You can send them to us on our phones. And FaceTime. Don't forget the FaceTime."

"I didn't forget you before and we're not going to forget you now," Bowie said, and then the first guests were at the door.

"Excuse me," Pearl said and turned on the charm.

The picture was taken for the paper. The guests were beginning to gather. The women looked at the beautiful home with varying degrees of joy for Pearl, while envious they had nothing like it. Then they'd eye the big, dark-haired man with Rowan Harper on his arm, wondering how such a shy, introverted woman had managed to snag such a glorious man.

A stranger drove by and then braked to look, wondering what was going on in there. There were cars up and down both sides of the street, leaving only a one-way lane in which to drive.

He was looking for a certain house number when he saw a car coming up behind him and moved on, noting the recent flood damage and thinking to himself that if it hadn't been for that DNA test kit he did on a whim, he wouldn't be here at all. He still hadn't come to terms with the fact that the woman he'd known as his mother was no relation, and the young girl who'd been his older sibling's babysitter was.

His not-real mother was recently deceased, and according to papers he'd found in her house, his birth mother's name was Janie Chapman. It was the DNA test he took and a lot of sleuthing that had led him to Blessings, Georgia. It might be just another dead end, or it could lead to people who knew her, but he wasn't leaving until he was sure. He was about to give up and go straight to the police station. He didn't want to, but if he wanted to find her he was going to need help.

So he left the area and headed back downtown.

———

About an hour into the party, Cora and Junior walked in. Bowie saw them come in and went to meet them. He nodded at Cora, then gave Junior a pat on the back.

"I hope it's okay that we're here," Cora said.

"Yes, ma'am. And Junior, good to see you up and about. Show your grandma around. Let her see what you helped build."

Junior hesitated. "I need to thank you. For letting me work and for dropping the charges. It was good to know you, too."

Bowie held out his hand. "It's been an honor to meet you, Junior. Stay on the right side of life, okay?"

Junior beamed as he shook Bowie's hand. "Yes, sir. I intend to do just that."

Then Pearl saw Cora and came toward her with her arms outstretched.

Bowie watched the two old friends embrace and thought how long it had taken for this to come full circle.

Later, when both Pearl and Ella were otherwise occupied, Bowie and Rowan snuck out and drove back to the trailer park. They changed out of their party finery, trading it for traveling clothes. Bowie pulled the motor home out of the parking place and then stopped in the drive so he could hook the Cherokee to the tow.

While Rowan was watching, she heard someone calling her name, and when she looked behind her, Reenie and her mother, Sheri, were waving them down. Sheri and Yancy had come the day after the rescue and thanked both her and Bowie effusively, so Rowan hadn't expected to see them again.

She smiled and went to meet them.

"I'm so glad I caught you," Sheri said. "Frank and Jewel said y'all were leaving today, and Reenie has been beside herself to give you this present but she wouldn't say why. They didn't have any in Blessings, so we drove all the way to Savannah to get it."

Rowan looked down at Reenie and smiled. "You didn't need to get me anything, sugar."

"But I did," Reenie said. "You have to bend over, though. I can't reach your high."

My high. Rowan looked down at the little redhead

and then at the serious frown between her eyes and, without thinking, knelt instead of bending over.

"Please close your eyes," Reenie said.

Sheri looked at Rowan and shrugged, but Rowan gladly obliged. Then she heard paper rustling and felt Reenie's knee against her chest as she leaned close and whispered in Rowan's ear.

"I didn't tell anyone you are really a princess. But maybe you could wear this for when you're living in your castle."

Then Rowan felt Reenie putting something on her head.

"You can get up now," Reenie said.

Still smiling, Rowan stood and put her hands on her head, trying to guess what was there. And then she felt the shape and the design, and took it off to look.

"They're almost diamonds," Reenie said.

Rowan's eyes were suddenly brimming as she put the tiara back on her head, then knelt once more and hugged Reenie as tightly as the day she'd held her above the water.

"Thank you, Reenie. I will treasure it always," she said, then kissed the soft skin of the girl's cheek before she stood.

She turned around to see if Bowie was ready, and saw him leaning against the shiny red motor home, patiently waiting.

"I see my brave knight awaits me, so it's time to say goodbye." Rowan touched the top of Reenie's head. "For the bravest girl I ever knew, I am making you a member of my court. I shall name you Lorene, Lady of the Water."

The glow in Reenie's eyes and the smile of wonder on her face were all Rowan needed to see.

A smile passed between her and Sheri, and then she turned and walked back to Bowie, not unlike the way Pearl had sailed to the door to let in her first guest.

Bowie saw what she was wearing, remembered the story she'd told Reenie to keep her from panicking, and shook his head.

"So she crowned her princess. You bewitch us all, Princess Rowan. Your chariot awaits. Are you ready for your next grand adventure?"

"With you? Always. Remember... 'Whither thou goest'..."

Bowie reached for her hand. "...'I will go.'"